THE OMEGA
NETWORK

*Also by Thomas Locke
in Large Print:*

The Delta Factor

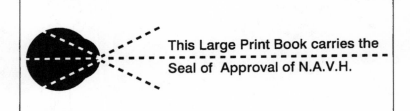

This Large Print Book carries the
Seal of Approval of N.A.V.H.

THE OMEGA NETWORK

A THOMAS LOCKE MYSTERY

Thomas Locke

Thorndike Press • Waterville, Maine

Published in 2001 by arrangement with Bethany House Publishers.

Thorndike Press Large Print Christian Mystery Series.

The tree indicium is a trademark of Thorndike Press.

The text of this Large Print edition is unabridged. Other aspects of the book may vary from the original edition.

Set in 16 pt. Plantin by Christina S. Huff.

Printed in the United States on permanent paper.

Library of Congress Cataloging-in-Publication Data

Locke, Thomas.
    The Omega network / Thomas Locke.
        p.   cm.
    ISBN 0-7862-3579-9 (lg. print : hc : alk. paper)
    1. Organized crime — Fiction.   2. Conspiracies — Fiction.
    3. Florida — Fiction.   4. Large type books.   I. Title.
PS3562.O236 O47 2001
    813'.54—dc21   2001045058

FOR GARY AND CAROL

"Now faith is being sure of what we hope for . . ."

"People will spend a tremendous amount of money in casinos. Money that they would normally spend on buying a refrigerator or a new car. . . . You can also expect crime to go up precipitously. Believe me, the casinos will make money for the state and the companies, but they won't be a bed of roses either. . . . As somebody who lives in Palm Beach, I'd prefer not to see casinos in Florida, but as someone in the gaming business, I'm going to be the first one to open up if Floridians vote for them."

> *Donald Trump*
> *Chairman of* The Trump Organization
> *Interview in* The Miami Herald
> *March 27, 1994*

"Bad money drives out good."

> *Gresham's Law*
> *Thomas Gresham was*
> *both an economist and*
> *Prime Minister of Great Britain*

1

"Talk to me."

"What about?"

"I don't care." Carlotta dragged deep on her cigarette. The tip cast a ruddy glow on her drawn features. "You're a sailor. Tell me about tides. Moon watches. Kelp islands."

"There's no such thing as a moon watch," Chase said, trying to ignore the rack between their two seats in the unmarked car. The rack that held the pump-action shotgun and the wooden baton as chipped and frayed as split stove wood. "Kelp grows in the Pacific, not the Atlantic. And the tides haven't changed in a hundred million years."

"Tell me about something nice," she said, her voice as hard as her eyes. "Something normal. Anything. Just so long as people are happy and nobody gets killed."

"This was not the conversation I was hoping to have," Chase replied, "when I asked to come up for a visit."

"You said you wanted to see how I was keeping. What I was doing with my life. Not to mention that last letter, telling me how excited you were to see what it was like to be a cop in the big city."

She made a jerky little circle with the cigarette, taking in the battered District of Columbia housing estate, the weed-infested yards, the chain-link fencing, the broken glass, the blackness unbroken by streetlight or signs of life. "Welcome to the big league."

"Thanks a lot." He squirmed in his seat.

"What's the matter?"

"This vest itches like crazy. Do I have to wear it?"

"It's not the vest," she said, turning back to the night. "It's the bullet you're afraid it might stop."

He stared at the woman who had been one of his two best friends. "Is this really Carlotta I'm talking to?"

"You see anybody else in this car?"

"The same Carlotta who collected butterflies and cried when we lost the game to Radley High?"

"We should've beaten their tails from Cocoa Beach to Miami. I still say they got to the ref."

"Yeah, I guess it really is you," Chase said. "So, what happened to you along the way?"

"I happen to love what I'm doing," she replied. "I'm not particularly fond of waiting, though, and I don't like getting shot at."

"Oh, great. Like, other than that, Mrs. Lincoln, how did you enjoy your night at the theater?"

She lit another cigarette and watched him above its glow. "I'm doing something important here, Chase. Finally. I spent my time in files and I had to fight like a tiger for them to get a chance at the action. Now I'm here. And I really do feel like this is vital."

"First female detective in DC narcotics," Chase recalled. "When I got word I was so proud I could've burst."

"Sometimes I feel like we are all that stands between the way of life you and I knew as kids and total anarchy. I like doing something valuable with my life. Contributing something. Upholding the American way and all that."

The car's atmosphere was acrid from her nonstop smoking. Chase replied, "I'm glad you're doing it, then, because I sure couldn't."

She turned from her constant searching of the empty night. "It was a relief hearing you wanted to come visit. Some of us were beginning to wonder if you'd ever wake up again."

Chase did not need to ask what she meant. "Like who was worried?"

"Like Matthew for one. Not to mention his Aunt Eunice. Colin for another. Every time they called, they'd say you were still

9

cocooned away in that life you'd made for yourself. Your job, your house, your boat. Back and forth from one to the other, never letting anybody get close to you again."

She inspected him through the smoke and the gloom. "You finally decided to pull your head out of the sand, Slim?"

He shrugged, not surprised to hear that they had been talking about him. Matthew was the third in their little band, friends since childhood. Colin had been a sometime friend from the early days, older and too much a loner to enter their group permanently, but always on the fringes. "I'm not sure."

"Then why did you want to come along?"

"Just to see," Chase said. "Your letters were getting, I don't know, a little bizarre. Like you were growing into somebody I didn't know anymore. I just wanted to see what was happening to you."

Her gaze remained steady on him. "Sorry you came?"

"No," he said, and almost meant it.

"Good. Besides, with my partner out of the action for a while, I could use a little company."

"What happened to him?"

"He got shot three days ago." A hard pull on the cigarette. "Sometimes I wonder if maybe he took a bullet meant for me."

"Don't talk like that."

"Sorry." Another pull. "Anyway, I was glad to get your call. I had started wondering if you were ever going to stop moping over that girl and get back to living."

"I wasn't moping, Carlotta."

"I don't know what else to call going into hibernation for over a year." She examined him in the darkness. "Sabine was an awful choice. You're well rid of that one."

"I hate that," he said, more tired than angry. "It really gets me how everybody seemed to know Sabine except me."

He and Carlotta had become friends soon after his family had moved to the east coast of Florida, basically because nobody else would have anything to do with them. Back then, before growth around Cape Canaveral had really caught hold, Cocoa Beach had been just another sleepy resort used mostly by Florida locals. Cocoa Beach was just far enough north to catch the tail end of major chills. Because it was out of reach of the Bahamas, it also had both colder and rougher waters than places like Palm Beach, Miami, and the Keys. Northern tourists had tended to head for Fort Lauderdale and points farther south.

Chase's family had moved down from

11

New Jersey when he was nine. Back then, Cocoa Beach was just waking up from its long slumber as a sleepy backwater. Back then, the shoreline belonged mostly to the crabs and the fishermen and the sea birds. Back then, Florida was still the South, a land more in tune with Georgia than Jersey. Neighbors knew everybody's families, grandparents, business, and futures. Back then, newcomers were still strangers, and not almost everybody.

He and Carlotta Krepps and Matthew Pembroke had arrived at Cocoa Elementary the same September, outcasts and friendless. Carlotta's father was some mental giant who worked with NASA and had little time for a daughter who was already four inches taller than he was, could name every starting player on the three Florida NCAA basketball teams, and positively hated math. Her mother had divorced both father and daughter and moved back to Washington.

After that, Chase's mom and dad sort of adopted Carlotta. She spent more time at their house than at her own. After her dad's heart attack, though, Carlotta had been shipped off to Washington, to a mother who scared her to death.

That event had occurred three days after Chase's sixteenth birthday and marked the first time in his life he had ever mourned. He and Carlotta had never been anything except friends, but he had never known the true value of friendship until after she was gone. They had stayed in touch through letters and calls and summer visits, growing apart yet somehow still remaining close.

She brought him back to the reality of the night with a whispered, "Put on your jacket."

He craned, searched the darkness, saw nothing. "What is it?"

"Nothing yet. But it's almost time."

Chase slipped on the dark blue windbreaker with the yellow Day-Glo police emblem stamped both front and back. "You're sure you're not going to get in trouble?"

"Just stay close. And if anybody asks, you're visiting from the Cocoa PD."

"You always were one for bending the rules." He forced an uncertain smile. "Guess you haven't changed that much after all." Chase snapped up the blue windbreaker, reviewed the little she had told him about what was going down.

The ACLU already called it the ultimate desecration of constitutional rights. The local residents called it their last hope. The SWAT teams called it Prime Time. And tonight was to be the first Washington strike.

The trial runs had all been up in Chicago,

13

home to the biggest projects and the highest square-mile murder rate in America. Chicago project residents had been complaining of noises in the night, which was nothing new. That the noises had started coming from automatic rifle fire, bazookas, rocket-propelled grenades, and antitank missiles certainly was.

So city officials had requested a warrant. Not for one dwelling. For the entire project. Blanket permission for an apartment-to-apartment hunt for weapons.

The first Chicago raid had managed to cover only three project buildings. Four hundred and sixteen apartments.

It had netted eleven tons of weapons. Eleven *tons*.

Carlotta hissed him to full alert, stubbed out her cigarette, slouched down behind the wheel, and pointed at shadows that separated themselves from the wall and began drifting toward the towering barracks-style housing units.

He whispered, "Who are they?"

"SWAT. Not long now."

The tension hummed in his ears like a salt-encrusted pylon back home. Chase tried to hold himself as steady as he could, determined not to show his oldest friend just how scared he really was.

Then the night erupted.

Spotlights. Megaphones ordering everyone to open their doors immediately. Running feet. The crashing sound of doors being battered down. Shouts. Screams.

Shots.

One shot led to a dozen, then a moment's silence, then screams louder than before. Through it all rang disciplined voices, disciplined even while raised to shouts of their own. Calling back and forth, trained to handle the panic and the confusion and use it to their advantage.

Chase found his voice. "What are we waiting for?"

"This is not our deal. They just let me come along in case something's found. They're not after drugs. They're after guns."

"You told me." Chase watched a pair of armored prison trucks pull up. Immediately SWAT-uniformed officers were frog-marching figures toward the waiting doors. "When you said a weapons search, I thought it was like knock on the door, ask politely, go home. Guess I should've known better."

A light flashed their way, a shadow figure hustled over, and before the man arrived Carlotta was already out of the car. "Find something?"

"Could be," he said, sounding smug. "Could certainly be."

"Jack, this is Chase from Cocoa Beach. This is Detective Jack Sproul, does all our coordination with SWAT. Don't ask me why, they trust him. Spread the word, Jack. Chase is up to have a look at how it's done in the big city."

"How it's not done, you mean." The man reached out a hand. "Cocoa Beach as in Florida?"

"The one and only."

"You guys need a big-city detective down there, give me a shout." He turned back to Carlotta. "Okay, this way."

Jack led them at a trot back toward the central building, talking as they went. "Pretty much what you'd expect on the first couple of floors. One apartment's full of people cheering us on, asking us to line up the suckers and just blow them away. Next one's got an arsenal that'd make the military jealous. Then this one guy, he says there's something big up on the top floor."

"Crack house," Carlotta said, breathing easy despite her gear.

"What we thought. But he said no, *really* big. So we take a squad and go racing up top, and what do you know, pay dirt."

They hit the stairs and raced up the five

flights, past scores of families all out waving and shouting and laughing, like it was some kind of long-overdue party. On each landing Chase caught glimpses of weapons. Piles of handguns next to bigger piles of rifles and semiautomatic weapons. Boxes with lids torn off to reveal ammo and plastic explosive and grenades. Missile launchers stacked like green pipes along one wall.

By the top floor Chase was breathing hard and trying not to show it. He fought to keep up with Carlotta as they passed through another grinning throng. One lined black face said, " 'Bout time you got here. Ain't but ten years too late."

"Right here," Jack said, stopping in front of a battered-down door. "Wait, here's one batch." He bent over a plastic trash can, plucked out a twenty-gallon plastic bag. "Crack. Already vialed."

"*One* batch?" Carlotta asked.

"Almost too good to be true, ain't it. Found like two dozen little kids, oldest couldn't be more than eleven or twelve, all of them bent over these long tables loading vials."

"A factory," Carlotta said. "That's why they were on the top floor."

"Didn't want to leave the kids anywhere they could run," Jack agreed. "Got three, maybe four hundred kilos of the stuff in there. And something else. Come on."

The apartment reeked of grime and old sweat and something so acrid it burned Chase's nostrils. Fear, maybe. The first room was lined with crouching little kids, most of them so burned out their eyes looked permanently fogged over, all of them caught in a long row of plastic cuffs. A couple of policewomen were working their way down the line, trying to get them to talk, not having much success. The kids were all too beaten down to care.

The room contained three long trestle tables, each stool centered by a pile of vials and a swivel lamp and a little mound of crack rocks. Two policemen photographed the room while others, wearing surgical gloves, swept up and tagged the evidence.

They walked down a narrow hallway, the walls so filthy Chase narrowed his shoulders and kept his hands in front of himself so he wouldn't touch anything. The kitchen was absolutely black with ancient grime. The next room was wall-to-wall mattresses. The third door was closed. Jack swept it open with a flourish. "Bingo."

Inside were two of the hardest faces Chase had ever seen.

One was Hispanic, the other white. Both

eyed the intruders with disdain, playing it cool, not the least troubled by getting busted. Jack said, "Found them trying to kick off the wire mesh they'd stuck up to keep the kids from jumping. And to our surprise and joy, it wasn't the crack they were holding back here, trying to get rid of."

"How's it going, officers," the Hispanic guy drawled, the cuffs turning his casual act into a two-handed wave. "Nice night for a raid."

"No," Jack went on, ignoring the banter. He bent over and lifted an alligator briefcase with solid gold buckles. "It was this."

"What's inside?"

Jack asked the policeman inspecting the room, "You dusted for prints yet?"

"All yours."

He set it on a table, snapped the locks, and opened it to reveal bundles of hundred-dollar bills and a pair of computer diskettes. "Makes you wonder, don't it."

"Hey, that's private property," the white guy said.

"We have a search-and-seizure warrant that covers the entire project," Carlotta replied, not even looking his way. "This grants us the right to hold anything that might be attached in any way to illegal activities. Are you telling me there is a legal way for this much money to be in this place?"

"Absolutely," the white guy said.

"We were just here visiting my cousin," the Hispanic said.

Carlotta felt around the edges of the case, found the catch, released the false bottom, found two more diskettes and more bundles of hundred-dollar bills. "Tell me about it."

"Hey, here's an idea," the white guy said. "Help yourself to the proceeds, my pal and I will just take a little stroll, how does that sound?"

"Like attempting to bribe a police officer," Carlotta said, searching the sides and top of the briefcase with care. Something about her flat tone told Chase she received such offers all the time. "I'll pretend I didn't hear that one."

"I want to see my lawyer," the white guy said. "Right *now*."

"You're welcome to give him a call, once you've been processed." She looked at Jack and said, "Go ahead and book them."

"Hey, lady, you know what? You're history," the Hispanic sneered. "Say bye-bye to all your nice friends."

2

"Down-home politics is a murky business. It's like the Everglades, dark and dank and full of deadly surprises."

Lieutenant Governor Lamar Laroque turned from perusing the view through his wall of glass and examined his lone visitor. "The animals that do best here are the ones that hold fast to their primitive roots — snakes and gators and bottom-hugging catfish. Animals that thrive on mud and stink and devouring the unwary. Those are the kinds that dominate these reaches, Mr. Rochelle. Animals that despise the cold, cruel light of day."

Despite his elegant appearance, the gentleman seated at the oval conference table did not seem the least perturbed. "Then it is important for us to have a guide through these treacherous waters. Especially at a time like this."

"It is important to have a guide, *Governor*," Lamar corrected. "Then we understand each other. Good. That's real good. I like a fast learner." He eased himself down into the high-backed leather chair behind his desk. "My family hails from Pensacola. Have you ever had the opportunity to visit there, Mr. Rochelle?"

"Not yet, but I intend to."

"Oh, indeed you must. Despite our reputation as a grits-for-breakfast sort of town, there's a lot to Pensacola besides the Alabama cracker tourists and the military."

The lieutenant governor of Florida was a trim man in his mid-fifties who wore tailored seersucker suits and bow ties and handmade striped cotton shirts. He gave a self-deprecating chuckle. "As a matter of fact, we are the oldest settlement in America. St. Augustine may indeed be the oldest *continuous* settlement, but Pensacola was first settled by de Luna in 1559, long before St. Augustine was ever a glint in that other Spaniard's eye."

Sylvan Rochelle, president and chief executive of the Omega Development Corporation, smoothed an imaginary crease from his gabardine trousers. He spoke a cultured, slightly accented English. "I confess that my business interests have kept me somewhat occupied at the other end of your lovely state, Governor."

"Yes, I have been watching with great interest your growing domination of the Miami luxury condominium market. Well, someday

22

I hope you will come and be my guest on Santa Rosa Island, sir. I do believe you might find yourself a reason to look farther north." Gray eyes flashed a hint of high humor. "Up here, our own legacy is as rich as that of Miami, and much older. Why, when Andrew Jackson, our very first territorial governor, arrived in Pensacola, he was shocked to the core by what he found. His wife, Rachel, wrote to a friend, and I quote, 'I feel as if I were in a vast howling wilderness, far from my friends of the Lord.' They tossed in the towel and went home after just two months. Their successor managed to hang on quite a bit longer and left only after he had embezzled the town's treasury." The smile broadened to reveal perfectly white-capped teeth. "As you can see, we have a lot to offer people who know how to do business the Florida way."

"It sounds as if I might feel perfectly at home there," Sylvan Rochelle replied.

"Indeed, sir, that is why I mentioned it. And I might add that it is a pleasure to speak with someone who understands the facts of doing business as well as you."

Laroque rose and ambled back to inspect the vista. From his twentieth-floor office he had a glorious view out over the older capitol and the green Tallahassee landscape, all the way to Lake Jackson in the shim-mering distance. To his mind, the state's pair of capitol buildings typified Florida — a graceful antebellum manor of tall windows and vast Grecian pillars, utterly dwarfed by the twenty-two-story modern addendum erected directly alongside. The match dam-aged the city's skyline but suited him just fine. He kept an office in both, just to re-mind himself of what Florida truly was — a living, breathing marriage of the old and stately with the new and garish.

"We're running into some opposition to your casino project, Mr. Rochelle," he said, turning from the window and fixing his gray-eyed gaze on the visitor. "Nothing we didn't expect. You see, there are in truth types of Floridians. The new up-and-comer you know all about. The old-timers, now, they're crackers who have just barely man-aged to emerge from the swamps where they breed. Their small-town mentalities have been a blight on this land ever since they first settled here. They are opposed to prog-ress of every kind."

"I understand your governor remains ada-mantly opposed to casino gambling," said Rochelle with a shrewd gaze that belied his boyish features and stylishly unkept brown hair. Sylvan Rochelle was surprisingly young for the power he wielded. Not yet out of his thirties, he had arrived on the Florida property scene nine years earlier with an impressive bankroll and an eye for only the most luxurious of projects. His most recent Miami condominium development sported fifty stories, gold-plated bathroom fixtures, and an eighty-million-dollar price tag.

"He is the worst possible example of what we're up against." Lieutenant Governor Laroque showed anger for the first time. "That so-called enlightened cracker is constantly pushing for stricter legislation on new developments. Then, because he's succeeded in slowing down the state's income, he goes hat in hand to the federal government for funds to clean up the Everglades. Have you ever heard of such nonsense? Who in their right mind would give a second thought to a swamp? Not to mention the damage he is doing to an already depressed job market."

"And now this."

"Exactly. He considers gambling to be a sin." Lamar snorted. "In this day and age. With cruise ships like yours leaving every night, full to the brim with people willing to spend ninety dollars just to ride out to international waters and gamble."

"And yet he seems not to lack support."

"Only because the people do not yet realize how bad things truly are." Laroque examined Rochelle, glad now he had insisted that the man's slick willie of a lawyer wait outside. Business such as this was best conducted in private. "The Florida populace simply need to be educated, you see. They need to hear how people are now fleeing the state. They need to see that Florida is being overtaken by other states. They need to be shown how their job market is going to shrivel up like an overripe fruit, ready to fall from the tree and leave them stranded and helpless, their families hungry. Then they will listen to reason."

"And this I understand will be your task."

"Exactly. Given the proper, ah, stimulus, I can assure you that no one will champion your cause with greater fervor or more success than I."

"Help us with the passage of this bill," Rochelle replied calmly, "and we shall offer payment in full."

Laroque turned back to the window in order to hide his flash of triumph. "Three weeks to the final vote," he mused. "A lot to be done in such a short time."

"I trust you did not ask me up today in order to tell me the task was too much for you." It was only in the eyes that the man's experience showed. Such hardness came neither swiftly nor easily. "Or to quibble over details."

"We are both too busy to waste time on such mundane maneuvers. No, your lawyer Mr. Sorrens and my assistant have been at it day and night." His hands locked behind him, Laroque raised up on his toes, searched the distance. "I specifically asked you up here today, Mr. Rochelle, for two reasons. Firstly, because if I am to throw my weight behind your proposal, it is important that we begin to be seen publicly together, starting with the pair who are soon to present themselves here and who hopefully will neutralize one of our staunchest opponents. And secondly, because I intend to tell you exactly what I plan." Lamar Laroque wheeled about, returned to his chair, seated himself, and leaned across the desk. "And exactly what I want in return."

"You think your boss is crooked?"

The sky was pristine blue, the late morning sun almost too bright, the field green and clear and a world away from the projects. Chase sat beside Carlotta, waiting his turn at bat. He had been drafted onto the precinct's softball team to replace Carlotta's partner.

"Bosses," Carlotta replied under her breath, her eyes glued to the action on the field. "No cop works for just one person. Not even the commissioner. That's one of the problems, too many chiefs playing politics instead of fighting the bad guys."

"Who are the bad guys, Carlotta?"

"Good question. You have to understand, there's a lot of gray area."

"Spoken like a true rule bender."

"And this gray area can grow pretty big."

"You mean, some of the narcotics cops are dealing drugs?"

"No. Not often, anyway. But drugs are only half the problem. The other is the money. There's so much of it, Chase." She waited through a cheer for a solid hit, yelling along with the rest, not really seeing the game. "Politicians looking at multimillion dollar reelection campaigns put pressure on the commissioner to take it easy on a big contributor. It filters down."

"You're saying you're on the take?"

"Not me. But then I don't have kids in school or a mortgage or sickness in the family to worry about."

A guy at the end of the bench called down, "You're up, Carlotta."

Chase joined in the cheers as Carlotta selected a bat and walked to the mound. She had always been a big girl. Not fat. Just big. Throughout junior high they had traded off, one week she was an ounce heavier or an inch taller, the next week it was him. She had ended up only an inch or two behind. Her hands were broad and strong, and her wrists were thicker than his. She wore size-ten men's hightops. All the same, she was attractive, with dark brown hair and freckles and an athlete's confident grace as she strode out toward the plate.

The other team made the mistake of closing up their outfielders in anticipation of an easy out. Carlotta responded by hammering the first pitch fifteen feet over the center fielder's head.

When she had rounded the bases and grinned her way through the cheers, Chase told her, "I've seen pros drive a golf ball shorter distances than that."

She sat down beside him, caught her breath, then surprised him by asking, "You ever wonder why we never tried to get something going?"

Chase shrugged. "I guess I always thought you were off limits. You know, sort of like a sister."

"Yeah, me too. When I was little —"

"You never were that."

"Littler, then. Back then, I was afraid that

if Paul or Anna caught us playing around, they might have banished me to Siberia."

Paul and Anna were his parents, both now gone. Siberia was what she had always called her dad's house, and not because of the air conditioning. "They would have never done that."

"Maybe not, but it was a risk I wasn't ready to take." She wiped her face, leaned forward with elbows on thighs, asked, "Where was I?"

"We don't have to talk about business if you don't want to."

"I want. There's something I need to ask you to do, and I need you to understand why before I ask."

"Like what?"

"Let me work around to it in my own way, okay?" Another swipe at her forehead, then, "The DEA estimates that the cocaine trade in this country alone is worth twelve billion dollars a year. That's a billion dollars a month, month after month after month. Last year the Colombian cocaine trade grossed more money worldwide than Italy's national budget. It's big, Chase. And it's getting bigger."

"My head doesn't count that high." To Chase it seemed as though an invisible cloud had passed before the sun. "So you're saying your boss has gone over to the other side?"

"My boss's boss, really. I used to think it was impossible," Carlotta replied. "Now I'm not so sure. It may be he's just blowing with the political winds, but some of the things that are happening really make me wonder. Like, his total drug strategy is, as soon as there's a chance to bust somebody, go ahead. Even if it means losing the possibility to take out somebody bigger. It leaves us feeling like the big-time boys are always there, always out of reach. The superintendent, the head of narcotics for D.C., well, maybe it's just all for headlines. You know, count the busts, put the big numbers up on a chart. But in the past couple of weeks we've come so close, Chase. Not to the drugs, to the money guys. They get that big, they don't hardly ever touch drugs or guns anymore. They've got a hundred others to do that for them."

The softball game swirled around them like forgotten theater. Chase heard the laughter and the chatter and the cheers, saw the happy sweating faces, watched the inning unfold, but could not make it register against what he was hearing. "The superintendent is stopping you from going after the big guys?"

"There's always some reason. Something that won't bring the house down on his head, something that looks perfectly reasonable on paper."

"Such as?"

"You'd be surprised." Carlotta sounded extremely tired. "Just two weeks ago it was that the trail led out of our jurisdiction. Down your way, as a matter of fact."

"Miami?"

"Probably operating out of there, but what we'd heard put the situation a little farther north. Anyway, the super pulled the plug, refused to give us permission to follow through. I took it on myself to draw up a report, pass what we knew on to the local DEA office in Orlando, and suddenly it was D-Day all over again."

"Orlando?" That was getting too close to home. "The big guys were doing something near Orlando?"

"My super went totally off his rocker," Carlotta said, so caught up in the memory locking her face stone-hard that she did not hear him. "Threatened to suspend me for not following proper procedure. I played all innocent, told him I had no idea any such report to fellow law enforcement agencies had to go through him. He sort of bought it. But I've had the feeling he's been watching me ever since."

"So get out," Chase said. "What do you

need this aggravation for?"

"I might be doing that sooner than you think," she said quietly. "Getting out."

"You're quitting the force?"

"Here, I want you to do something for me." She scanned the scene, reached for her nylon sports bag, unzipped it, rummaged carefully so that it fell open and he could see inside. "Will you keep these for me?"

Inside the bag, she had pointed to four computer diskettes. "Are those copied from the briefcase you took in the raid?"

She shook her head. "Originals. I tried to copy them, but there's some kind of protective coding that stopped me."

"You just took evidence?" He looked from the bag to her face and back to the bag. "You're that worried about something going on in your department?"

"By this afternoon at the latest, some slick lawyer is going to be camped upstairs, lodging complaints and insisting that his client's property be returned. My superintendent is going to do exactly what he asks. I know it because I've seen it happen before." Her gaze pleaded with him. "Please, Chase. With my partner laid up I don't know who else to trust."

He reached over. "All right."

"Keep them in the bag. Hand carry it back on your flight." Her face was creased with concern. "I hope I'm doing the right thing, getting you involved like this. Promise me you'll be careful."

"Chase Bennett, lethal at fifty paces."

"I'm serious, Chase."

"I know you're serious. You've taken serious for your middle name. I haven't seen you crack a smile since I got up here."

She rearranged the worry lines on her face. "How's that?"

"Awful."

"Sorry. It's the best I can do right now."

He slid the bag under the bench. "Did you tell me you were leaving the force?"

"I can't talk about that right now." The inning ended with a cheer. "Thanks, Chase. I knew I could count on you."

There was a discreet knock at the door. Laroque checked his watch, said, "Right on time," and rose to his feet.

The door opened to admit a stunningly beautiful brunette who smiled a beckoning hello toward both men. "Mr. Governor, this is Bartholomew Tadlock and Linda Armacost."

"Good grief, Sabine, you know Barry doesn't need any introduction. Not around these quarters. Come in, come in, both of you."

A balding, portly man sported a suit cut far

too stylishly for his ample lines. He approached with a broad grin and outstretched hand. "Good to see you again, Governor."

"Barry. How nice of you to join us today." The lieutenant governor gave the newcomer's hand a hearty shake, then steered him around to where the other man stood waiting. "Mr. Rochelle, may I introduce Senator Bartholomew Tadlock. He is an attorney by profession. His district encompasses Brevard County, which includes Cocoa Beach." He turned to where a middle-aged woman in a navy dress stood nervously waiting to be noticed. "And you must be Ms. Armacost, the new president of the Brevard County Chamber of Commerce. Hope you had a good flight."

"It was just fine, Mr. Governor. It's a pleasure to meet you." The words came out stiff with nerves.

"The pleasure is all mine, I assure you, Ms. Armacost. It certainly is nice to see Brevard's chamber showing the wisdom to bring in some new blood." He led her forward. "Please allow me to introduce Sylvan Rochelle, formerly of Geneva, Switzerland, and now a resident of Miami." He walked back behind his desk, waved a welcoming hand, said, "You all know my personal assistant, Sabine Duprie. Pull up chairs, everybody, and make yourselves comfortable. Join us, won't you, Miss Duprie."

When everyone had settled, the lieutenant governor went on, "As you are no doubt aware, Mr. Rochelle has proven himself time and again as one of Florida's most astute and successful real estate developers. When everybody else was running for cover and predicting the bottom had fallen from the market, Mr. Rochelle single-handedly turned the Miami luxury hotel and condominium market around. What you might not be aware of is the fact that our bankers were too all-fired scared to back him on his first two projects, so Mr. Rochelle paid for them all from his very own pockets." Lamar Laroque paused to make sure that message had sunk in deep, then added for emphasis, "In cash."

Barry Tadlock had not stopped grinning. "I believe you run a couple of cruise liners that have their home port in my district, Mr. Rochelle."

"Four," Sylvan corrected. "Two casino day cruisers with a six-hundred-passenger capacity, and two recent additions. These larger vessels sail to the Bahamas and the Caribbean. We are also negotiating to acquire three more."

"Seven vessels," Barry Tadlock mused.

"That would make you the largest cruise-ship company operating from Cocoa Beach. I don't believe the information about your new purchases is widely known. May I have the honor of briefing the press?"

"No you may not," the lieutenant governor replied, the kindly tone belied by the steely glint in his eyes. "And to set the record straight, everything we discuss here today is strictly confidential. Nothing, and I do mean nothing, is to go further than these four walls. Is that clear?" When he had received dutiful nods from the pair, Laroque turned toward Sylvan. "Perhaps you would care to proceed, Mr. Rochelle."

Sylvan Rochelle reluctantly pulled his gaze away from Sabine and said, "As you may know, I am actively involved in the movement to bring casino gambling to Florida."

Barry Tadlock shifted uncomfortably. Lamar Laroque raised one languid hand. "Barry, please. I am well aware of your father-in-law's violent opposition to this matter. I also know how this has chained you to a stand which I am not sure is in Brevard County's best interests. If you will please just hear Mr. Rochelle out, I think you may find yourself with the ammunition you need to turn this situation around." He gestured toward the elegant young man. "Mr. Rochelle?"

"In our opinion, the current motion to legalize gambling has the best chance of passing if the dangers voiced by the opposition are met and overcome, rather than simply challenged with argument," Sylvan Rochelle continued.

"At least in the beginning," Lamar Laroque murmured.

"Exactly. Further down the line, when we have proven ourselves, such things can more easily be altered. For the moment, however, the Omega Development Corporation has withdrawn its intention to build casinos near every major city. Instead, we have decided to build *one* casino."

"Are you listening, Barry?" Lamar Laroque's voice carried a honeyed burr. "You too, Miss Armacost. This is real important what our Mr. Rochelle is saying."

"One casino," Sylvan Rochelle repeated. "Situated at a midpoint where it may serve a large portion of Florida's population."

"Here comes the good part," Lamar Laroque beamed. "Tell them what you're planning, Mr. Rochelle."

"Not just any casino," Sylvan Rochelle replied, "but a *giant* casino. One of the largest in the world. Fifty acres of sculptured gardens and grounds, four thousand hotel rooms, one hundred and seventy thousand square feet of gambling on three levels, and eleven thousand employees."

"Now tell them where this dream might go," Lamar Laroque said.

"Orlando would have been interesting, but we feared opposition from Disney. Yet such a central location would be essential."

"With good road connections," Lamar Laroque interjected. "Like the Bee Line from Orlando and Tampa, and 95 down to Miami and up to Jacksonville."

"Cocoa Beach?" Barry Tadlock's eyes were on full alert. "You're talking about Cocoa Beach?"

"The operative word here is maybe," Laroque cautioned.

"Brevard County is one of several regions under consideration," Rochelle hedged.

"Eleven thousand employees," Laroque repeated. "Gambling's the most labor-intensive business in the world. High-paying, too. Think what that would do for your county." A longish pause, then, "Now take a guess what your major stumbling block might be."

"Grey Spenser," Barry said. "My father-in-law."

"The man has gone from being just another noisy troublemaker to a major thorn in our side," Laroque said, no longer smiling.

"He is organizing these church groups all up and down the coast, rallying opposition to legalized gambling. Those are becoming as pesky as a hive of bees. It's time to knock out their king bee, Barry. And for this we need your help. Now."

Barry looked vastly uncomfortable. "I don't —"

"Our first-phase investment," Rochelle interrupted, "would be close to three hundred million dollars."

"And eleven thousand jobs," Lamar Laroque repeated. "Now don't you think that's enough of a reason to put a lid on that troublesome old man?"

"I would also feel more comfortable knowing my casino's legal affairs were being handled by someone of stature within the local community," Sylvan Rochelle continued.

"Which means you, Barry," Lamar Laroque said, rising to his feet. "Now why don't you run on home and see if your daddy-in-law might be willing to soften his tone a little. Just until after the legislature has its vote. After that he can go back to banging his little tin drum."

Arriving back home that night was like slipping out of somebody else's clothes.

Chase drove the Bee Line from the Orlando airport to Cocoa Beach in record time. He pulled into his darkened driveway, cut off the engine, and sat listening to the night. Crickets and sea breeze and rattling palms, a hooting owl trying to scare up dinner, music from the diner down at the corner of his cul-de-sac. Home sounds. Far removed from the shouts and the screams and the gunfire he knew he would carry for a long time to come.

Chase stepped from the car, popped the trunk, and stopped. He stood looking down at the bag containing Carlotta's diskettes. For some reason he felt hesitant about picking it up, carrying it inside his home. As though the act itself would be a commitment, an entry into the unknown. He pushed the thoughts aside, scooped up everything, shut the trunk with his elbow, and walked toward the house.

His father had built their home three winters after their arrival, and they had moved in on Chase's twelfth birthday. It was made of white oak clapboard, tougher in this climate than the nails that held it in place. The roof was cedar shingle, weathered by seventeen years of rain and wind and salt to a dry gray crown. The interior walls were cork, the floors heart of pine, the cabinets and furniture fashioned by Chase and his father from a variety of local woods — elm and birch and even a little willow, left to dry for four solid years before they used it to frame the glass-fronted bookshelves in the main hall.

They had still been building and working and planning together when the semi had crossed the temporary markers where the city had been reconstructing the causeway and pushed both his mom and dad into a watery grave. Ever since, Chase had been meaning to get back to the unfinished work, but never had. It had taken him almost a full year to move down from his old garage apartment and into the main house, and he had only done it then because of all the locals nosing around, hinting at how such good space was going to waste when so many people would love to rent it from him. Nobody else was ever going to live in his parents' house. Not while he was alive.

Chase left the lights off, maneuvering through the house by memory and the glimmer of illumination coming through the big picture window. Beyond stretched the Banana River and farther still the carnival lights of Merritt Island. When they first moved in, stars had provided the only nighttime illumination. Now the island alone supported a population of almost ten thousand people, a fifth of Cocoa's total.

Chase's father had operated a dry-goods store in an old-fashioned strip shopping center, one of those stores that stocked a little of everything, if only the customer knew where to look. He had shown the remarkable good sense to sell out when Home Depot started its growth-through-acquisitions spree. Chase and his mother had worried long and hard how his father, who always started work at five and finished by personally closing the shop six nights a week, would adjust to doing nothing. Within a month they could scarcely remember a time when he had done anything else.

Chase had inherited his father's quiet manner and his mother's love of people, his father's flexibility and his mother's sense of humor, his father's love of wood and his mother's love of water. That was why they had waited an extra year to build, waited until they could afford a lot with water frontage, even when it meant settling for a smaller home. What was the use of a bigger place, his mother had constantly urged, when all she'd want was to be somewhere else? She had filled the walls with her pictures of water birds and her seashell collages and the entire house with the sound of her laughter. It had been a happy home. The rooms still echoed Chase's lingering loss.

He pulled the telephone out onto the back porch and made his five-hundredth mental note to see about buying a portable. His problem was, he didn't really care for phones. But he needed to make this call.

There was scarcely time for the first ring to finish before a rough-edged voice said, "Narcotics."

"This is Chase Bennett. Can I speak to Carlotta Krepps, please."

"Chase, yeah, hey, that was some catch you made in the ninth."

"Is that Jack?"

"The one and only. Hang on a sec." The phone clicked to hold. When it was picked up again, the background noise had died to a low murmur. "Carlotta's not here, Chase. Didn't she tell you?"

"I'm back in Cocoa Beach, just this second walked in the door. Tell me what?"

"Don't know all that much myself. I've been calling her house every hour since she left, but there hasn't been any answer. As of five this afternoon she's down as having been put on administrative leave."

A cold knot of foreboding coalesced just below his rib cage. "What is that?"

"Vacation, internal investigation, witness

protection or dead, take your pick."

The knot tightened. "Dead?"

"Bad joke. Well, not totally. Fellow last year in vice got into something over his head, the Internal boys passed it around that he was on admin leave for a week or so, then it turned out he'd gotten caught in the middle of a deal, only he was on the wrong side at the time." The voice lowered a notch. "Carlotta didn't say anything to you?"

"She took me to the airport, dropped me off, said she was late for work." By now the knot had turned to stone and was pinning him to the chair. "What's going on up there?"

"All I know is there was some major flak upstairs right after she showed up this afternoon. I mean major. Something about tampering with evidence, I dunno. Didn't sound like Carlotta, she's always been tops at stuff like that. Anyway, she stormed out of here not a half hour later, didn't say a word to anybody. Then the brass were down here, heard she was gone, and sort of went berserk. I mean, it was a good time to be elsewhere. Then the lieutenant comes in, says she's out on indefinite admin leave and be ready for a visit from Internal Affairs."

Chase thought of the nylon bag at the back of his closet, tried to think of something to say, could only come up with, "If you hear anything —"

"I was about to say the same thing. Carlotta's told me a lot about you. Sounds like you two were pretty close. I think a lot of the kid, been sorta looking after her since her partner took a hit."

There was a rise in the level of background noise, and suddenly Jack's attention was elsewhere. "Gotta go. Look, it's probably nothing. Carlotta's first rate, she can take care of herself. Give me a call sometime tomorrow, I'll let you know what I've heard."

3

It was lunchtime Saturday before hunger and an empty larder drove Chase from the house. He had spent the morning on the phone. Every fifteen minutes or so he had tried Carlotta's home, calling so often he had long since memorized her answering machine's message. Two calls to Jack Sproul had proven equally futile.

He decided to try a new restaurant, something he often did before taking clients. The newcomer was an up-market riverside place of striped awnings and wicker furniture and lots of glass. Chase walked in with his worries and a double armload of newspapers that had been delivered while he had been in Washington, sat down, spotted an approaching waitress, and felt his entire world focus upon the moment.

Her short bouncy hair was somewhere between brown and red and gold, a shade he had never seen before, not even thought of. She was what people now called full-figured. Casually stylish baggy clothes and a tall frame, not much shorter than his, kept her from looking heavy. Her eyes were not just gray, they were many grays, dark at the rims, then progressively lighter around the pupil. They were big eyes, held open wide, like a porcelain doll.

As she reeled off her list of salad dressings, he decided she was not sad, not really, more like watchful. Solemn. A woman of many depths. Then she caught him off guard by asking which dressing he wanted, and he had to reply. "The middle one."

She nodded solemnly, as though understanding all that was not yet said between them. "It took me a month before I could even pronounce half of them."

"Which one do you go for?"

"I'm just a country girl," she replied. "I keep a jar of homemade ranch back in the fridge."

"I'll have some of that."

"My private store?"

"I'm a big tipper," Chase said. "Why don't you have on a name tag like the others?"

"Because my name is my own," she replied. "I choose who I give it to, and when."

"You don't end your little spiel with, my name is whatever, don't hesitate to call me and all that?"

"Nobody ever listens to that stuff unless they're trying to put the moves on. If they insist, I use whatever name comes into my head."

"Except . . ."

"Right. Except the one I'm not going to say to you."

"Yet," Chase amended. "Will you at least tell me what you're doing here? I mean, there's a lot more than waitress written in that face of yours. And I've got a hunch you're not really a country girl."

She opened her mouth, closed it, breathed out the denial he was afraid she would give him, and replied, "I'm going to school nights, studying finance and banking at SFCC."

SFCC stood for South Florida Community College, a local school gradually building a statewide name for its business department. "A banker," he said. "I hadn't expected that."

"Why not?"

"You look like you want to see everything. Drink it all in." He held his own gaze steady, although it was hard. Something in her eyes left him feeling naked. "I would have thought you'd be studying something like art, use the painting to make room for whatever you're going to see next."

"You don't know me at all." Not spoken in protest, though. An observation.

"You don't know how rare it is to find

somebody who really wants to see with their heart as well as their eyes," he persisted. "Especially around here."

This time she did not object. "This is home for you?"

A trace of accent, but he couldn't tell from where. He nodded, reluctant to disturb the flow of conversation by asking. Instead he said, "Most of the Cocoa Beach locals keep a permanent tourist mentality. They don't want to see anything except what's nice. They work to strain out everything bad before it hits them."

"You don't like tourists, is that what you're saying?"

"That's not it at all," he said, the patience coming easy, wanting to be understood. "They've made this place come alive, brought it from the Civil War to the twenty-first century in less than twenty years. But it's one thing to take a couple of weeks off from real life, leave the pressures and the worries behind, soak in the sun, take time to heal. It's another thing entirely to fashion your whole life around that mentality."

"I think I see," she said, and it seemed to him that her gaze opened up even further. Down to the heart. Willing to accept him as someone more than just another bored customer out to spin whatever web would work.

"The locals aren't tourists," he said, and felt as though he was sharing his deepest thoughts with this stranger he had only known for what, maybe ten minutes. Feeling himself taking an interest for the first time in more than a year. Wondering if this was the girl who would finally, finally be strong enough and wise enough to lift the stone from his heart. "They pretend they are, though, and after a while they forget they're pretending. They start really believing that life can be made up of two-week romances, endless parties, everything that makes for a good vacation. They wind up unable to feel very much for anybody or hold on to anything for very long — a job, a family, a discipline, a commitment, whatever. Then one day they wake up and realize that it isn't as much fun as it once was, and they don't understand what's gone wrong."

"So you don't like it here." She leaned up against the booth's opposite side, parking herself, getting as comfortable as her job would permit. Totally involved now.

"I love it here. It's just —" And then the bubble rose, the first of those that he had been holding down for so long he had lost the words and could remember only the pain. "I just get lonely sometimes for somebody who could see it all with me and still be there after the vacation time is over."

She inspected him for a long, cautious moment. "All right."

"What is?"

"You were going to ask me out, wasn't that where you were headed?"

Suddenly it was difficult to find breath. "Yes."

"Dinner tonight would be fine, thank you." She pulled out her pad and pen and scribbled. She tore off the paper, handed it over, and said, "Here's my number in case you need to reach me this afternoon. Otherwise you can pick me up right here."

He read the sloping script. "Kaitlyn."

"That's right. Kaitlyn Picard. What's yours?"

"Chase. Chase Bennett."

"Is that a nickname?"

"No."

"Then it sounds very old and very family."

"It is. Both."

She smiled for the very first time, and Chase felt an unaccustomed lurch in his chest. She said, "I like your name, Chase Bennett. Seven o'clock. I also like my men to be on time."

His other car was a truck.

Chase drove over the 520 causeway and

into the sprawling big-little city of Cocoa. His truck was, to his mind, the perfect beach transport. The Ford had a rumbling V-8, four-wheel drive, comfortable cab, air conditioning, and just enough rust to have made it a bargain. The frame was solid, and the engine purred like a big cat. Chase was actually glad about the rust. It kept him from having to worry about upkeep. Here was a truck he could drive until it guzzled its last gallon, then walk away from it happy.

Linda Armacost hated it almost as much as she did his secretary.

Chase groaned at the sight of her car parked outside his office. The new chamber president seldom appeared around his Cocoa office, and since her arrival he had avoided the main chamber offices in Melbourne like he would ringworm.

She was headed down the stairs as he was coming up. Hiding his thoughts and his gaze behind his shades, he did his best to sound the eager employee. "Linda, what a nice surprise. What brings you up this way on a Saturday?"

"Something came up in Tallahassee yesterday. I needed a few things." Her briefcase was stuffed to overflowing with promotional brochures. She surveyed the truck. "I thought I told you to start driving one of the chamber vehicles."

"A Caprice is not a vehicle," Chase replied. "It's a boat with wheels. I like to keep my boats in the water where they belong. Besides, it's Saturday. Time off. Freedom from rules and regulations, remember?"

Sunlight glinted off her own dark glasses. "You've got to do something about that outer office of yours."

"We've been through this before, Linda. Don't go on any more about Troy."

"People are talking, Chase. You know I don't like it when people begin talking."

"They've been talking since long before you got here." Chase tried a coaxing tone. "Look, Troy happens to be the perfect secretary. He types faster than I can talk, remembers everybody's name and position, never has to be told anything twice, and he has a perfect attitude on the phone. Better than me."

"Troy also happens to be a man. A very big man."

"So? He can't help that."

"Try to see it from my side, okay? Let's say we happen to have this major player, he comes walking into your office expecting to be met by a totally professional team."

"Troy is a total professional," Chase insisted, and stopped himself from adding, "a lot more than you, sunshine."

"Wait, now, let me finish. So in the gentleman comes, checkbook burning a hole in his back pocket, ready to invest millions in our little community. And what does he find? A cheerful smile? A warm welcome?"

"Troy welcomes everybody terrifically well, he's got the patience of Job, and you need Ray-Bans to stare at his smile."

"No, what they find," she continued grimly, "is a seven-foot gorilla with lizard skin and white hair."

"Six-six," Chase corrected. "His skin got that texture from all the time he spent in Hawaii. And he can't help the color of his hair any more than you can. He's naturally very blond, and the sea has bleached it out."

"A surfer — no, let me correct myself — a *giant* surfer acting as secretary to our Vice-President for Regional Development does not fit with the image the chamber wishes to have portrayed."

"Troy stays."

"Over my dead body."

"Don't push it," Chase warned. "Troy stays. He is a good secretary and he is a good friend. He stays."

"We'll see about that."

Chase watched her storm to her car and

drive away, then sighed his way up the stairs to his office.

The county's regional development office occupied part of a U-shaped courtyard built in the late twenties, one of the first office centers in the village of Cocoa. Chase had been promoted to regional development officer the year Cocoa Village, as the old downtown section was now known, had undergone its face-lift. When the chamber decided to place this department closer to the county center rather than in the bigger city of Melbourne farther south, Chase had fought tooth and nail to avoid being encased in a modern glass and concrete structure. What they needed to show, he insisted, was continuity. What place better exemplified this than the oldest portion of Brevard County's oldest town? Moving into the newly renovated office had marked many things for Chase Bennett, including his relative freedom to act at will. It had also marked his ongoing battle with chamber officials who resented his independence and strived to bring him tighter into the fold.

Chase pushed through the outer door, paused, and admitted to himself that Troy Keeler was indeed a very big man.

He looked like a living, breathing Hulk, only more handsome. His skin had been

56

toasted a permanent golden brown by years of living in climates where rain was almost as rare as cold weather. His long white hair was held neatly in an authentic Navajo silver and turquoise clasp. His knit shirt bulged with sea-hewn muscles. Chase had never seen Troy in a tie. He doubted there were many dress shirts with a collar large enough to encircle that neck.

Seated behind his undersized secretary's desk, Troy Keeler stopped traffic. But those who were willing to look behind the man's incredible size and strength were struck by other facts.

For one thing, Troy Keeler possessed the kindest eyes and softest voice of any man they knew. Second, he was a man who radiated contentment. Despite his intelligence, he lacked the first ounce of personal ambition.

He was also a perfect secretary.

Chase took a breath of the air-conditioned comfort. "Did somebody change the days on me? Last I looked it was Saturday."

"I was out most of yesterday looking after the kids. Everybody's down with the flu except me. Came in for a couple of hours of makeup. How was Washington?"

"Interesting. Exhausting." Chase looked back out the door. "I just had a run-in with our new commander in chief."

"I know." Troy was also one of the few people Chase had ever met who could actually type at full speed and carry on a conversation at the same time. "She was in and out of here faster than a summer squall. Loaded herself down with copies of all the development and promotional material we have and took off."

Chase looked back out the door. "Any idea what's gotten her back up?"

"All I can tell you is when I asked her how it went in Tallahassee, she looked like the cat that swallowed the canary." He lifted huge hands from the computer keyboard and hefted a pile of envelopes. "The junk mail is on your desk. Two urgent messages. Matt was down here yesterday, said he needed ten minutes of your time."

His old friend Matthew Pembroke was now an up-and-comer in the state attorney general's office. Two years earlier his work had forced him to move his family to Tallahassee. "He's probably already headed back west. I'll call him Monday."

"Holiday," Troy reminded him.

"Oh, right. The other?"

"Miss Marie. Wanted to know why you hadn't returned her calls."

"What calls?"

"The ones that started about an hour after you left. I explained that you were up in Washington. She wanted to know how you would dare leave the state without asking her permission."

Chase had to smile. Marie Hale had been his ninth-grade science teacher, his mother's best friend, and the first true eccentric Chase had ever known. Her husband, a major real estate developer, had died young, some said driven to an early grave by his wife's skewed perspective. She remained one of his very favorite people.

"How urgent is urgent?"

"It took me ten minutes to convince her not to meet your plane last night. She said to tell you that if you were not over first thing today that you should expect not to be able to sit down for a week."

"Sounds serious." He flipped through his mail, announced, "I have a date tonight." Troy's silence finally made him raise his eyes. "You can lift your jaw off the desk now."

"I'm just surprised. And delighted. Chen will be very pleased." Chen was Troy's wife, a Hawaiian-Chinese pixie who worried constantly about Chase's preference for solitude.

"It's just a date, Troy."

59

"Your first in what, a year?"

"Not that long."

"Long enough."

Chase dug a slip of paper from his pocket. "You've heard me talk about Carlotta Krepps, haven't you?"

"The cop in D.C. Sure."

"I can't find her. Do me a favor, try this number every once in a while. If you get in touch, make sure everything's okay and ask her for a time when I can call her back, okay?"

"No problem. Anything wrong?"

"I'm not sure." He thought back to the night and the projects, memories which were both fresh and years away from the sunlight and the calm and the normality here. "I better go see to Miss Marie. Have a good weekend, tell Chen and the kids I said hello and I hope they're better soon. I'll see you Tuesday."

Miss Marie's house was something out of the mad scientist's guidebook to better living. The ceilings and upper walls were decked out with fishnet and seashells. Where the nets stopped the books began. Chase had figured there were maybe fifty books per yard of shelf; with more than four hundred yards of shelves running through the living room and kitchen and hallways and den and even the glassed-in side porch, that made twenty thousand books. He also knew the upstairs held two more rooms so full of books she could no longer enter them.

The living room held five pieces of furniture: two lumpy chairs, a desk, a television, and a computer. The computer worked. The television had not functioned since the year of her forced retirement from the Brevard County school system. That winter she had listened to the local newscaster mispronounce Czechoslovakia three different ways and blasted it with her late husband's twelve-gauge shotgun. She had subsequently made the weekend papers by suing the station for the cost of a new television, claiming their newscaster was bad enough to drive anyone around the bend. The school system had at that point decided it was time for a parting of the ways, despite the fact that she was considered one of Florida's finest science teachers and had sent an even dozen of her students to the lofty heights of MIT.

The den and the sunroom saw duty as her at-home lab, where she spent her days studying the ecological effects of industrial waste on local flora and fauna. The entire house stunk of ammonia and petroleum sludge. Chase found her bent over a test tube that boiled and smoked like something out of a fifties horror flick. "This place smells awful, Marie."

"So hold your nose." She gave a smile her best shot. "How are you, boy?"

"You're always cooking up something that either threatens to eat out my eyes or blow up in my face. Why can't you spend your time baking cookies and doing other things that grannies are supposed to do?"

"I hate sweets and I'm not anybody's granny. Is that what you came here for, to mess up a perfectly fine day?"

"You were the one who said it was urgent."

"A likely story." She shook her head and bent back over her apparatus. "You always were destined for no good."

"I thought you considered me your favorite."

"Favorite my left foot. The only reason I passed you was to get you out of my hair. What there was left, anyway, after you almost burned it all off."

"That explosion was an accident."

"Humph. As was the one that burst the pipes in the principal's toilet, I suppose."

He opened his mouth to deny it, as he had

since she had first confronted him fifteen years before. But today he let the grin show through. "I wish you could have seen it, Marie."

She turned, looked, sniffed, "Decided to come clean, have you. Had to happen, I suppose. Guilty conscience certainly does eat at a body. I always knew it was you. Ought to go back and flunk you for spite."

"It was your fault, really. You remember telling the class how high compression would increase the power of an explosion?"

"That is the one thing you took away from my class, was it? Well, I won't be blamed for this, nor for any other delinquent act you perpetrate."

"I stuffed six cherry bombs into one of those plastic tubes you stick on the end of a vacuum cleaner, you know, the kind to clean in corners." He looked around the room, decided, "Well, maybe you don't."

"You will not get smart with me, young man. You're not too big to spend the rest of the weekend standing up."

"Anyway," he said, "I plugged the holes up with putty, left just this one fuse sticking through. Then I snuck in, lit the fuse, and dropped that sucker into the principal's toilet. I started to run, but decided I should do like you always said, wait and study the results and make careful notes of all my experiments."

"Experiments," Marie sniffed, but she had stopped her work and was listening carefully.

"It was beautiful," he said. "The floor sort of buckled up, and this water spout knocked all the tiles out of the ceiling. That was all I saw before I dived out the window and went crawling through the shrubs."

She examined him. "That was just after the principal convinced the board to fire me, wasn't it?"

"The very next week."

"You always were a dear. Misguided, but still a dear." She glanced at the wall timer and pulled the test tube from the burner. "Well, the rest of this can wait. Would you like some lemonade?"

"If you're sure it's coming from the right jar."

"Come along, then." She sidled out from behind the lab table, wincing at the movement.

"How are you doing?"

"Is that a polite nothingness or are you really concerned?"

He watched her stump into the kitchen on legs that wobbled under her insufficient weight. "You know I mean what I say."

"Yes, sincerity has always been one of your most endearing qualities." She used both hands to jerk open the ancient Frigidaire. "I am not well is the true answer."

"Your arthritis?" She had suffered from swollen, painful joints for as long as he had known her.

"Among other things. I may well be forced finally to do as the medics have long been insisting and begin slowing down."

He accepted the glass, asked, "Do you need me to take you to the clinic?"

"Thank you, dear, but I have all the willing little helpers one old lady could tolerate. Besides which, all Doc Sutton does for me these days is look worried and give me more pills which leave me in a fog." She swiped at a wayward strand of gray hair with an impatient gesture. "No, I have something more important in mind for you."

Something in her tone caught at his chest. "The land," he breathed. "You've decided to sell the land."

"I have been approached by a buyer. Or rather, a lawyer representing someone who wishes to purchase the property."

"That's nothing new."

"This one was different." She motioned him toward the kitchen table. On it rested a single manila folder. "Do you know someone called Sylvan Rochelle?"

"The name, sure. Who doesn't?"

"I most certainly did not. Although he seemed surprised when I expressed ignorance. Rochelle is big in the real estate business, is he?"

"One of the biggest. He doesn't take on anything except major projects." He waited until she had eased herself down before seating himself. "The Miami papers sort of dote on him. They call him Florida's most eligible bachelor. He's in his late thirties, attractive, single, from an old Swiss family. Also rich. Very rich. He's got four liners docked in Cocoa Beach, and rumors have it, he's negotiating to buy more. That's why I know about him."

"His lawyers have offered me a positively ridiculous sum of money for Ralph's land."

Chase leaned forward. "Just how ridiculous are we talking?"

Marie shifted her glass to one side. "I remember the first time someone approached me. It was just after Ralph passed on. They offered me two hundred and fifty thousand dollars. I laughed in their face. That land was all I had left of Ralph. You know his last two projects had not gone well, and he had become badly overstretched. We barely managed to hold on to the house and the land."

She looked at him. "How much do you think it would be worth now?"

"Hard to say," Chase mused, and tried to stop thinking of all the people who would drool at the chance to counter-bid. "You've got, what, almost sixty acres? Usually ocean-front property is priced by the frontage foot. But yours is shaped like a triangle, broadening out at the back. Another bad point is the gas storage facility over by the port. Whoever built there would have to leave, oh, ten acres or so as woodland to block off the tanks. No matter how you hide it, though, something that big and the way it'll smell in the wrong wind will detract from the value. Still, you have that section that looks out over the inlet, so you could see all the liners coming and going —"

"A ballpark figure would do quite nicely, Mr. Bennett."

"Close to three million," he guessed. "Even in this recession."

"So much," she said slowly.

"Maybe more."

"Ralph had planned to build a nursing home there. He always hated how most of them were in dismal surroundings, as though being elderly and infirm meant that natural beauty was no longer appreciated. It was to have been a gift, a sort of tithe of the profits he never made, a project he was not given time to build."

Chase nodded. "I remember him talking about it."

"Yes, well, I didn't ask you over for a walk down memory lane." She straightened and announced, "I have been offered fifteen million dollars."

He spent a moment struggling for breath before declaring, "It's not worth that much, Marie."

"You know it and I know it, but obviously someone else disagrees."

"There's a catch," Chase said. "There has to be."

"I found that lawyer fellow to be positively infuriating," she replied. "Claude Sorrens was his name. He paraded in here and set out their terms as though I would leap to do his bidding."

"What are you going to do?"

"I have already done it." Marie reached for the folder and slid it across to Chase. "Read and sign, please, sir."

Chase opened the folder, began reading the local document. "You're making me administrator of the property?"

"Full authority to dispose of it as you see fit," she said firmly. "I have neither the energy nor the inclination to get to the bottom of this." She pointed at the bottom of the page with one curved and knotted finger. "The final paragraph spells out your own remuneration. I expect you to earn every last penny."

"Why are you doing this?"

"Because I want to know what's going on. I positively detest the notion that someone would seek to make a mockery of my husband's legacy by using his property for some evil purpose."

"You can't say that for sure."

"Chase Bennett, nobody in his right mind would offer me such a sum unless he had something fishy in mind. You know that as well as I do." The arthritic hand rose to point directly at him. "Now, I expect you to go out there and find out just exactly what they're planning. And put a stop to it once and for all."

4

Speak softly and drive a hot car.

That was the line he handed anybody trying to give him a hard time. Chase drove a sixty-nine sky blue Camaro SS ragtop with white leather interior. He and his father had spent two years bringing the old car back to within an inch of its original glory. After his parents' accident, the car had spent the better part of a year stored in his garage.

Chase loved the way that car sounded, like a motorized symphony when the dual carbs opened up and bellowed with delight. The Hearst shifter with the chrome-plated T-bar was probably as over the top as the saddle soap he used on the leather interior. Not to mention the wax and chrome job he gave it every month.

"Wow," was what Kaitlyn said when she stepped out of the restaurant's front door and saw the car. She gave it a slow walking tour, then asked, "Does the radio play anything except country?"

"Don't tell me you've got a hangup against rednecks."

"Not the people, just the music. There are too many songs that go, my girl's broke down and my truck's run off with my best friend."

"In your case I think we can make an exception." He closed her door, walked around, seated himself. "Where would you like to go?"

She seemed genuinely surprised by the question. "You're letting me decide?"

"If you like. Sure."

Kaitlyn thought a moment. "I've heard some interesting things about a place called Fisherman's Wharf."

He knew a moment's panic. "You want to go there?"

"I think it would be nice." She looked at him. "You said I could choose."

He searched for something, anything, but could only come up with, "But it's Saturday."

"So?" Her expression went through a gradual change. "What is this, old flame night at the local hangout?"

"No, no, nothing like that." Defeated, he started the car, knowing there was only one way to get the night back on track. "Fisherman's Wharf is fine."

The place was an old-style Florida restaurant, a fisherman's shanty built on stilts and reached by a long, narrow plank pier. It was weather-beaten and faded, and the Indian River waters lapped cheerfully at the pilings all day and all night. Twenty years earlier, an enterprising local had purchased the building, glassed in the deck where hand-drawn nets had dried, and turned it into a restaurant. Fisherman's Wharf now offered some of the most spectacular sunsets and the finest food in all of the Space Coast. The locals had swiftly adopted it as their own.

Chase led Kaitlyn across the planked walkway, opened the screen door, and winced when the owner smiled and said, "Chase, great, wondering if you were ever gonna show up. Back for more punishment?"

He glanced around, saw the coast was clear. "Put us somewhere else tonight, Ty."

"Can't do it, buddy. More than my life's worth."

Aware that Kaitlyn's gaze was on him, he leaned closer. "Please, Ty. This is important."

"Hey, I would, but like, I've grown fond of my own skin. I'd rather wear it than watch Eunice tag it to the wall. You eat here, Eunice serves you. That's how it is."

"Ty —"

Further argument was cut off by a great black woman swooping down and enveloping Chase in a massive hug. "Chase, honey, you done made my evening." She released him, turned, planted hands on hips. "And who is this?"

"Eunice, this is Kaitlyn." Subdued. Resigned. Already tired.

"Pretty name. Is that foreign?"

"Not on me," Kaitlyn replied. "But I think it came from Ireland."

"Um-hmmm." She gave Kaitlyn a friendly nod. To Chase, "Looks like a nice one, honey. Come on, you two. Got you a table out on the edge, you can watch the sun go down."

"Enjoy," Ty said, turning to the next couple.

On the way through the restaurant Eunice said over her shoulder, "I've known Chase since he was just a little towheaded runt. His momma and I used to work together. Ain't he growed up nice and tall?"

"Yes, he has," Kaitlyn said, her eyes a questioning blank.

"Has Chase here told you about his problem yet?"

"Okay," Chase said. "We're leaving."

"I don't think so," Kaitlyn said. To Chase, "Have you told me?"

"Here now, ain't this a nice table? Just set yourself right there, honey, you'll get the best view." She waited until they had slid in, then said, "Chase-honey's always carried a little extra around the middle. He's a skinny boy, but you get his shirt off, right there it all is, just hanging on like he swallowed his bicycle tire and been blowing it up all day."

"I don't believe this is happening," Chase said to the window.

"You can't call him fat. Naw. Boy's gonna stay tall and yellow-haired and good-looking all his life. Got that from his daddy, now that was one handsome man. Kept a full head of hair till the day he passed over. Chase is just a touch on the heavy side is all." Eunice gave a fruity chuckle. "Somebody must of been giving him a hard time, though. He was in here last Saturday, same as usual. Started asking me how many calories everything had. Steak, baked potatoes, salad dressing, ice tea. Didn't slow him down none. Boy just wanted to know. Got down to desert, he even asked me how many calories was in hot pecan pie with ice cream. Know what I told him? All there is, sugar. Every last one." She laughed at her own joke. "What y'all want to eat tonight?"

"I'll have the boiled squid," Chase muttered.

"You won't have no such thing. We got us some nice fresh-caught grouper. I'll have chef blacken it up and serve it with two baked potatoes and extra sour cream, just how you like." To Kaitlyn, "Is Chase-honey your special beau?"

Chase groaned.

"I'm not sure." Watchful. Observant. Not giving much away.

"Well, take it from me, honey. He's a good boy. Don't matter none, him collecting that little belt of fat. He just got him a healthy appetite." Another deep chuckle. "There ain't a thing wrong with a man that's got hisself a healthy appetite, now, is there?"

"No." To Chase's surprise, Kaitlyn smiled back. Really smiled. "Are you from here?" she asked Eunice.

"Sure am, honey. One of the few. Chase here is what we call a semi-native. Sort of a grafted-on Floridian." She reached over and ruffled his hair. "Anybody this good-looking we definitely claim as one of our own." Back to Kaitlyn. "What you gonna eat tonight?"

"I think I'll take the same as him, only with one potato."

"You'll like it. I'll see chef makes it up good and spicy." Another smile at Chase. "Y'all have a good time now, hear?"

When she was gone and the silence lengthened, Kaitlyn said, "So tell me about yourself."

"I think you've already heard too much."

"I really want to know." She waited until he raised his eyes. "Please?"

Under the weight of his embarrassment, the last eight years collapsed into a tale of four short sentences. "My folks died the year I finished college at Gainesville. I started working at the Brevard Chamber of Commerce straight out of college, and I've been there ever since. I guess you could call me a roving fixer. I love my work, and I love the people I work around, most of them anyway."

"But what do you *do?*"

"I told you. I fix things." His discomfiture eased as he explained, "Say a company's got internal vandalism, I help them hire local security they can trust. A manufacturer is looking for a site to set up a new plant, hire workers, get his people settled in a new town — I do all of that. A construction job is mired in paperwork — that one happens a lot — first I find out if the bureaucrat is on the level, and then I sort of usher things through. No bribes. I don't do bribes, and I don't bend rules. But a lot of it is neither, just overworked, hot-tempered people who get up each other's noses. Most of the time they're ready to do whatever's necessary, long as somebody with a cool head comes in and talks with them."

"And that's you," she said.

"Or say a building project is about ready to hit the skids. I see if I can bring together people who can make it work." He turned mildly sheepish. "I get a commission for some of those."

"What's the matter with that?"

"Some people here and a lot of other chambers think it's wrong. But our board made a position and stuck me in it. Well, they made a position for me is probably closer to the truth."

"A tailor-made job," she said. "That must mean you're really good at it."

"I am," he said. No false modesty tonight. "The banks kick up a fuss sometimes, on account of they would like to get the cut themselves. Then they turn around and try to hire me. I pulled their fat out of the fire a couple of times in this recession, though, when they were ready to lose big on some projects that were going wrong fast. Now they pretty much leave me alone."

"Bet your boss doesn't like you having this independence."

He cocked his head. She was listening. And she was perceptive. "She hates it."

"She?"

"Linda Armacost is the new chamber

president. Lives life according to a flow chart. Having a sort-of employee who pays her lip service but doesn't answer directly to her drives Linda straight up the wall."

"How do you handle it?"

"I stay as far away from her as I can. My office is in another building. Another town, for that matter. And there's a guy who sort of runs interference. Grey Spenser. He's one of the biggest employers in the county. Runs Spenser Construction Supplies, Spenser Groves, some other stuff. Or did, until he became so involved in fighting the state's gambling legislation. The second month Linda was on the job, she started harping to the board about me, and Grey stood up and said, 'Lady, the only reason that boy doesn't have your job is because he didn't ask for it.' "

"Must be nice to have friends in high places."

"Sure is. So what about you?"

More guarded now. "What about me?"

"Have you —"

A voice beside them boomed, "Well, hey there, old son. Scoot on over and let me park it."

This time the groan was audible. "Not right now, Matt, okay?"

"Hey, is that any way to greet an old

buddy?" A tall black with the even features of a model and eyes that shone like live wires looked down at Kaitlyn. "You're new."

"Kaitlyn, meet Matthew Pembroke, assistant state attorney general."

"Hi. I told you, Slim, shift the weight. Got a hot one for you."

"Matt —"

But he was already down and shoving Chase sideways. "Has he told you about the time I took him to the Melbourne African Baptist Church, little old towheaded thing sitting there in a whole universe of black faces, and it turns out there's a guest preacher that Sunday, fellow shows up with a chest full of live snakes?"

"Not yet." Kaitlyn had returned to her watchful caution.

"Funny how I never could get him to come with me another time." He looked up, beamed a model's dazzling smile. "Aunt Eunice, my favorite woman in the whole wide world, how're you tonight?"

Eunice gave him a frown the size of a skillet. "What're you doing here, bothering these nice folks."

"Thank you, Eunice," Chase said.

"They asked me to sit here, didn't they, Kaitlyn — did I say that right?"

"Close enough."

"This here's a nice lady Chase is with for a change," Eunice snapped. "He don't need no help from you."

Kaitlyn looked at Chase. "For a change?"

"Figure of speech," Matthew said. "Old Chase has only been with one bad girl, far as I know, and I guess I know him about as good as anybody. Isn't that right, Slim?" He turned back to Eunice. "I'll have whatever they're having."

"I'll buy," Chase offered. "Long as you eat it somewhere else."

"Uh-oh, offering a bribe to a state official, that's a big no-no. You ought to know better. Good thing I'm not on duty."

Eunice asked, "You want me to throw him out?"

"Yes," Chase said.

"No," Kaitlyn said. "This is interesting."

"Hear that, Slim? Girl's got taste." To Kaitlyn, "Thank you. Eunice could toss a full-grown bear fifty yards with one hand tied behind her back."

Eunice humphed her reply. Matthew smiled at Chase. "My compliments, old son. I do believe there's hope for you yet." Then he asked Kaitlyn, "He told you about Sabine?"

"Matt," Chase moaned, "this is our first date."

"No," Kaitlyn replied. "He hasn't."

"Sabine Duprie," Matthew said with evident relish. Stopped to wink as Eunice came back and set down their water glasses. "Name like that brings to mind all sorts of stuff. Swampy bayous, toads big as my hand, slimy critters that eat bugs and croak all night."

"Her father was old Louisiana French," Eunice explained, looking down at them, clearly in no hurry to be elsewhere.

"So she said, anyway," Matthew corrected. "Only I wouldn't trust anything that gal said to have even a nodding acquaintance with the truth."

"Her parents were divorced," Eunice explained to Kaitlyn, ignoring the stream of patrons who had to weave their way around her. "Her father lived up north somewhere."

"Raiford State Prison, I imagine," Matthew offered. Then to Chase, who was holding his head, "You got a headache, Slim? Need Eunice to hustle you up an aspirin?"

"I never did like that girl," Eunice ruminated. " 'Specially after she hurt my boy. Huh. What a passel of worry and woe that woman was."

Chase continued his slumping slide farther down in his seat.

"Sabine was a vulture, only she hid in a size-six dress," Matthew said.

"Had all them lovely ways," Eunice agreed. "Nice dark hair, big brown eyes, pretty legs. She did have pretty legs, didn't she, Chase-honey."

Chase muttered something about not having noticed.

"Humph. You can go sell that one down the street." To Kaitlyn, "Hurt him bad. Real bad. Made his poor soul bleed for, my goodness, must've been over a year."

"You didn't like her long before that," Matthew said.

"I saw what was coming. Whole world could see it."

"Except me," Chase muttered.

"That's 'cause you were under a spell, old son," Matthew said cheerfully. To Kaitlyn, "Gotta watch out with old Slim here. Exterior may look pure Florida cracker, but down deep he's just an old romantic fool."

"Boy's got a heart too big for this world, and that's the pure and simple truth," Eunice said.

To Chase's permanent surprise and gratitude, Kaitlyn lowered her head so that she could catch his eyes and said quietly, "Sounds good to me."

The whole table held its breath for a moment, all caught up in seeing the birth of something new. And good. Finally Eunice turned away. "Let me go see if chef's fixing that fish up proper."

The moment dissolved into the relaxed happiness of strangers who find themselves becoming friends. Kaitlyn asked, "How did you two meet?"

"I came down here to live with Eunice when my momma got sick. Slim was the only kid I couldn't outrun," Matthew replied. "Not all the time, anyway. We raced against each other all through junior high and then high school, figured the battle wasn't over yet, so we went to Gainesville together and kept on there."

"Matthew was an alternate to the U.S. Olympic team one year," Chase said. "Two hundred and four hundred both."

"Only reason Chase didn't make it is he got all caught up in sailing. Slim's the only man I know who's gotten my wife out on the water. I suppose Jesus could too, but He hasn't asked her yet."

"Matthew showed up here the same year I did and picked on me from the day I arrived," Chase said. "The only reason I ran was because he promised he'd beat me up if I didn't."

"Couldn't see all that talent go to waste," Matthew said, winking at Kaitlyn. "Imagine my surprise when this little blond-headed kid pops out of nowhere and proceeds to run my poor hide right into the ground."

"I hated to fight," Chase said simply. "Only way to stay out of trouble was to run."

Kaitlyn asked Matthew, "And you're a lawyer?"

"Matthew is the youngest assistant AG in the history of the state," Chase said. "Won his first fifteen cases in a row."

"Should've won that next one too," Matthew said. "Guy walked on a technicality, went out, committed another felony, now I got him locked up for ten to twenty."

The owner appeared at Chase's elbow. "I almost forgot. You got a call here a couple of hours ago. A Miss Smith."

"This is like trying to eat in Grand Central Station," Chase said.

"Lady said it was important," he replied. "Something about the briefcase and extras she showed you. Since when did you start using this place as your office?"

Chase was already on his feet and moving for the front. "Be right back."

Matthew watched his friend move off. "Sure is nice to see a light back in that boy's eyes. Been quite a while. Can't remember the last time he's been out on a date."

Kaitlyn inspected him with a frank gaze.

"You think a lot of him."

"Let me tell you what kind of guy Chase Bennett is." Matthew leaned both elbows on the table, took on a conspiratorial tone. "There was this school church group we got involved with back in the early days, started by a fellow named Grey Spenser, that's a name you'll be hearing a lot of around these parts. Most of us stayed in touch down through the years. Anyway, Chase had been back from college about a year, still settling down at the chamber, people were just getting to know Chase the man instead of Chase the boy who went off to college. Then these two older guys, people we'd met through that group, they went into major crisis. We're talking ground-zero-type family battles, lawyers, the works.

"Colin Poyner, he was a master sergeant, served in Vietnam right there at the very last. Troy Keeler, well, Troy was a drifter. Lived for a while in Hawaii, came back with a cute island girl as a wife. Turns out these two fellows had started spending a lot of time in bars together. Staying gone all the time. Some fights, some women. It was getting worse."

Kaitlyn asked, "You know this much about everybody here?"

"Only the ones that count." He sipped his

water, said, "So the church gets together, tries to reconcile husbands and wives, tells these two fellows to find other company and stay out of the bars, even called a couple of prayer meetings. Good-hearted, but it didn't amount to a whole lot. Then Chase steps in. Doesn't tell anybody, don't guess many people even know what he did."

"But you do."

"Heard about it from Troy's wife. She's friends with Mildred, that's my wife. Anyway, Chase hunts these two guys out, starts spending time with them only place he can, in the bars. That got the church people talking, let me tell you. Chase doesn't pay it any mind, though. He just keeps on doing what he's doing.

"After a while, Chase learns that Colin worked with wood before he joined the army. So Chase pulls some strings, gets him a job as a carpenter with a local builder. Troy, now, that guy didn't have much going for him but an easy manner and a good heart. So what does Chase do but hire Troy as his very own secretary. Turned some heads, that one did, local chamber official with a blond giant for a secretary. But Troy made good on it. Went to night school, learned to type and handle a computer. Doesn't have a shred of ambition, probably doesn't even know what the word means. But he's the best secretary in the county, he's loyal to Chase, and his marriage is solid."

A shadow appeared above their table and a deep voice demanded, "Where's Chase at?"

"On the phone," Matthew said, exasperated. "Now if you'll excuse us, we were having a conversation."

Eunice glared at him, then asked Kaitlyn, "Is my boy bothering you?"

"I'm not sure," she replied.

"Well, if he starts in, you let me know, you hear?" To Matthew, "You best watch yourself, mister."

"I was just telling her what a nice guy Chase is."

"Boy's got a heart of pure gold. That's all you need to say." To Kaitlyn, "You look like a nice girl. That's good. Sure would be nice to see him settle down with a nice girl." Then she flung back at Matthew as she sailed off into the kitchen, "You best be watching your p's and q's, mister. You're not too old to get a piece of my mind."

Matthew subsided into silence. Kaitlyn watched him awhile, then asked, "Why are you telling me this?"

His dark features were as mobile as they

were handsome. "Because Chase Bennett is the best friend —" Then he straightened and wiped his features clear. "Here he comes."

Chase picked up the restaurant's counter phone, pulled its long cord free, pushed through the front door, and moved around to the relative quiet of the narrow side porch. He dialed the number on the slip, knew it was not one he had for Carlotta. But the voice that answered sounded like hers. Muffled, tired, maybe drugged, but still Carlotta. Probably. Since he wasn't totally sure he read off the name there by the number, "Miss, ah, Smith?"

"Don't say who this is." The words came out in a blurred rush. "Do you recognize my voice?"

"Of course. Where are you?"

"A hospital. Do you have the disks?"

"Yes. What —"

"Listen. You heard about my suspension?"

"Jack told me."

The voice sounded hoarse from strain and something else. Like she was talking around a mouthful of wadding. "They gave it all back."

"What?"

"The briefcase and the money. Can you believe it? Just handed it back, even before the guy's lawyer appeared in court. When they saw those disks weren't there, brother, was there ever a stink. Then I got home, and my place had been taken apart. Professional job. Every pillow, every mattress, every chair seat, all cut to shreds and the stuffing torn out. I called it in as a burglary. Had to. If I didn't report it, they would've known I'd taken the stuff. But the detective that came by took one look around and asked, who's after you?"

Chase leaned on an old hardwood banister, trying to take in what she was saying. With the sun making riotous colors along the horizon, the air filled with the scents of water and good food, laughter and chatter and the tinkle of cutlery on china floating through the nearby door — what he was hearing just didn't mesh. "Did you say hospital?"

"I'm coming to that. A couple of hours after the police cleared out of my place, I went for a bite, and somebody tried to run me down. I only saw it coming because by then I was all hyped up with nerves. No lights, just this car roaring out of nowhere straight for me. I jumped and rolled and they didn't get me, but I messed up my shoulder and my jaw on a wall. Didn't even notice it at the time. I was too busy running."

"Messed up how bad?"

"Don't worry about it. I checked myself in under an alias. Used an ID we had made up for some undercover work a while back."

"Do you want me to come?"

"No." Harsh and definite as she could make it. "Stay away from here. I'm going to hide out for a while. And, Chase, listen. If anybody comes by, I didn't send them. Whatever they tell you, they're not from me."

"What's going on, Carlotta?"

"I wish I knew. But I'm okay. I'm staying here awhile, it's safe and they want to check out a couple of things. Soon as I'm out, I have a friend up —" A pause, then, "Never mind. Someplace I can be safe. I should be there by the end of the week. It may be a while before I contact you again."

He felt as though he were living in two worlds, one of friends and a peaceful sundown and a date with a beautiful woman, and the other of darkness and chaos. "What do you want me to do with the disks?"

"I don't know." Another pause, then, "Looks like the white guy we picked up in the raid was a courier. Shouldn't have been there at all, went by just to pick something up from the other guy. Probably money. That's what I'm guessing. Just don't tell anybody else about this, okay? Not a soul."

"What about Matthew? He's here having dinner with me."

A long pause, then, "Don't be too upset if he can't help."

"What are you talking about? Matthew is a friend."

"He also happens to be a lawyer."

"What difference does that make?"

"Forget it. Just the cop in me that's talking." A silence. "I rather it stay just between us, though. There's nothing Matt can do to help me out of this mess, and it'd only be one more person who knows. Plus he might feel like he's got to bring in the feds."

"He might be right."

"Yeah?" Her voice was raw with worry. "And can you be absolutely certain he'd come up with somebody we can trust?"

Chase sighed an okay. "Who do you think is after you?"

"Who isn't? Look, I've got to go. If I come up with an idea for what you can do with the disks, I'll call you. Take care, Chase. You're a pal."

Chase carried his worries back to the table. He remained locked in his thoughts as Eunice appeared with a tray, swung it onto the fold-out table, and lifted three plates in front of them. Matthew took one look and said, "Did I order this?"

Eunice said to Kaitlyn, "My nephew's been a finicky eater since he was in diapers."

"That's libel. There's no call to libel your own kin." He used his fork to lift up the fish, inspected the bottom, asked, "Why is it all burnt?"

"You like, I'll go back and tell Chef you called his best blackened fish burnt." To Kaitlyn, "He's the only boy I ever seen pick his string beans up one by one." Eunice held up an imaginary bean, squinted her nose into a frown, and turned her fingers from side to side. "Then he'd line them up on his plate like little soldiers, wouldn't start eating till he'd inspected every one."

"Caterpillars," Matthew explained. "Got to be extra careful. One of them could sneak up, disguise himself like a green bean, and then where would you be?"

Kaitlyn took a bite, proclaimed, "Delicious."

Eunice beamed down at her. "Y'all enjoy it now."

Chase ate without tasting, felt eyes on him, looked up to find both his companions looking his way.

"Something on your mind?" Matthew asked.

It was right there on the tip of his tongue,

to tell him about Washington and Carlotta and the conversation, but Carlotta's warning held him back. "A little bad news."

Matthew nodded as though he understood perfectly, said between bites, "Had something I needed to tell you about, Slim. Kaitlyn, you mind if I talk three minutes of business?"

"Not if you don't mind me listening."

He smiled his approval, said to Chase, "Caught wind of a whale of a case, charges to be filed in Melbourne next week. Insurance fraud. One of these incorporated doctor-medical groups down here been billing a company for renting wheelchairs. Got it all worked out with a local wheelchair company. They bill insurance companies or Medicaid for a power chair, then give these old folks a regular push-starter." To Kaitlyn, "See, power chairs go for four thousand a year, non-motorized you can buy for something like eight hundred. They're pocketing close to a half-million a year. Perfect scam."

Chase tried to show interest but could not push aside the swirling commotion in his head.

"These old folks don't check their insurance payouts," Matthew continued, "don't know enough to complain about not getting a power chair. Not most of them, anyway.

93

But we had this one old gal, a retired accountant. She calls us up last year and says maybe we ought to check it out. I mean to tell you, we were on that one like hogs on the trough. Got all six doctors with their John Henrys on the fake orders. Seeing these patients pushing themselves in and out of the clinic time after time, no way they're not gonna know what's happening."

Suddenly Chase was hit with a thought as powerful as a searchlight. It split the chaos of his mind with lightning clarity. Everything was tied together. Matthew, Kaitlyn, Marie and her property, the night, the weekend, Carlotta, even this story about the doctors, everything. The thought made no sense whatsoever, but it was too powerful to ignore. It gave him strength to focus. "You're telling me six Cocoa Beach doctors are about to be brought up on felony charges?"

Matthew gave Kaitlyn a self-satisfied beam. "Told you there weren't no ticks on this man." To Chase, "You got it, old son. And guess who the doctors have chosen as their defending attorney."

His sense of prescient focus tightened even further. "Not Barry."

"None other." To Kaitlyn, "Bartholomew Tadlock looks like a world-class lawyer, and he talks a good game. Good enough to get him elected to the state senate. But not a second time. Too many people have figured out he's got less bite than a toothless dog. He also wins about as many cases as the Dolphins have shutouts. Barry gets most of his work by being in the right place at the right time."

"Barry is also Grey Spenser's son-in-law," Chase explained.

"Your ally on the chamber," Kaitlyn said, then to Matthew, "and the one who led the church group."

Chase looked at Matthew. "You told her about church?"

"Yeah, old Grey thinks about as much of Barry as I do," Matthew said. "Which isn't a lot." To Chase, "Looks like the level of medical care in some of our correctional institutions is about to take a major step up. That is, unless you can do something to change things."

"I'll talk to them."

"Didn't hear this from me, you understand. Wouldn't do any of us any good to have the press hear how the prosecuting attorney had been giving advice to the defendants." To Kaitlyn, "The AG's office isn't supposed to warn defendants they've hired Bozo the Clown for their lawyer. That's what those fancy law schools call a major no-no."

"Losing six doctors in one fell swoop would be a total disaster to a town our size, especially one playing host six months a year to a national convention of elderly people," Chase explained, trying hard to hold on to the here and now.

"Even if those jokers do deserve being locked up for a short lifetime." Matthew set down his fork. Somehow he had managed to inhale his entire plate while talking continually. "Well, I'm giving a policy speech tomorrow, that's why I'm not back in Tallahassee playing catch with the kids. Got to go polish my act. Good to meet you, Kaitlyn. Congratulations, Slim. Looks like you found yourself a keeper."

When he was gone, Kaitlyn said, "I feel like I've been sitting across from a whirlwind."

"Yeah, Matthew's something."

"Now I see why you were concerned about bringing me here."

He looked at her, felt once again the rise of chaos. Too much, too fast, and none of it handled well. Especially this first night with Kaitlyn. "Have I lost it?"

"Lost what?"

"You. Us."

Time stretched to agonizing slowness before she reached across and took his hand. A look from those wonderful eyes, then, "They really care for you. Do you know how rare that is?"

He refused to let the hand go. "Does that mean I get another chance?"

She nodded slowly, her eyes locked on his. "If you like."

"I like," he replied. "A lot."

5

Chase greeted the next morning as he often did, coffee in hand, strolling through his postage stamp of a backyard, looking out over the water, studying the wind and sky, putting plans for his day in order. Sometimes praying. But not so often now as a year before. Back then, he had prayed daily, asking for something, one particular thing, hoping against hope for a gift he wanted more than anything, almost more than life itself. When it did not come, prayer and a lot of other things lost meaning.

Chase took another sip from his mug and decided that the weatherman had it right for once. The wind would drift feather light around the compass for much of today, then tomorrow it would take the bit between its teeth and blow strong and steady from the sea. No sailing today, but tomorrow for sure. It was a sign of spring's arrival in central Florida, this tentative warm spell followed by a blustery nor'easter. Chase checked his watch, flicked his remaining coffee out over the river, and headed in for tie and jacket before driving to church.

January and February were the uncertain months in central Florida. Sometimes winter forgot herself and tried to enter the state. But down deep she knew she did not belong, and soon enough would tuck away in flustered shame.

March was the month of change, with high ocean winds and rowdy surf and temperatures all over the place. Sailing in such days required an iron grip and steady nerves. Then with April came spring, and the many Florida worlds all began to change.

The nicest thing about spring was that the Florida population shrunk by half. Come the first muggy days of late April, Indiana and Ohio and Vermont license plates would clog the northbound lanes, the snowbirds fleeing as fast as their Dunlops would take them. The land would smolder for a few days, giving just a taste of the steamy summer to come. The locals usually slept through it all. Then everything would cool off for a final spring fling. Those were the best days of all. People emerged from their beds and greeted neighbors as if they were rising from a winter's hibernation. They smiled across supermarket counters, silently congratulating each other for having made it through another winter invasion.

The pace of life eased. Tension slipped from foreheads and voices. Folks wished each other a nice day and meant it.

On his way to church, Chase pulled in at the local beach health center, hoping that a Sunday morning would make for a quick in and out.

The clinic was a freestanding structure of plaster, concrete, and reflective glass. The interior was refrigerated to an uncomfortable degree and decorated with typical doctor's office sterility. Even on an early Sunday morning, the overly large waiting room was crowded with patients.

He crossed over to the receptionist's window. "My name is Chase Bennett, I'm with the local chamber of commerce. I need to speak with one of the doctors."

The receptionist, a brassy-haired retiree who wished she no longer had to work, did not even look up. "I'll take your name, and you'll have to wait," she said by rote. "The doctors do not accept appointments. It's first come, first served. The wait is about an hour and a half today."

Chase leaned through the window and spoke as quietly as he could. "I'm not here because I'm sick. I'm here to try to keep your bosses out of jail."

At that she jerked her head up and examined him through sequined frames. "What did you say your name was?"

"Bennett. They'll want to see me. I promise."

A few minutes later, a white-jacketed young man with angry dark eyes opened the side door. "Mr. Bennett?"

"That's right."

"In here." The doctor waited until the door had closed behind Chase before demanding, "What's this all about?"

"Your lawyer is Bartholomew Tadlock, am I right?"

Unease joined anger in the man's gaze. "I don't know what you're talking about."

"Of course not," Chase agreed, irritation clipping his words. "Look, so far as I know, Bartholomew Tadlock has never won a major court case in his entire life. In case you're interested in staying out of jail, you need to think about getting yourself a different lawyer. And if you tell anybody I said this, I'll deny it."

Angry eyes darted nervously. "Bartholomew Tadlock came highly recommended."

"Sure he did. By guys who've used him on real estate deals, not to defend them in criminal court." Chase found he could bear to stay no longer. "If you want a second opinion, check with his father-in-law, Grey Spenser."

As Chase opened the door, the doctor said defiantly, "I haven't done anything wrong."

Chase let the door slip out of his fingers and allowed a trace of his anger to show. "It's guys like you and your partners that give Florida medicine a bad name. I went to a conference in Atlanta last year, know what they called this place? The Beirut of American health care." He opened the door a second time. "I'm only sorry we need you too much to let you sink."

Chase pulled into the church parking lot, climbed from the truck, greeted his friend Colin Poyner with, "What is that hanging around your neck?"

The man's habitually grim expression was longer than usual. "A noose."

Chase turned his grin toward Colin's wife, Samantha. "You trying to make that man fit for society?"

"Shoot. Take more than a tie to do that." She stood on tiptoe to buss Chase's cheek. "How you been keeping?"

"Fair to middling."

"I heard it's better than that," Colin said. "I even heard talk about a certain young lady you been wining and dining."

"News travels fast."

"That sort does," she agreed.

"Lady had some sort of funny foreign name," Colin offered. "What was it again?"

"Kaitlyn," Chase said, and felt his heart kick to higher gear just from saying the word.

Colin rearranged the heavy lines of his face into a smile. "Look at the boy. Says the gal's name, face lights up like the harbor lights."

Samantha nodded approval. "You about ready to come out of your shell?"

Chase started to deny it, then decided on honesty. "Maybe so."

"It's time you did," Samantha went on. "You been pining over that other gal for too long. She wasn't worth it."

"I wouldn't have traded her for day-old chum," Colin agreed.

Chase inspected his old friend, dressed in ancient but freshly pressed khakis, passingly clean lace-up boots, and a white shirt from a bygone era. The tie was canted slightly to one side, the knot bunched up under the collar. His hair was plastered down with a liberal dressing of oil. It was a testimony to his wife's love and patient attention that he had given Sunday dress a try at all. Chase asked, "How have you been keeping?"

Ancient shadows passed over his eyes like clouds scuttling across a wind-torn sky. "Enduring."

"Not good," Chase interpreted.

"A cowboy is born with a broken heart. You ought to know that by now." Colin swiped at his hair, the simple movement causing his muscles to bunch and knot under his shirt. "Least I'm not drinking."

"Thanks to you, Chase," Samantha said quietly, then slipped her hand into her husband's. "Come on, honey. Let's go find us a seat."

Chase started up after them, then stopped. "Save me a place, I'll join you in a minute."

Grey Spenser was stationed at his usual spot by the steps leading up to the church's main entrance. His hands were full of leaflets, and people skirted a wide circle around him. Grey Spenser was too powerful to be totally ignored, so most tossed overloud howdies his way as they scurried past. But few approached. To strike up a casual conversation with Grey Spenser these days meant having their ear bent out of shape. Especially on Sunday.

Still, he stood there. Isolated by his fervor for a cause others had long since given up on. Determined to do all he could with what he had.

To his surprise, Chase felt drawn toward Grey, a gentle inner urging to walk over. He knew the man's arguments like a litany, ones heard so often they meant next to nothing anymore. Still he went, for reasons he could not for the life of him understand. "How're you, Grey?"

The beefy, aging man started, unaccustomed to being approached so casually there before church. Clearly he had come to take his isolation as a permanent state. "Not so well, Chase. Not so well. A third group's declared their own campaign. Know how much they've already collected? Four million dollars in official contributions. In just one week."

Chase nodded as though he understood it all. For the past four months Grey Spenser had put his businesses aside and worked on nothing but the statewide campaign against casino gambling. Organizing support drives, speaking all over the state, debating the issue on television, spending hefty amounts of his own hard-earned savings on brochures and advertisements and posters and ammunition. He sometimes forgot that others did not follow the battle as closely. "Who're the players?"

"Two big groups have been pushing hard for almost six months now. The out-of-state companies are pressing for a 'select number' of casinos, they call it. Efforts in other states have shown them that going for a specific number like twenty or thirty improves their chances of having gambling legalized. The local hotel owners hate the plan. They've gotten together and back a proposal to put gambling in every big hotel throughout the state."

"What's the third?"

"Eh?"

"You said there was a new proposal."

"Oh, yeah. An outsider, but he's gaining fast. Proposes just one giant casino for the whole state. Bigger than anything ever built. Give everybody a chance to watch and see how it's run, what effect it has on the region, that sort of thing. All of a sudden he's getting a lot of attention. Got some big names behind him, including the lieutenant governor. Idea has a lot of appeal to the fence-sitters, plus he's known as a high-class developer." Grey's expression was grim. "Looks bad, Chase. Before Rochelle got involved, I thought we had a fairly solid chance of defeating the legislation to legalize gambling. Again."

"Did you say Rochelle? Sylvan Rochelle?"

Grey's gaze sharpened. "You know him?"

"Not really." Chase thought that one over. "Do you know where he wants to put his casino?"

"Hard to say. Doubt if Miami would be the location, though. Certainly nowhere too far north. He'd probably try for some place on the coast with a low crime rate, maybe a sluggish economy, somewhere not in the absolute first league so he can point at it later and say, look what I've done for this place, just think what I could do somewhere else."

"And you think this proposal will pass."

"Looks that way." It was not like Grey to sound so downtrodden. Defeated before the battle began. "We're seeing our support leak away like water through a sieve. It's the sort of compromise that a lot of folks can live with, especially if this one casino goes somewhere other than their hometown." Grey lunged, managed to stuff a pamphlet into the hands of someone who had strayed too close. "It's tragic is what it is. The fight's come down to where, not whether."

"But it won't be just one."

"These people I'm trying to organize," Grey sighed, "they won't say it, but they see the battle as already lost, and one casino looks better than a couple of hundred. So they'll stick their heads in the sand until this governor is defeated and somebody else comes in who'll throw his weight behind a full opening of the state to gambling. Then they'll all gather round and moan and argue how on earth this horrible situation ever came to pass."

"What about the governor, won't he try to stop it?"

"The governor is just one person," Grey replied in a tone that suggested it was an argument he had been forced to call upon too often. "A powerful person, but one person just the same. If the voices surrounding him are all urging him to let gambling in, there is a chance he's going to settle on this compromise. Right now he is beleaguered and isolated both by the legislature and by his own party. They see jobs, he sees moral decay and crime and danger to society. Which means this compromise of Rochelle's is looking better and better to everyone."

The final stragglers hustled by, and Grey checked his watch. "Guess we better go in."

"Sorry to bother you on a Sunday morning," Sabine Duprie began, which was a lie, but an acceptable one. Seldom did a weekend pass without at least one conversation between them.

"Not at all, my dear. Not at all." Lieutenant Governor Lamar Laroque carried the portable phone into his study and closed the door behind him. Something about her tone said this would be a conversation best carried out in private.

Sabine Duprie was, in his eyes, the perfect

number two. She was utterly without an agenda of her own, as far as he could tell, except her ambition. Which was fine with him. He liked ambition, especially when it was as unbridled as he suspected Sabine's was. Her lack of a personal cause meant she was free to blow with whatever wind he decided was politically correct at the time. Her ambition meant she was willing to go along with whatever strategy he decided on, so long as she felt there was something in it for her.

Sabine Duprie had collected enough mannerisms to appear highly polished, at least for the first hour of any encounter. That too was fine with Laroque. The current world of politics thrived on twenty-minute meetings and overnight friendships. She was a smooth dresser, flashed a bright smile, and talked a patter as slick as Teflon. Nothing stuck to her. Nothing.

On the other hand, Sabine was genuinely loathed as a hired killer by most of the other capitol staff. This too suited him down to the ground. She was all his. Sink or swim, her career rested on him and him alone. And she was smart enough to know it. Her loyalty was assured.

Lamar settled in behind his desk. "What can I do for you, my dear?"

"I received a call from Rochelle's lawyers. They went by Marie Hale's place yesterday afternoon."

"Yes." This was all according to plan. Lamar searched the far wall. Why did she sound so disturbed?

"She . . ." A moment's hesitation, an indrawn breath, a crack in the unbreakable shield. "She has turned over all responsibility for the land to someone else."

Lamar squinted into the unseen distance. Not good, but not a disaster. "She's an old woman, as I recall. Not in the best of health."

"That's correct." Another pause. "Her trustee is Chase Bennett."

"You know him." It was not a question. Her tone made it clear.

"I did. We haven't seen each other for," another pause, "about a year."

His forehead creased in thought. This was something new, a relationship that had left its mark. Sabine Duprie was known as someone who prowled the Florida straits with remarkable appetite and rarely left her prey unscarred. It was widely speculated that the two of them were having an illicit affair. Laroque did nothing to deny the allegations, though he appreciated her abilities far too much to damage her usefulness with anything so fleeting as sex. "Tell me about him."

"He's with the Cocoa branch of the Brevard County Chamber of Commerce." She tried for brisk efficiency, almost made it. "Chase is, well, he's sort of a wild card. His official title is Vice-President of Development, but it doesn't really cover everything he does. He basically is left free to roam at will."

"A troubleshooter," Lamar suggested, trying to get a fix on both what she was saying and what lay behind it all. "A problem solver."

"That and more. He's managed to salvage a couple of major land deals that almost everybody had given up on. He knows almost everybody in the area. People listen to him."

"Intelligent?"

"Yes." Definite on that at least. "And perceptive."

And holding some power over his assistant. An added value, perhaps, or, "A danger to our plans?"

The hesitation returned. "I don't know. He, well, once he gets an idea in his head he can be very stubborn."

"Forceful," he probed.

"He has a lot of influence locally," she hedged. "Unofficially, of course."

"Of course," he agreed. "Perhaps it would be a good idea to inform our allies in the area of this development. Sound both Barry and that new chamber president out."

"Linda Armacost."

"See how they think this might affect our plans. Be circumspect. Play it casual."

"Of course." Trying for casual herself. Not succeeding.

He started to ask her directly, demand an explanation, but decided to hold back. There would be ample time for such questions, and it would be better to ask them in person so he could observe her reaction. "Then I shall bid you a pleasant day, my dear. Thank you for calling."

From the outside, Cocoa's First Baptist Church looked like a windowless warehouse planted too close to the road. From within, however, all was light and friendliness and communion. Despite its size, it was a locals' church, and almost everyone knew almost everything about everybody else. It was Chase's ideal Sunday meetinghouse, too far from the beach to attract more than a handful of tourists, frequented by people of all ages, a cheery, happy place.

Chase remained locked in thought through most of the sermon, caught up in wondering and worrying, until some word or another worked through to his mind, caught his attention, and drew him away from his internal struggle to focus on what was being said.

"We have not been called to march in a dress parade," the pastor was saying. "We have not been called to stand in our finery and watch the soldiers and the workers and the marchers and the musicians pass before us. We have, all of us, been called to go and do."

Chase found himself sitting up straighter, not sure why, but sensing a message intended for his ears. And mind. And heart.

"Are you satisfied with a sugar-coated faith? Fine. Then the call to arms, *your* call to action, will go unanswered. I am not asking whether or not you are saved. I am asking whether or not you are ready to take the next step. To become a willing servant. To grow beyond who you are and become who you are called to be."

The pastor was blessed with a face that would remain young to the grave and a body that was too active to ever hold on to excess weight. In person he was quiet and calm and a bit diffident, carefully weighing his words, listening more than he spoke. In the pulpit, however, he showed a more passionate side.

"Are you burdened this day? Then let us who are not so troubled be there for you. But when the Lord lifts these burdens from you, let them go. Do not be tempted to hide in a despair which is no longer truly there."

For Chase, church was usually a comfortable time. A chance to sit in a welcome island of peace and let down his defenses. Knowing that his pains and his worries seldom followed him inside. Rarely taking much notice of what was said from the pulpit. Whenever the pastor let go like this and challenged his complacency, he usually took solace from the smirks and head shakes that were passed around the parking lot afterward.

But not today.

"Some are no doubt looking at me and asking, who on earth would hold on to sadness? Friends, let me tell you, there are few easier hiding places than a sadness which no longer hurts or a burden which is no longer heavy. We find ourselves with an ideal excuse to remain weak and comfortable, ideal because it spares us from being condemned.

"Few would criticize us for not going forward, while they think that staying put is so hard. No one, that is, save the One who knows our heart. The One who understands how tempted we are by complacency."

The pastor lifted his Bible. "We are told in Revelation that the Word of God is both bitter and sweet. I challenge you now to accept the scroll when it is passed to you. Eat it. Swallow it. Take it deep within you. Grow in the Word. Accept the task assigned you, whatever it may be.

"Go. And *do*."

Once home, Chase headed for the phone even before taking off his tie. Allowing no time for doubt or fear or hesitation. He dialed the number on the slip of paper he had left resting there, felt a teenager's jangled nerves when Kaitlyn's voice answered.

"It's me," he said. "The goof who blew it last night."

"Hello." A thoughtful pause, then, "You didn't blow anything."

Relief flooded through him. He settled down on the rug by the phone, asked, "Would you tell me something about yourself?"

She replied with a calmness that gave him the impression she had almost been waiting for the question. "Like what?"

"Something about your past. Something you'd never want anybody to find out."

"Something secret," she said quietly.

He nodded to the receiver. "Exactly like that."

"Why?"

"Because I feel so exposed to you right now." Something about her, even across the telephone wires, brought out an attitude he had never known himself capable of. Not just honest, no, an *easy* honesty. As though there was no reason not to give her anything but the straight truth. "Sort of bruised and skinless. You've seen so much of me, and all I know about you is the finished product. The beautiful girl with the watchful gaze."

"How is it," she said, "that you seem to know what I need to hear?"

"Tell me," he said, quieter now.

She remained silent for a time, then said, "Can you come by here this afternoon?"

"Your house? Sure."

She gave him the address. "Three o'clock. Bye."

The address she had given him was for a riverside road on Merritt Island. Chase drove past expensive houses in shades of pink and coral, counting the numbers until he spotted her in front of a white-frame wooden house set on shoulder-high stilts. Chase pulled in, emerged from the car, stood looking at the structure. "I know this place."

"My grandfather built it the year he married," Kaitlyn said.

"I've driven past it, I don't know, dozens of times. It's always been one of my favorites. A piece of living Florida history." He looked at her. "I had the impression you had just moved here, didn't know anything about Florida."

"Both true." She started forward. "Try to be quiet."

Something caused him to hesitate. "If someone's asleep, maybe I should come back later."

"If you want to know my secrets, this is where we have to start." Kaitlyn reached out a hand. "Coming?"

She led him across a springy, well-trimmed lawn, their footsteps lost to a chorus of crickets and birdsong. Quietly they climbed the back stairs and entered a broad, screened-in porch. Kaitlyn let the door swing back softly behind him, then started toward a door set into the far corner, well removed from the rest of the house. She pushed open the door, gave him a searching look, then turned and entered.

In the room was a cadaver.

Chase stopped at the doorway, unable to go farther. The air was so close and so foul that his lungs rebelled from drawing breath. The figure on the bed looked and smelled ten days dead. Only the face and hands emerged from the covers, and they were a bloodless white. The skin was so dry and translucent as to appear spray-painted over delicate bones. The man's cheeks and eyes and even his pale lips were sunken caverns.

Kaitlyn sat on the edge of the bed. "Grandpa?"

Eyelids fluttered like frail birds, then opened to reveal eyes of palest blue. Toothless gums smacked together, then a voice croaked, "Hey, gal."

"I've brought somebody to meet you." She motioned him forward. "This is Chase."

He forced himself to step closer to the bed. "Hello, sir."

Eyes tracked toward him, but did not hold. "I been asleep long?"

"Chase is my friend, Grandpa. My good friend."

The eyes wandered back, struggled to focus, but only for a moment. "Awful tired, gal. Think maybe I'll rest."

Kaitlyn sat there, watching the old man's cheeks flutter with each gasping breath. "He has good days and bad days. Mostly bad."

"You and your folks look after him?"

"My dad, mostly. Mom refuses to enter this room. I help when I can. We have a retired nurse who comes two hours every morning and afternoon. We pay a college student to sleep on a cot outside his door every night. And we have a housekeeper. All that is still cheaper than a nursing home bed."

"But the work," Chase murmured.

She did not deny it. "Grandpa knew he was going a year or so back. That's when we were still up north, and he was here. He called Pop and broke down over the phone. Begged Pop not to make him die in a nursing home. Pop had never heard him cry, never heard him sound scared before. He thought about it for a couple of months, then decided we needed to move down here. Mom was furious that he would even consider it. Pop had decided to take early retirement, and the last thing she wanted was to spend her days looking after a dying old man who she'd never really liked all that much."

Kaitlyn sighed. "It's been hard on her here. Really hard. Recently she's been spending more and more time back at our home outside Chicago. I guess that's why I've been able to forgive her for everything."

"Everything like what?"

"Another time," she whispered, her eyes still on the slumbering form. She patted the thin arm, then rose and walked over to him. Kaitlyn looked long and deep into his eyes, searching the depths of him. "Thank you for coming."

"How has your mother hurt you?"

She gave him a glimmer of a sad smile. "One secret at a time, okay?"

Chase followed her from the room. He stood by the screen, let her lean on him for comfort and support, felt the intimacy between them. Kaitlyn breathed long and deep, as though clearing the room from her mind and spirit, and leaned her head back. He raised one arm to her shoulder, felt the strength and resilience and the mystery. So much he didn't know. So much he wanted to share.

"Will you let me take you sailing tomorrow?" It was out almost before he realized he had spoken.

She stepped back. "You have a boat?"

He nodded. Amazed that he had said it, and that he had said it so easily. One of his own passions so freely revealed. "It may be kind of rough. There's a front moving in, and there's almost always a wind preceding. Sometimes a strong wind."

Another of the deep gazes, as though searching for something. "What is your boat's name?"

"Windward Lass. I bought her used, decided to keep the name. Some people say it's bad luck to christen a boat twice."

"I like it," she said. "Somehow it suits you."

"Will you come?"

"I don't work tomorrow morning, so I can come over as soon as I finish helping with Grandpa."

A thought struck him then, a realization of something left undone. A matter he suddenly wanted to take care of before meeting her tomorrow. Something that required the early morning, before the beach came alive to another day. "Perfect."

"So much to you, Chase Bennett," she murmured, watching him. "So many layers. So many surprises."

6

He ate breakfast standing at the bulkhead behind his house and watching as dawn painted the distant horizon with great streaks of pink and gold. The breeze was fresh and steady, a perfect day for sailing. He shivered with anticipation.

Chase loaded the truck and joined the first traces of morning traffic. His heart hammered and his hands sweated, but not painfully. Not any longer. He needed to lay a ghost to rest, to have the task over and done before meeting Kaitlyn.

It was time.

He pulled into the Jetty Park lot, the attendant's cabin still locked up tight, the vast acreage empty save for three silent campers drawn over to the far wall. Chase cut the engine and for once let the memories flood back. Not fighting them, not any longer. Letting them come. Welcoming them as he welcomed the familiar sounds of surf and the gulls.

Crazy to have stayed away from this stretch of beach for so long. Crazy to have lived a whole year isolated and locked up with memories of a woman who could not ever love him.

Sabine's looks were so compelling it had taken a while for him to realize what might lie beneath the surface. By then it had been too late. He was already drowning in love.

Two years later, he finally forced himself to look beyond that glossy dark hair, that sculpted figure, that perfect face. Two years of being used, two years of hoping he could change things around, make her see that she really would be happy with him, really could open up and receive back the love he ached so much to give to her.

But finally the eyes had given her away.

It had happened on a pristine March day, just over a year ago. It had been one of those special moments when central Florida stood apart from the rest of America and watched in befuddled satisfaction as another late winter storm invaded and captured everywhere but here. The weather had been cool enough to demand a sweater, the wind brisk, the sky so clear they could see to infinity.

He drove her to the jetty shore, and they walked an empty beach, she down from Tallahassee for some meeting or other, he immediately clearing the decks to make time for her. The velvet box was in his pocket.

He had gone ahead and bought the ring, hoping for a moment like this. Spent the whole week scared and excited, scarcely able to eat. Long hours with the box open in front of him, dreaming of all it would mean to slip the diamond on her finger.

Sabine swung his arm as they walked along the hard low-tide sand. She chattered brightly about work and problems with the lieutenant governor's staff and her new apartment, never letting up, hardly pausing to draw breath. He walked alongside her, desperately yearning to take her in his arms, squeeze her to silence, tell her all the things that had swirled about in his mind and heart for so long. So very long. About marriage and children and a life together.

But he caught himself, just as he opened his mouth. He had a sudden electric vision, an absolute certainty that stopped him before he started.

He saw with wrenching clarity what would happen — the sudden irritation, the pulling away, the accusation that he had spoiled their morning together. Again. She wasn't ready for all that and he knew it, so why insist on bringing it up? He had heard the words before, a tragic litany that had ended numerous recent visits. But he had always returned to hope as soon as the hurt had dimmed, believing still he had a chance, a prospect of seeing all that change. So the next time he had always spoken again, because he could not help but open his mouth and let out at least a little of the steam his heart was generating.

But this time he turned toward Sabine, and the words were simply not there. Instead, he had searched her face, hunting desperately for some way to claw back the reinforced steel door to her heart.

And finally, finally, he saw her eyes. Saw what was not there. It was as if some invisible hand were holding his head and forcing him to look, look beyond what he *wanted* to what actually *was*.

Those eyes were brown and big and perfect as the rest of her, but lifeless as a showroom doll's. Dead. Forever empty.

It's not me, he realized in that moment of seeing beyond the hope his love had been creating. It's her. And that's the way she'll always be. Here in front of him stood a woman truly incapable of ever giving herself as he would like to give in return. Not now, not ever.

Never.

The word tolled through his being with such force that it threatened to shatter him into a billion pieces and fling his life to the winds. Chase turned back to the beach they shared only with the birds, his mouth gaping, his lungs unable to fill themselves around the balloon of sorrow that expanded and threatened to seal him off from within.

Never.

This time it was she who jerked him around. "What's the matter?"

He stood there, struggling to find the power to speak the words, looking back to her face and to his surprise finding fear in it. Real fear. She sensed the change as well. That gave him the strength to say, "I've got to go back."

"But I'm not ready."

The same words, a different meaning. Too late. Chase made his fingers go limp, plucked his hand free, felt the years and the effort and the hunger and the yearning all pulled away, all cast seaward on a breeze suddenly strong enough to tear even hope from his heart. Leaving only emptiness. Leaving only a great looming vacuum of sorrow and regret.

He turned and walked away.

"Chase!"

The scream was almost enough to turn him back. Almost. But now he knew. He understood. With Sabine there was nothing for him but unanswered need. He kept walking down the empty beach, wondering dully how anything that hurt so bad could feel so right.

Chase walked up and over the empty crosswalk. To either side, the dune grass and sea oats were flattened into dusky, silken hillocks by the wind. The ocean was frothy and empty, the gulls wheeling and crying their endless song to the wave's rumbling music.

He slipped off his topsiders and walked down to the water's edge. The wind searched his soul with probing fingers, drawing open all the compartments and crannies he had grimly held shut for so long. Chase raised his hands to the morning sun and had a sudden sensation of a second wind rising, far stronger than the one that plucked at his hair, blasting through his wide-open heart, clearing away all the dust and cobwebs and unwanted burdens.

When the cleansing was over, he turned and walked back over the dunes. Walked into a future he was now ready to meet.

Lamar Laroque found he had been waiting all morning for the call. He brushed aside Sabine's pleasantries and demanded, "What have you learned?"

"It's not so good." The discomfort of yesterday had been joined by something else. "For one thing, Chase has strong connections with our primary opponent."

Fatigue. That was it. She sounded exhausted. This was as worrisome as the news. He faced an antagonist who was capable of causing his unshakable assistant to lose sleep. "Not Barry Tadlock's father-in-law."

"Grey Spenser. Yessir, that's what Linda Armacost claims. She doesn't like Chase, not at all. Claims the only way he keeps his job is with Spenser's backing. And something else. He's done something to make Barry absolutely furious. I couldn't make out exactly what it was, but it doesn't appear to have any direct connection with our plans."

Bad and getting worse. "Can he be fired from the chamber?"

Again that unusual hesitation. "Armacost would certainly like to see him gone. But I'm not sure that would be the way to handle this."

"What are you saying?"

"He might just get stubborn and fight all the harder."

Laroque bore down hard, searching like a cornered ferret. "Think carefully, my dear. Did either of them state explicitly that

Chase Bennett is opposed to legalized gambling?"

A longish pause. "Not that I recall."

"What about your own contacts with him."

"I don't recall," she said slowly, the uncertainty loud and clear, "that the matter ever arose."

"Then we may be growing excited over nothing. Here is what I want you to do. Call Rochelle's deputy, have him make a direct approach to Bennett, sound him out. In the meantime, I want you to arrange a little get-together. Make it for the end of this week, cancel whatever is necessary. We'll have a presentation and a luncheon, yes, that should do it. Invite a number of the development officers from the regions supposedly under consideration. It doesn't really matter who, just so long as this Bennett is present. Give me an opportunity to sound him out and impress him with just how major an issue this is."

"You want me to call Chase?"

He narrowed his eyes. "Is that a problem, my dear?"

"No," she said. Quiet. Resigned. "Of course not."

"I'm certainly glad to hear it. Because we must maintain absolute control over this situation. I'm sure I don't have to tell you what a crucial time this is. Chase Bennett has unfortunately placed himself directly in our path. He must be monitored. And if he proves himself to be a nuisance, then he must be dealt with."

The marina was home to a strange blend of people and attitudes and lifestyles. Many of the berths were taken by half-million-dollar floating fantasies, boats polished from stem to stern. Pilot cabins rigged like Starfleet Command, sporting every navigational aid known to man. Such boats seldom left dock for more than a weekend at a time. Their owners entertained on aft decks, leaving the doors to the main cabins open wide to offer a continual cooling breath of air conditioning. Men dressed in blue blazers and foulards, women in elegant sailor outfits by Chanel and Dior.

Many neighboring berths were occupied by modern-day buccaneers. More often than not, these boats were their owner's only home. They lived on society's borderland, unlisted, unstamped, unchecked, undocumented, untaxed. Their boats were decked out in worn rigging and sun-bleached wood and hand-me-down sails. Their best clothes were often the only remaining clean pair of cutoffs and a shirt with both sleeves. Their conversations were liberally sprinkled with references to bars halfway around a globe marked not by cities but rather by islands and water-currents and warm weather. Their charts were salt stained and bore countless interlocking rings from coffee mugs spilled in heavy seas. Their eyes had the clarity of people used to infinite horizons.

Chase slid his cooler out of the truck, slammed the tailgate, took three steps down the gangplank, and was halted by an angry voice. "One minute there, Bennett."

Chase released a low groan, raised his chin, said to the sky overhead, "Not today, okay?"

"Yes, today, right now, this very minute." A tall, fleshy man with slightly bulging blue eyes rocked toward him. He was dressed like one of the sailor boys from the pages of GQ. But not even the fancy nautical sweater could hide the belly's bulge nor the way his jowls quivered with each step. "You've gone too far this time, Bennett."

Chase set down the cooler. "Come on, Barry, give me a break. It's a beautiful day, there's a great wind —"

"Now you listen to me." He shook one finger in Chase's face. "I'm going straight to the board tomorrow, tell them how one of our chamber employees has stolen clients away from me."

"Barry, you know as well as I do that you would have made an absolute shambles of that court case."

"I am going to demand, and I am going to receive, your instant dismissal."

"The town can't afford to have a half-dozen doctors sent to jail all at once, Barry."

He glared frostily at Chase. "And just what, may I ask, gives you the —"

"Chase! Hey, buddy, been looking everywhere for you." The sun was suddenly cut off by a vast looming mountain of muscle and leathery tan. And smell. "Got a problem with my motor, man. Think you could take a look at it for me?"

"In a minute, Conrad."

With a nervous glance at the towering menace in grease-stained cutoffs, Barry Tadlock raised the finger once more. "Now you look here, Bennett. I'm thinking seriously of pressing —"

"Listen, man, this is urgent." The sweaty giant sounded like a bear with a cold. He took a step closer, until he was all but crammed up against a cringing Barry Tadlock. "I got to catch the tide."

"You'll be well advised to keep your distance from my clients in the future, Bennett."

Barry Tadlock cast another nervous glance at the bearded menace and tried his best to stalk off, muttering, "You haven't heard the last of this."

Chase watched him waddle away and said thoughtfully, "The best thing you can do with that motor of yours is to sail out about ten miles and chuck it over the side. And the tide doesn't change until midafternoon."

"Hey, man, don't complain." Conrad's face split into a broad grin. "I saved your bacon, didn't I?"

Chase grinned back. "Yeah, I owe you one."

"Just give me the name and number of the lady waiting out by your boat, man, and we're even."

"Kaitlyn's already here?" He hefted the cooler. "You're a pal, Conrad."

"She's a nice one, that lady. Believe I'd try to hang on to her, if I was you."

Chase waved and trotted down the uneven gangway, breathing the dependable fragrance of seaweed and swamp and diesel and brackish water, intensely conscious of loving this seabound world. He loved the sound of the halyards beating on masts like tin drums keeping time to the breeze. He loved the gulls, their cocky swagger and their white plumage and lonely cries, echoing the call of

133

every sailor's heart. He loved it all, the coming, the sailing, the tinkering, even the leaving. He was content to be the occasional sailor, let the water serve as a well of peace and beauty from which he would continue to draw for all his life long.

He turned down his jetty, saw Kaitlyn standing at the very end, her back to him, looking out over the water to the marsh island beyond. She had one hand raised, her fingers outstretched, straining to touch a lone gull that rode the wind just out of reach. From where he stood, it looked to Chase as though she held the rising sun perched upon her hand.

He set down the cooler, captivated by the moment and the morning and the beauty of her. Chase walked forward, heard her crooning talk to the gull, trying to coax it closer. Then he spun her around, catching a fleeting glimpse of her startled face before he wrapped her in his arms, so caught up in all he felt at that moment as to be beyond words, afraid even for her to see what he was sure would show in his eyes. He held her tight, felt her relax into his embrace, felt two cool hands rise to trace intricate patterns up his back and into his hair. Felt the warm fragrance of her sighed breath. Felt the surging fullness pour into his heart.

And heard a raucous cheer erupt from the boats around them. He opened his eyes, saw a couple dozen of his chums whistling and shouting, leaning on halyards or pilings, grinning with the abandon of people who knew the value of a smile. And he knew that there could have been no better place, no better way to know the rightness of them together, than here, his very own haven from the storm.

The tree-lined bay sparkled like a cauldron filled with multicolored jewels. Blues and greens gleamed overbright in the sunshine, the birds soared like winged creatures from some distant mystical land.

Wind feathers coursed the water, miniature ripples where blustery currents touched down. Only a landlubber thought of wind as a constant. A sailor knew that wind was never singular. *Winds.* Like the threads making up a sheet. *Winds.* The smaller the boat, the more responsive it became to the small spurts of stronger wind. Watch a small-boat sailor, see him continually track from one puff to the next, making faint course adjustments all the time. *Winds.*

From behind the safety of his Ray-Bans, Chase examined Kaitlyn. She wore an oversized sweatshirt over Lycra shorts, leaning into the wind, supporting her weight on her arms like an excited little girl about to jump from her seat. Brown-gold hair filtering the breeze, eyes full of new experience and pleasure and a far-seeing gaze.

And suddenly it was not enough just to watch her, to observe, to remain detached. "Do you know much about boats?"

"Almost nothing," she replied, happy to turn to him, happy to share with him the joy in her eyes. "I've always loved the way boats look out on the water, but for one reason or another I've only been out a couple of times in my life."

He slid the dark glasses off so that they dangled around his neck. "This is a thirty-six-foot sloop," he said, knowing much of what he said would not be retained, but wanting to say it just the same. "It has a partially retractable keel, which is rare on a boat this size. It was especially designed for shallow drafts, so it could sail where a lot of other larger boats would go aground. An east-coast boat for east-coast waters. Someday I'd like to take it up the entire Inland Waterway, all the way from Florida to Nova Scotia."

There he stopped, astounded with the ease of sharing something he had held on to in secret for so long. Kaitlyn nodded slowly, as though taking it in deep. "That sounds like a wonderful trip."

Chase turned his face to the wind, squinting as though checking clouds. "Every time I come out here, especially after work, I spend an hour or so changing my mental clothes. Putting aside all the stuff that doesn't fit here on the water. Letting my muscles remember and get me moving with the sails and the weather and the currents. Not letting anything in from outside."

He kept his face turned upward and away until he felt a soft warm hand settle down upon his own. He turned back to find smoky gray eyes open and there for him.

"Thank you for sharing all this with me," was what she said. But her eyes and her touch said more. Much, much more.

The wind freshened, blowing straight and cool from the sea. A stand of nearby Australian pines moaned a continual warning of the coming storm. On the horizon, great looming hordes of dark nimbus marched toward land, their tread a muffled thunder. The coming rain scented the wind water sweet as they headed south toward the marina and safety.

The first fat drops finally arrived as Chase made the stern line fast. He stripped the sails, silently reveling in the fact that Kaitlyn stayed right there beside him, sheltered in a rain slicker he had bought for someone else. Someone who had never come out with him on the boat, no matter how often he asked and begged and pleaded to share with him this great and glorious part of his world. Now it seemed as though the boat and the slicker and the moment had all waited for Kaitlyn's arrival.

When all was done they shared a smile, a sense that something greater than just a sail through rising wind had happened here today. Then Chase felt a change in the gusts, looked forward to see a solid wall of water moving toward them. He reached for the soggy sail bag, taking enormous pleasure in seeing Kaitlyn grab the cooler without being asked, and together they jogged toward the truck.

He hefted the sail bag, took the cooler from her and set it into place, then turned to her. Saw how she stood chilled yet still unfazed by the weather, still happy with the day and the moment and the time they had shared. Her upturned face rain streaked yet cheerful. Hugging herself for warmth, yet content to stand and let him look into her eyes, quietly accepting the good with the bad. And once more his heart grew too big for his chest, pressing him into expressing what he felt with something more than words.

He wrapped his arms around her, felt her trembling from more than just the wet, saw how she had hoped he would do just what he had done, saw how she welcomed him with a gaze that held both heartache and hope and the wisdom of experience. He lowered his face to hers, tasted lips both cool and warm, welcoming him, melting and opening until he could not tell where he ended and she began.

Then the squall hit, a torrent so heavy it almost blew him off his feet. It turned his slicker into a funnel that trapped the rainwater and sluiced it down his back. They drew apart with a shared shriek, laughing at the silliness of running for cover when they were already soaked to the bone. But they dived into the truck's cab, slammed the truck door closed, turned on the motor, and switched the heater on full. Then he was helping her take off the slicker, sliding out of his, then reaching out and meeting her reaching for him, hungry now, straining toward him, eagerly sliding back into an embrace which was as much hers as his.

7

He was still toweling off, the steam from a long, bone-warming shower swirling about the bedroom, when the phone rang. He bounced down the hall, stopped his whistling in midflow to pick up the receiver, and almost sang a hello.

"Chase."

The one word was enough to rock him to his foundations. The voice quieter than he recalled, but unmistakable. "Yes."

"This is Sabine."

He reached to the side wall for support. "I know who it is."

"Some hello." Trying for a pout. When he gave no response, the voice brightened. "Lamar is planning a little conference here in Tallahassee, very exclusive, very high-powered. I told him about you. He wants you to come."

So much of her was contained in those words. Exclusive and high-powered were two of the biggest magnets in Sabine's universe, so she assumed they appealed to him as well. Supposedly she had gone out of her

140

way to get him in. Doing him a favor. Putting him in her debt. Why? "Lamar as in the lieutenant governor?"

"Do you know another?" There was an edge to her voice that he did not recall. It kept slipping out, showing itself and then vanishing. Had he not been so trained to listen for every nuance in Sabine's tone, he probably would have missed it. Back to all brightness, she continued, "He wants to have you join them on Friday morning. The meeting will be followed by a luncheon. You're invited to that, too."

"Friday's tough, Sabine." Automatic response. He had no interest in traveling to Tallahassee to play the power games, even less interest in seeing her again. Especially now.

Tough was the best way to describe how she came back. "This is important, Chase. I went out on a limb to get you a place, and now the LG is expecting you. I'm sure Linda Armacost, your new president, would be most willing to help you shift things around, make room in your schedule."

"In other words, it's an invitation, but I don't have any choice whether I accept or not."

"Hey, do we have to talk to each other like this?" Little girl pouting prettily, big eyes beckoning even though he could not see. "I thought I was doing you a favor, Chase. I mean, a little gratitude wouldn't hurt, would it?"

Once upon a time that tone would have melted him completely. Now it sounded false and manipulative and left him feeling only heartsore and very nervous. Suddenly all he wanted was to be finished with the conversation. "Thanks, Sabine. What time do I need to show up?"

"This will be just great, Chase, you'll see. A big step in the right direction." Brightness and something else. Relief? "Hey, maybe we can get together afterward, chat about old times. Ten o'clock, the LG's office on the nineteenth floor. Until then."

Chase hung up the phone, grabbed it and the slip of paper off the stand, sank to the floor, and dialed before he had a chance to think. Said with vast relief when Kaitlyn answered, "I just wanted to make sure you were for real."

"I'm real, all right. What's the matter?"

"Bad shock. I'm getting over it. Just let me hold on to you for a minute, okay?"

"Sure." There was the sound of a chair scraping, her settling. "Do you want to talk about it?"

"Sometime, but not now. It's all a little raw."

"I know how that is." Sympathy gave her voice a dusky burr.

A *genuine* sympathy. Chase knew it was wrong to compare, knew he could not help it. "Thank you, Kaitlyn."

"For what?"

"For making room for me just now. I needed to hear the sound of something real."

A pause, then, "I had a wonderful time today, Chase Bennett. I never knew how much fun you guys were having out there, messing around on your boats."

"You can't imagine," he said, "how much it meant to have you out there with me."

"Funny, isn't it." She sounded so intimate it gave him a shiver. "I don't know you at all, and yet I feel as though we've been together talking like this for years and years."

"You know me," he said, without understanding why.

"Maybe I do," she answered quietly. "All better?"

"Much. Thanks. Really."

"You're welcome. Really. Now my advice to you is to have a big bowl of chicken soup and a glass of milk and then go to bed. When I was little and something hurt my feelings, there was nothing that made me feel better faster than soup and milk and a good night's sleep."

"I can't understand how anyone could hurt your feelings," he said. "Not ever."

"Good-night, Chase," she sighed, her voice a gentle caress. "Sweet dreams."

"Matt?"

"Whatever it is, the answer's no. I'm busy." The head jerked up in irritation, then, "Chase? Chase Bennett? That you, Slim?"

"There wasn't anybody in your outer office."

"Come in, come in, grab a chair. Sorry about that welcome. I'm due in court in a half hour and I'm not ready."

"I called your Tallahassee office, they said you were down here again. I can come back later."

"Shoot. Later for you might mean next year." He went back around his desk. "Doesn't matter anyway. I know the guy's guilty as sin, the judge knows it, the jury knows it, the guy himself knows it. But the arresting officers made so many mistakes they'll be used in the next policeman's manual to illustrate what not to do when making a bust. What can I do for you?"

"I need ten minutes, Matt."

"Sure, sure, ten minutes I've always got for an old buddy." He eased back in his chair as far as the coiled tension would allow.

"What's on your mind?"

"You remember Carlotta?"

"The albino amazon? The girl that beat me arm-wrestling five times in a row? My number two best friend until she got swept away to the wilds of D.C.? What kind of question is that?"

Chase pulled the four diskettes from his coat pocket. "She's gotten into some kind of trouble. Big trouble. I can't say more than that. I guess she'd say I shouldn't be talking to you at all, but I'm worried. I think there might be something important on these."

Matthew eyed the disks, made no move. "What's in them?"

"I don't know."

"I mean, is that material evidence in a criminal case? And if so, does it have anything to do with drugs?"

"I don't know," Chase repeated, then flashed back on the D.C. projects raid, the little kids crouched against a wall, the wastepaper baskets filled with little glass vials. "Possibly. No, probably."

"Then I can't help you." Flat, hard, unbending.

"This is Carlotta we're talking about, Matt."

"You just wait right there," he said, holding up one rigid finger. "Are you telling me that if I hear you out and start involving myself I might help Carlotta out of a mess she's gotten herself into? Or am I just digging myself into the same doggone hole?"

"Now you're talking like a lawyer and not like a friend."

"Lawyering just happens to be my profession, in case you haven't noticed. And I just happen to be involved in a major investigation I've given two years of my life to." Matthew was genuinely hot. "We go to court in three months, maximum four. Their lawyers are the best money could buy. If I'm caught within a mile of tainted evidence, it's all over before we even get in the door."

Chase stood. "I'm sure Carlotta would understand."

"Don't get sarcastic with me," Matthew snapped, rising with him. "This is big, Chase. It's our chance to go after the top guys."

They both started at the knock on the door. An eager young black woman poked her head in and said, "You are now late."

"I know. Listen, something's come up. I want you to go on over there and start things moving. I'll be along directly."

Dark eyes widened to the size of saucers. "Me?"

"You can't do any worse than I would.

That judge is going to tear a piece the size of Texas from the hides of those two lamebrain cops. All we're gonna do is be witnesses at the wake."

"That mean you couldn't come up with anything?"

"Clarence Darrow himself couldn't win this one. Now get." When the door closed behind her, he said, "Where was I?"

Chase saw desperation mixed with defiance on Matthew's features and found himself unable to hold on to the anger. "The last time I saw Carlotta, she told me how much she'd like to go after the big ones herself," he said quietly. "Go on to your court case, Matt. Then clobber the power players."

The defiance softened into naked appeal. "Anything but this, old son. Anything."

A skinny stranger with slicked-back hair and a thousand-dollar suit was standing on Marie's front porch when Chase pulled up. He started across the lawn before Chase had even cut the motor. "Mr. Bennett, what a pleasant surprise. I was planning to go directly from here to your office. My name is Claude Sorrens, and I have the pleasure of representing the Omega Corporation. Perhaps you have heard of us."

Chase pointed at the gray sedan parked in

the drive. "Is that Doc Sutton's car?"

The slick little man was not pleased with the reaction. "There is a doctor with Miss Hale," he replied irritably. "I didn't manage to catch his name. I wanted to discuss with you —"

But Chase had already left him speaking to a hole in the air. He leaped up the front steps and through the door. "Marie!"

A voice from the front parlor called back, "Is that weasel still camped outside on my lawn?"

"I believe proper decorum for a doctor's visit is a little less shouting and a lot more relaxing," another voice snapped.

Chase found her stretched out on an old daybed and adjusting her clothes while the gray-headed doctor repacked his black bag. "Are you all right?"

"Ralph's shotgun is upstairs under the bed. I want you to go out there and wing that buzzard of a lawyer. Won't disturb me in the least if you inflict a little permanent damage."

"You'll do no such thing." Doc Sutton snapped his bag closed and straightened slowly. "I did not drop everything to rush over here and watch either of you make more work for me. Besides which, I hate doing gunshot wounds."

"What happened?" Chase demanded.

"A pain," Marie Hale snapped, hating all weakness, especially in herself. "I was being an old fool, calling the doctor."

"You are less a fool than anybody I know." Doc Sutton patted Marie's shoulder. "Two pills twice a day. I'll be back on Friday morning. Until then, you are to rest. No lifting, no standing for long periods, and no working in the lab." Before she could reply he stumped over and grabbed Chase by the arm. "Come along with me, son."

When they emerged on the front porch, the lawyer started toward them but stopped abruptly when Doc Sutton raised his hand and said, "I don't know who you are, but I do know nothing I have to say to this young man has anything whatsoever to do with you. So you just keep your distance."

Chase waited until the man had sulked his way back over to his low-slung foreign car, then demanded, "Tell me."

"Not good," Doc Sutton replied. "There. How's that for straight talking?"

Chase did not bother to mask his shock. "I thought she was doing okay. Usual aches and pains, but nothing out of the ordinary."

"Son, that lady's heart sounds like a Maytag chewing on a pair of old tennis shoes. She's been surviving for years on will alone." He made stiff-legged progress down the front steps. "Walk with me to my car."

Chase forced himself forward. "What can I do?"

"Nothing you aren't doing already. All her daily needs are seen to, she's got friends and family enough for that. Her sister may be moving in, much as Marie is against it. I refuse to get involved in that one. My feeling is, if the lady wants to live alone and die alone, that's her business."

Die. "Is it that bad?"

The old man peered out from beneath bushy eyebrows. "I think it's time you prepared yourself for the worst, son. Or the best. Marie Hale has long since made peace with herself and her God. If her time has come, her time has come. That's all there is to it."

Chase swallowed around the burning lump that had settled in his throat. "I just wish —"

"I know you do, and so do I. The world will be a poorer place, and that's a fact. But I'll tell you a secret forty-seven years of doctoring has taught me, son. Life goes on. Accept death as a part of it, and don't let a day pass without putting at least a little bit of goodness into it. You hear what I'm saying?"

Chase could do little more than nod.

Doc Sutton patted his shoulder. "You've been a good friend, son. She's proud of you and so am I. She tells me you're gonna be handling that Miami legal lizard over there, him and his friends."

"Try," he managed.

"That'll be a weight off her shoulders, sure enough." Another pat, then the doctor opened his door and climbed in. He looked up, nodded once, repeated, "Proud of you, son."

As soon as the doctor had driven off, the lawyer appeared at his side. "Perhaps now we can discuss the matter of —"

Chase took time for a pair of breaths before turning, but what remained in his eyes was still enough to force the lawyer back a step. "This afternoon. My office. Five o'clock," Chase said, his voice low with the strain of control. "And if you ever come within a mile of this house again, I'll see to it that Omega has absolutely no chance whatsoever of setting foot on her land. Is that clear?"

Kaitlyn read off the street sign as they turned into his cul-de-sac, "Willow Green Place. A lovely name."

He had picked her up a half hour ago, just driven over from the office after an exhausting meeting with the sleazeball lawyer. Wanted nothing more than to talk with her, feeling an incredible lift when she opened the door to him and smiled with genuine delight. It had come to him then, unbidden and unexpected, that he wanted to share his world with her. Everything. Including his home.

He stopped in front of the low-slung bungalow and looked at the front yard with its riot of color as though seeing it for the first time. "This is it."

Slowly she emerged from the car. "What a beautiful yard."

Chase circled around to her side. "My mother was really into gardening. She OD'd on petunias and azaleas, actually named each of the palm trees. Dad did the lawn, she did the flowers."

"And you've kept them up."

"Sort of. Nothing like they were. Gardening down here can be a full-time job if you let it."

The sound of another car turned him around. He felt a steely touch of anticipation when he saw it was Matthew. Regret, too, knowing the evening's plans were about to be drastically changed. But glad just the same.

Matthew's first words were, "I made a mistake, okay?"

Chase looked at him. "Am I really hearing this?"

"Don't make it any harder than it already is." Matthew's forehead was bunched with the same tension that tightened his voice. "I need to be there for you and Carlotta."

"Yeah, that's right. You do."

"So are we going after punishment, or after the bad guys?"

"It's great you stopped by," Chase said. "You remember Kaitlyn?"

"Sure. Hi."

She nodded his way, asked Chase, "Should I be going?"

"Not unless you want to," he replied. Not needing to think it out. "I have a problem. A big one. It's what was on my mind the other night. I'd like you to hear about it."

"All right," she said. No hesitation. "If you think I can help."

"You already have," he said. To them both, "Come on inside."

He took a few minutes to show her the living room, the view, but he felt her holding back. "We'll do this another time, just the two of us, let you really get a feel for the place."

She understood him perfectly. "I'd like that," she replied.

"Great, just great," Matthew said, grinning broadly. "You know how long I've been waiting to hear Slim here show an interest like this? About half a lifetime. Kaitlyn, you are a genuine miracle worker."

Chase got them drinks and sighed his way down to the couch. "This has been some day."

"Tell me about it," Matthew shot back. "And I've still got a long drive ahead of me tonight. What say you just give me the bare bones."

Chase fished out the diskettes he had carried with him all day, not knowing where to leave them, glad finally to hand them over to somebody else. First he explained to Kaitlyn who Carlotta was, then sketched out the night raid in D.C. and the day that had followed.

When he finished Matthew made no move toward the diskettes. "I can't take them."

"Why not?"

"I can't even touch them. If I did, I'd have to turn them over to the D.C. authorities. Matter of fact, we're not even having this conversation."

"You've got to help me, Matthew."

"I'm doing all the helping I can by not seeing them, believe me. Now stick them someplace else before they get officially noticed." He waited until Chase had reluctantly placed the disks back in his pocket before continuing, "Look here, old son. There's a couple of things they teach us folks in the AG's office that you need to hear. Part of the problem with evidence is, if it's been obtained in any illegal way, it is bad evidence and nothing will ever make it good." He pointed toward the unseen disks with his chin. "What you've got there is the very definition of tainted evidence."

"So what am I supposed to do?"

"Wait, now, I'm just getting started, and you know what happens if you stop a lawyer in midflow. We puff up like a blowfish and explode." He glanced at his watch, shook his head, and went on, "Okay. The trail of evidence that leads back to this tainted item — all that is tainted too. Which means nothing that is collected along the way can ever be good, even if it is legal up to a point. If the defense can tie it to a tainted origin, then it is all tainted. You see where I'm headed?"

"No."

"I don't know where these disks came from or what they contain. I've only got your word that it was gotten from a legal raid, and even if it was, there are two big problems you've got to face. The first is, anything I get off of these disks, no matter how valuable, is tainted. Control is your problem here. Custody and control of the evidence, to be exact. The police lost control when Carlotta gave it to you. The defense would accuse you of tampering. Which means if we take this from you and use it in a case we might be preparing, the defense could have the whole thing tossed out of court. You say the big players might be down here in Florida?"

"That's what Carlotta suspects."

He spent a moment staring through Chase's jacket, then shook his head. "I'm sorely tempted, old son, but I can't do it. We're working on a couple of cases of our own right now, one of them involving the feds. Major league stuff. The defense would just jump all over this like kids on a trampoline." He propped his feet on the nearby stool and went on. "But the other problem is the real kicker. That search-and-seizure warrant they used in that raid was quashed."

"What?"

"Law enforcement groups all over the nation were watching this one. The idea of an area-wide warrant was just the ticket, far as we were concerned. It was a way to get one leg over the fence, really hit them hard. But the ACLU took it to court and had it declared invalid. The judge ruled the warrant was overly broad. The D.C. police have had to release all suspects and return all evidence."

"Which means," Case said slowly, "that my having this is illegal."

"Having it, receiving it, keeping it, showing it to me, us sitting here talking about it," Matt agreed, his voice growing bitter. "Not that I'm in all that much of a hurry to call the cops. I tell you, old son, this is a sorry business these days. You ask me, what those ACLU folks did was just plain *wrong*. Our criminal justice system has been perverted. We're protecting the bad guys instead of helping their victims. You know how many weapons they found in that bust?"

"A lot."

"Dang right. Twelve *tons* of weapons, including a hundred thousand rounds of high-velocity ammunition and some stuff the feds didn't even know was in the country. Not to mention six hundred kilos of crack and other stuff. All this in a project the government built to give homes to people who couldn't afford any of their own. And most of 'em wanted the raids to happen. Folks actually stood around out there cheering the cops on."

"I remember," Chase said quietly, his mind filled with the sounds of that alien night.

"I don't suppose you realize just how unusual it is to have folks in a project cheer the cops. When they started the hearings, they had three hundred people come forward and offer to be witnesses for the police. Three hundred people. You know how much trouble we go to in areas like that to find even one person willing to testify? I mean to tell you, old son, those folks are scared. Like they say, the only law you can rely on in the projects these days is the law of gravity. But did the ACLU give a thought to all those people terrified to walk out their own front door? Shoot, no. They're too busy trashing our judiciary system, claiming all along they're out to protect people's rights."

Chase fingered the disks. "So what do I do with these?"

"Whatever it is, you'll have to do it on your own. Unless you want to wait and see if Carlotta shows up."

"I've waited as long as I can, Matt."

"Well, my advice to you — strictly off the record, you understand — is try and find out what's on those disks. Then, if it's for real, go and help somebody who's on the chase. Don't tell them anything about where you got it. You're just a concerned citizen who happened across this incredible find, and you want to offer what help you can." His features creased into a field of furrows. "And watch your back out there, Slim. There's some awful bad people out there doing awful bad things."

When Matthew had left and they were back watching the night settle in over the waters, Kaitlyn asked, "How much do you know about computers?"

"Next to nothing."

A pause, then, "Maybe I could help."

He looked at her. "You mean it?"

She was already rising to her feet. "I said maybe. Let's go back to my house, and I'll tell you for sure."

8

The house was very quiet when they arrived. Kaitlyn's mother was in Chicago. Her father was meeting with his church support group. The college student they paid to come over nights was reading in the living room.

"I really want to show you around the house," she said, leading him around to the back. "But not tonight, okay? Not while your mind is full of other things."

"Fine with me," he said.

Kaitlyn's room was at the opposite end of the back porch from her grandfather's and was probably once intended as maid's quarters. It was crowded with a desk, two bookshelves, a narrow brass bed, and a computer terminal on a separate little table with wheels. With a porch chair drawn up into the doorway, there was not enough room left for them both to stand up. As she switched on the computer and sorted the diskettes, he glanced around. The room was painted a creamy pastel that matched both the curtains and the bedspread. The walls were unadorned save for a single poster of a sunset. The whole room smelled faintly of her.

"This is nice," he declared.

"Okay," she said, already intent on the screen. "I'm loading a program I use to unscramble other people's files. It comes in handy sometimes, lets me take data from different sources."

He looked over her shoulder and saw only a long row of capital letters and dots. "I was talking about your room."

Her glance carried a message of uncertainty. "Maybe we should concentrate on this."

He sighed his agreement and watched the screen copy out the instructions as she typed. "I don't know what we have, and I don't know how to enter, so I'm playing it carefully."

She popped in one of the disks, keyed in, and the screen ranked up a single short ribbon of letters. "Okay," she said. "It looks like we have a program here." She read the screen for a moment, then shook her head. "It's missing the command code. That's the entry point, telling the computer how to enter the program files."

Chase nodded his acceptance of the information, feeling as lost as he usually did around computer types.

She popped out the disk, slipped in the second, read the screen, nodded. "Again, the way this has similar codes for the files, I'd say it was more of the same program. Also without the command code."

"What does that mean?"

"Well, say, if your man was taking information from one place to another, maybe they needed to carry the program too so that it could be read off another computer. But he leaves off the command code as extra insurance. People do that sometimes, wiping off that file or carrying it separately, as a sort of insurance for confidentiality. But I don't really need the program to translate a file, so I'm putting these two aside." She flipped out that disk, slid in the third. The screen went through a bewildering array of changes as she typed lightly on the keys. "Interesting."

"What is?"

"There's only one file here. Let's see if I can read it." She tapped more keys, the computer appearing to ask her questions which she quickly answered, and suddenly the screen was filled with hieroglyphics. "Uh oh. Encoded. I was afraid of that."

"You'll have to be a little clearer than that."

"The file is encrypted. That means it was

put on the disk in a certain way for security reasons. See, the computer has stored the data in a different language. It means that you need a special pass-code to find out what is written here." She popped out the disk, put in the last one, went through the same process. "Four files this time." Again the back and forth with the computer, and another screen filled with gibberish. She turned back to him. "I'm sorry, Chase. I'm not good enough to take this any further."

He was more aware of her closeness than what the screen displayed. "It doesn't matter."

"Yes it does. What you need is a hacker." She turned back to inspect the illegible screen. "Somebody who breaks codes. A computer freak."

"You know people like that?"

"No." She turned off the computer, pushed it away. "But I might know somebody who does. A friend works security at Crystal City. Someone I know through church. Sort of."

Chase filed the church information away for another time and pulled a face. "Not Miami. Please. I'd rather spend a weekend tending sheep in Outer Mongolia."

"There are three places on the East Coast where hackers gather," she said, ignoring his

163

complaint. She called up something on her computer, read off the screen, reached for her phone. "A place in New York, a shopping center near the Pentagon, and Miami's Crystal City Mall."

"Isn't it a little late to be catching somebody at the mall?"

"Not Sal. I have to work all this week, but hopefully he'll see you without me." She finished dialing, put the phone to the ear, asked him, "How does your schedule look for tomorrow?"

Wednesday morning, Lieutenant Governor Lamar Laroque was hosting members of the Florida Cattlemen's Association when Sabine poked her head into the conference room and said, "The call you've been waiting for."

He was up and out of his streamlined leather chair before she had finished speaking. "Excuse me a moment, gentlemen. This won't take any time at all."

He took the phone from Sabine, motioned with his head for her to seal the room, said, "Laroque."

"Sylvan Rochelle here, Governor."

"Morning, Mr. Rochelle." Cheerier than he felt. "How's the weather down your end?"

"I hadn't noticed. All right, I suppose."

Laroque had learned to probe other people sharp and fast, but behind Rochelle's faintly prissy air were walls he could not fathom. Rochelle continued, "We have a problem."

"We shall always have those, I'm afraid." Maintaining the lighthearted tone. Motioning for Sabine to pick up the earpiece and listen in. "One must always take time to enjoy the finer things of life, no matter how hectic, that's my motto. We are enjoying an absolutely gorgeous spring day up this way."

"I am happy for you." No sign of irritation, just a slight thickening of the faint accent. "My attorney spoke with this Bennett person yesterday."

"Why, that's just splendid."

"Not splendid at all. It appears we may not be able to tie our land deal up as swiftly as we had hoped."

"What did Bennett say?"

"According to my attorney, he said hardly a word. Just listened to the repeated offer and said he would be in touch."

Laroque raised one manicured hand and smoothed back his silver-white hair. "I'm afraid I don't understand. Offers like yours don't just grow on trees."

"My thoughts exactly. In any case, my attorney has managed to get hold of the agreement between the Hale woman and this

Bennett. It is, in his opinion, ironclad. Even if the Hale woman dies, Bennett retains sole responsibility for disposal of the property, and following that, is to be made head of her trust."

Even if she dies. The casual way he spoke those words suggested it had been considered as an option. Lamar nodded once, accepting it as confirmation of something he had long suspected. And probed further. "And if this Bennett fellow happens to meet with a dire end?"

"Responsibility passes to the lawyer who drew up the agreement."

A light dawned. "The same one who passed you a copy."

"Exactly."

"I see." Returning to the heartiness of earlier. "Then we know where we stand, don't we? I am to be meeting with this Bennett gentleman on Friday. I suggest we hold off on any further action until we have an opportunity to see whether our Mr. Bennett is open to some form of gentle persuasion."

Lamar exchanged pleasantries, hung up the phone, looked out his wall of plate glass, and said conversationally, "It appears that our meeting on Friday is becoming increasingly important." He mused a moment longer, then went on, "I want you to call our allies on the Space Coast. Explain to them that Mr. Bennett appears to be standing in the way of their area being seriously considered as a possible site for this new casino. Do not go into too great detail, they don't need to know all the ins and outs. Simply give them proper cause to soften this Mr. Bennett up on our behalf." Then he glanced over at his assistant. "My dear, is anything the matter?"

She shook herself awake. "No, nothing."

"You have turned positively green." He walked over and laid a hand upon her shoulder. "Now is not the time for you to be turning squeamish."

"I'm fine. Really." She looked up at him, her gaze more confused than he had ever seen. "Do you really think he would —"

"Who, Rochelle? He is a businessman. A professional. He would only do what is necessary. No more, no less." He inspected her. "Do you have a problem with that, my dear? Because if you do, now is most certainly the time to inform me."

"No, no, I understand. It's just . . ." She let the words hang in the air and pushed herself to her feet.

Lamar held the door for her, fastened his politician's smile back into place as he entered the conference room, made a mental note to watch her very, very carefully on this one.

Miami was about as similar to the rest of Florida as Havana. Miami was the place all of Florida's bad children were destined to wind up, according to their parents' threats. Miami was connected to the rest of Florida by the slenderest of threads, called interstates — threads that most of the rest of the state would gladly cut if they only knew how. It was said that every single banknote of twenty dollars or higher in Miami bore traces of cocaine, so much was snorted through the rolled bills. Nowadays, when Floridians said they had to go to Miami, they did so with a wry face and accepted the sympathy of their neighbors.

As far as Chase was concerned, the best thing about the Crystal City shopping complex was that it was situated both at the northernmost edge of the Miami sprawl and relatively close to the interstate. He spent a quarter hour searching for a parking space in the crowded lot, then twice that long getting lost and redirected inside the mall. Eventually he found the maze of cramped administration offices and waited in an airless cubicle until he was collected by Kaitlyn's contact.

Chase followed the man down to the security offices, then halted abruptly in the doorway. "Good grief."

"This is just one weekend's haul. Maybe a little more than usual since Monday was a school holiday. That's why we're a little late sorting." The Crystal City security chief led Chase through vast and bewildering piles of merchandise. "We give it back to the shops today, they rack it during the slow time tomorrow."

Chase skirted a pile of sport bags and gym shoes taller then he was. "It looks like a fire sale at Sears."

"Yeah, got a lot left to do. Sure you need to talk today?"

"I need to find out about this stuff as soon as I can."

"Well, on account of your being a buddy of Kaitlyn's." His name was Sal, a burly man not much over five five, hair grown long and tied back in a bushy ponytail, dressed in surfer's T-shirt and denim drawstring pants. Not exactly what Chase had imagined for the head of security at the Crystal City Mall. "How's Kaitlyn doing, anyway?"

"Wonderful." He followed Sal past pile after pile of tagged merchandise, everything from designer drawers to full-size color television sets. "People just walk out with this stuff?"

"What you see here is the downside of the consumer society," Sal said. "People run out of dough, they figure the world owes them one, so they come in here and walk off with whatever they need. That's the adult lifters. The teens have a different line."

"Which is?"

"Oh, pretty basic. They want it, they take it. Parents are too busy with the treadmill to teach them ideas like right and wrong." He pointed at three officers sorting through a mass of CDs. "We call these flat diamonds. Biggest headache of our business. Kids go for them constantly. The record companies did this survey a while back, turns out they sell more when the CDs are actually out there on display instead of kept back behind the counter with the display boxes all empty. Don't ask me why. All it takes is for one kid to show up at school with the newest hit album from Spitball or Red Death or whichever group's got the hot song of the moment and claim they stole it. Doesn't matter whether they did or not. Claiming they did it is in, see. Gives them class. Makes them up like shopping mall buccaneers or something."

"Status," Chase offered.

"Yeah. And it eggs everybody else on, see. The next week, we get maybe fifteen arrests from the same school, all part of some clique. It's a well-known pattern, we call it the herd syndrome. All traced back to one kid who probably bought the CD and thought it would be cooler to say it was stolen."

Sal passed through another room full of multicolored backpacks and sports clothes. "Same here, only a lot more multiple offenders, out for stuff they can sell easy. They're a different breed. Broken home, probably messed up on crack, sometimes gang connections. We caught one kid yesterday with almost four thousand dollars' worth of stuff on him. Eleven years old. Knew exactly what to pick up, only went for quality items. First time we'd seen him, so we called around. Found out he'd been picked up the week before over at Liberty City. That day he had almost ten grand worth of watches in his pack, still got off with a warning. Most cops are reluctant to bust anybody that young. The paperwork would choke a moose." He led Chase through another doorway. "Come on in here."

The office was jammed with five desks buried under avalanches of forms. All four walls were papered with wanted posters, most of the faces around thirteen or fourteen years old. Chase let himself be pointed into a creaking chair.

"I guess Kaitlyn told you we met at a retreat center last year. Most of the people there were couples, Kaitlyn looked a little lonely, so my wife sort of adopted her. We've stayed in touch ever since. She's a good kid."

"Yes she is."

The eyes probed hard. "You and she getting together?"

Chase met the gaze. "I'd like to. We're still in early stages yet."

"She's been through a hard time. Harder than she deserves."

Chase searched for something to reassure the man, settled on, "I respect her. Very much."

That was enough. The gaze lightened, and Sal said, "Kaitlyn told me you're after a hacker."

"Somebody I can trust. Totally."

"Yeah, that's what she said. I spoke to the guy I told her about, and he's willing to see you. No promises, but he'll talk. He was a regular around here a few years back, here and a lot of the other malls around south Florida. Seemed like we were bringing him in almost every weekend for a while. Always after computer stuff. Software, magazines, printers, modems, circuit boards, that kind of stuff. Finally got himself sent off to a correctional institute for juveniles, did maybe six months. Ended up coming to faith while he was in." The gaze returned to full bore. "You have any problem with that?"

"No."

"I tell you, seeing what's happened in his life, I sure wish more of these kids would give it a chance. Anyway, he works a straight job with a software company these days, hasn't been in trouble since. Spends his free time out here, trying to talk to the kids before they get in worse trouble than they already are. His name's Trig. Trig Adams. If anybody can help you, guess it'll be him."

It was late enough in the afternoon for most schools to have let out, so the Crystal City shopping mall was a two-storied chaotic din. A young girl played truly awful show-tune renditions on a revolving piano, while around her spread hundreds and hundreds of tables, all full. The entire ground floor's central atrium was encircled by food bars. The floor was ceramic tile, the ceiling steel and glass, the noise deafening.

A girl appeared at his elbow, her face aged somewhere around eighteen but her body stuck in early-teen gawkiness. She popped onto her toes and said something that was swept away in the pounding racket. He yelled, "What?"

She raised her voice. "You've got to learn to lip read if you're going to spend much time in this place. Are you Chase?"

"Yes."

"I'm Steffi. This way." She led him into the center of the din.

The young man wore a black turtleneck under a chain-knit sweater that stretched down to his knees. His eyes were clear green and cautious and very intelligent. He watched Chase approach with a measuring gaze. Steffi plopped into a free chair, pulled her legs up like pretzels, announced loudly, "This be him."

The gaze was unrelenting. Chase forced himself to hold it, remain calm, and wait. Finally a hand snaked out. "Let's have them."

It was Chase's turn to wait and inspect. Trig was having none of it. "Either you trust me or you don't."

Still he hesitated, wondering what Carlotta would think of him handing the diskettes over to somebody like this.

"It's no big deal to me one way or the other," Trig said. "But Sal said it was urgent."

"It is."

"Ooooh," Steffi chimed. "Big doings from the world of big business."

"It's not like that," Chase said, struggling with himself over how far to go. "They tried to kill a good friend of mine to get these back."

Trig's eyes crept up a notch. "Who's they?"

"That's why I need to know what's on the disks. To find the answer."

"Outstanding. A mystery." Steffi bounced up and down in her seat. "I just love mysteries."

Trig just sat and waited. Reluctantly Chase reached into his pocket and handed over the disks. Trig swiftly made them disappear and rose to his feet. "Do a little shopping, take in a movie, whatever you like."

Chase was impressed despite himself. "That fast?"

"We'll go out to the car, use the notebook." Steffi did not appear able to stand still. She danced in place as she pointed to her companion's lumpy backpack. "Ready for every emergency."

"Meet you back here in a couple of hours," Trig said. And then he was gone.

By the time they met again, the mall was winding down for the night. Which meant they could talk without shouting.

"Two of them aren't anything," Trig told him, tossing the pair of disks on the table. "Out-of-date programs, sorta gives you an idea what level these guys are operating on."

"Moron," Steffi agreed. "Barely above ga-ga and spit bubbles."

"This kind of user, he'll go into the store, pick out hardware because it's expensive, wear it around like a gold Rolex. Doesn't have a clue what it'll do, doesn't really care. Probably got himself a five-thousand-dollar Pentium notebook with active-matrix color, can't hardly find the power switch."

" 'Course the good news is," Steffi added, "his encrypted data was easy to crack."

"Piece of cake," Trig agreed. "Like hiding treasure under a tree with a yellow ribbon around the trunk."

"So you found something," Chase said.

"You could say that," he replied, and reached into his shirt pocket.

"And behind door number two," Steffi sang, "ta-da, the deluxe washer-dryer with a lifetime supply of bath oil."

Trig hefted the first disk. "Names. A couple of them were familiar. The rest, I dunno, maybe I've heard of them, but I can't remember where. Anyway, each of them has a little data strung alongside. They want this or that, looks like. Some notation too, now I've forgotten the word."

"Lame duck," Steffi offered. "A lot of them had it written beside their name. That they were lame ducks. Poor little things, can't walk proper."

Trig offered the disk, asked, "Does that mean anything to you?"

Chase accepted the disk and replied honestly, "I don't know."

He was more reluctant to release the second disk. "This was the surprise. Illegal access codes. Lots of them. More than lots. Plus another list of names, this one with contact times and prices. You know what this stuff is worth?"

"Oodles," Steffi said.

"I don't even know what you're talking about," Chase said.

"Big money. No, delete that. Bigger money. An illegal access code goes for around thirty thousand dollars today. Say you've got fifty of them here. At least. I didn't bother to count. Say a mil and a half as an easy base."

"Plus a death warrant," Steffi added. "Yours."

"I can't believe you were walking around with this," Trig said.

"Ahem," Steffi said.

"Oh, right." Reluctantly he handed it over, had trouble letting his fingers open.

"Give the toy to daddy," Steffi said. "That's a nice boy."

"Some days it doesn't pay to be on the right side with God," he said, releasing his grip.

"Yes it does," Steffi corrected.

He sighed. "Yeah, well, anyway, keep a tight lid on this."

Chase slid the disks into his own pocket, felt them burn his skin. "Keep a lid on *what?*"

9

"You're talking about a whole different world," Trig told him.

"And a whole different vocabulary," Steffi added. "You know what a hacker is, right? Well, a phreaker is, like, a phone hacker, somebody that uses computers to hunt down phone codes. A shoulder surfer's somebody that hides near phone booths, uses high-powered lenses to watch people key in their credit card numbers. A cell operator takes these stolen numbers from phreakers and shoulder surfers and sells them to people wanting to make long distance calls on the cheap."

"Small-time cell operators work from phone booths," Trig said, taking the lead. "Any time you drive along a busy downtown street, find fifteen people waiting to use a phone, it isn't because this is the only one in town. What it is, the maid from Nicaragua hears from her sister's husband's best friend that there's this guy who'll let her call home for five bucks, talk as long as she likes. She stands in line, gives him the number, he keys

179

it in with the stolen card, she talks and talks and talks. Bigger operators rent an apartment, set up in a garage, have maybe ten lines going out, ten different stolen numbers. Place could have upwards of a hundred people milling about, shouting over the lines to Pakistan, Argentina, wherever."

The shopping mall continued its winding down. A few kids came racing through, their shouts and footsteps echoing off the distant ceiling. One by one the shops began rolling down their shutters. Chase sat and listened and tried to learn, not overly concerned about the hour. The later he started back, the lighter the traffic. Lighter traffic was a major plus. Fewer macho studs playing bumper tag, less chance of running into somebody using a gun instead of his turn signal. The pleasures of an evening drive in Miami.

"Even that's minor league compared to what you've got," Steffi added.

"Right." Trig pointed at the diskettes in Chase's jacket pocket. "Your second disk is broken down into four files. A few credit card numbers, chip codes, some PBX codes, and even a list of suppliers. Must be a big buyer, to get access directly to the phreakers. That surprised me. But I can't figure it out any other way. You've got a guy's label, you know, his nickname, then his phone number, then a day and time to call. Has to be a phreaker."

"I'm pretty sure," Chase replied, "that I haven't understood a word you've just said."

Steffi gave an exaggerated sigh. "Back to first grade, Trig."

"Okay, look. We're talking about different ways of making money off phone systems — by getting hold of different kinds of numbers. First of all, say some shoulder surfers have collected a few credit card numbers. They're probably all clean, haven't been used, or not much. You pay top dollar for clean numbers, but ten times that for a PBX access code."

"A hundred times," Steffi corrected. "Maybe more."

"Right. A PBX is a private bench exchange, you know, inside a big company. They've got an 800 number for people to call in, okay? Then their employees, they get a private access code. This lets them call in, punch in the private code, then call out again at the cheaper corporate rate — instead of having to pay hotel rates or pay phone rates or car phone rates, whatever."

"I feel like you're talking a completely different language," Chase confessed.

"Not just you," Trig replied. "These big companies, they buy these feature-rich

CPEs, that's customer premises equipment, then the exchange is inside their company, okay? And *all* CPEs are sold with the access code set at 0000."

"They ought to be using more than four numbers," Steffi added. "But it's all the suits are able to remember without having it stamped on their foreheads."

"Right. The fewer the numbers, the easier for a phreaker to random-access it. A good phreaker can random-access a four-digit sequence in less than a day. But that's not the only problem. A lot of these companies, they leave their access code set where it was when the exchange was installed. You know, at 0000. Why? Because they don't have idea one about their own equipment."

"Sometimes you don't even need the code," Steffi said. "The first hacker that moved onto the telephone lines was this guy called Captain Crunch. He took a whistle from the cereal box, blew into a frequency modulator, found out it was set at 2600 megahertz. That's the level of all numbers on the touch-tone phones. So he started calling 800 numbers, then blowing the whistle into the phone. If there was a touch-tone access code, it automatically switched him into the system."

"The telephone companies finally worked

that out," Trig said. "But the legend lives on. There's an underground electronic magazine now called 2600, where phreakers teach each other the tools of the trade." He looked at Steffi. "I've forgotten something."

"Chip codes," she sang.

"Right. You've got a file for those as well. What happens is, phreakers sit on the sides of freeways with radar guns, sort of like electronic vacuum cleaners. They wait for an expensive car to drive by and shoot it. If somebody is using a mobile phone, the gun intercepts the signal and reads off the phone's private access code."

"You can buy a gun like that for about three hundred dollars these days," Steffi said. "If you know where to look."

"Mobile phones constantly transmit their access codes whenever they're being used," Trig explained. "It's implanted on an internal chip. Change the chip code, and the cost of the call is billed to somebody else."

"Not to mention keeping the call secret," Steffi added.

"Yeah, say the police are watching for calls from a certain mobile phone. What they do is order the central exchange to record all conversations coming from that access code, okay? But if the chip code has been changed, then the police don't know which number to watch."

"You're talking about drug dealers, aren't you?" Chase looked from one to the other. "You used to do this?"

"Hey, it started out as a game," Trig said. "It does for a lot of these kids. They do it because it's a challenge, a sport they can play at home on their computer. Then somebody comes in, offers them money for doing what they'd do anyway. They don't know who the buyer is, and most of the time don't want to know."

"But the buyers are the drug lords, right?"

Trig nodded glumly. "You can only keep your head in the sand for so long. That was what woke me up as much as getting caught ripping off stuff. They have people around here a lot of the time, looking for phreakers they can hire."

"Vultures," Steffi said. "That's what they're called because that's what they are."

Trig motioned with his chin toward Chase's pocket. "But that wasn't stuff meant for vultures. Too much, too heavy. That was a major sale. Right to the top. Somebody able to lay down a suitcase full of cash."

Chase looked from one to the other. "What are you saying?"

"Watch out," Steffi said, both still and serious for the first time that night. "Some-

184

body is gonna be looking for you. Somebody bad."

"Somebody you don't want to meet," Trig
agreed. "And if you do, somebody you won't
meet but once."

Chase pulled his truck up alongside the
telephone booths flanking the mall exit. Despite himself, he was more than a little
shaken by what he had learned. He dug
around in his pocket and came up with
Carlotta's hospital number. He dialed,
waited, and then when the operator answered instead of his friend, he had to fish
for a moment to remember the name she
had used. "Miss, ah, Smith, please."

"I'm sorry," came the standard reply. "Miss
Smith has been released."

A faint tingle of alarm. "Can you tell me
when?"

"Just a minute." A pause, then, "Miss
Smith left yesterday."

"Wasn't she supposed to be in for a while
longer?"

"What is your relation to the patient,
Mr. . . ."

"Bennett. Family," he replied, deciding he
had as much right to that title as anyone in
her life just then.

"Yes, Mr. Bennett, I have you down as

next of kin. I wouldn't have any idea about her treatment. The only notation here is that she checked herself out. You'll have to call back tomorrow and speak with her doctor. That's, let's see, Dr. McTirney."

Chase made a note, thanked her, dialed Carlotta's home number from memory. With each unanswered ring he felt the hollow space in his gut growing larger and colder.

He hung up, tried her precinct, got a deep-voiced black man who demanded abruptly, "Who's this."

"Chase Bennett. I'm a friend."

"Yeah, well, Carlotta hasn't been around for a while."

"What about Detective Jack Sproul?"

A pause, then, "Who did you say this was?"

The alarm went off in his head, louder this time. "Charles Benson. I'm a friend of theirs from," a breath, "Atlanta."

"Benson, Charles," he growled, slow enough to be writing as he spoke. "Jack isn't here either."

"Could you tell me when he starts his shift?"

Another hesitation. "Jack ain't been around for a while either."

Chase felt his guts twist another notch.

"Jack Sproul has been put on administrative leave too?"

Anger deepened the voice. "That's departmental business. You got any further questions, call back during regular office hours, talk to the lieutenant responsible for community affairs." The receiver went down as if it had been hammered.

Chase stood there with the night spreading out unbroken around him, powerless to move, unable to think of anything else he could do.

The phone's insistent buzz woke him from a scattered sleep. He fumbled, caught the phone on his third sweep of the bedside table, mumbled, "This had better be good."

"I let you sleep as long as I could," Kaitlyn said. "I'm supposed to be at work already."

He rolled over, opened one eye, found himself unable to focus on the clock. "What time is it?"

"Almost seven."

Chase groaned.

"What time did you get in last night? Don't you ever check your messages?"

"After one. And I was too tired to bother."

"I couldn't sleep, I was so worried. What happened?"

"Give me a minute, okay?" Chase groaned

his way to his feet, padded to the bathroom, splashed water on his face, wondered why fatigue left him feeling so numb. He stumbled into the kitchen and picked up the extension. "Okay, I'm back."

"What are you doing?"

"Making coffee."

"Talk while you're working. I have to go."

Chase gave her the bare bones, which was still enough to jolt him awake, just remembering it all. He stumbled over some of the terms, gave up, did his best to sketch out what he understood.

"There's something you're not telling me," she said when he finished.

"Two things," he agreed, surprise managing to filter through his lack of sleep. How could someone who did not know him at all know him so well?

"So tell."

"Are you sure?"

"Chase Bennett, either you tell me right this instant or I am personally going to come by after work and give you a piece of my mind."

"I might like that." Smiling in spite of himself.

"Chase, please, okay? And fast. I'm late. Really."

He told her about Trig's final warning. As

he did so he spooned coffee into the filter, poured in water, was relieved to find his hand remaining steady. Then he told her about not being able to find Carlotta or Jack.

"That worries you more than the warning." An observation, not a question.

"She wouldn't tell me where she was going from the hospital. I don't have any way even to find out if she's okay."

"I could come by your office after work," she offered. "Take you to dinner or something. Maybe together we can come up with an answer. Or at least a reason to hope."

Chase felt the unseen knots easing in his shoulders and belly. He was not alone. "You," he said quietly, "are a real friend."

He felt fragile but fairly alert by the time he showered and breakfasted. As he was preparing to leave, Chase remembered he had not checked his messages. He stood knotting his tie and smiling over Kaitlyn's messages, one every hour, passing through impatience and on into irritation and from there into genuine worry.

Then he was jolted by a different voice. Angrier and more strident. Furious, almost. "Chase, this is Linda Armacost. I have spoken this evening to," a pause to check her paper, then, "Sabine Duprie, personal assistant to the lieutenant governor. She has informed me and Barry Tadlock of your handling of the Marie Hale property. Frankly, I am shocked that you would put yourself in a position of even *appearing* to block such a potentially important deal for Brevard County. I have just spoken to Barry, and we are contemplating bringing you before the board on charges of conflict of interest. If you are even the least bit concerned about keeping your job, I suggest you meet me and Barry in his office at ten o'clock tomorrow morning. Be on time."

Grey Spenser called himself one of the hunter-fisher breeds. Which meant he liked tall tales and dawn trips with buddies to the back of beyond, and counted among his oldest pals two of the finest flytiers in the world. At home he tended toward topsiders with loose soles, went to fancy restaurants sporting string ties with turquoise catches, and kept a pair of over-and-under twelve gauges on the wall of his office to scare off, as he put it, "All the time wasters and fast talkers who're out to sell me what I don't need and don't like and don't want to hear about."

His office operated at a level of barely

controlled bedlam, directed by a voice so loud that most staffers found their boss by cocking one ear and following the loudest noise. When interviewed by *Enterprise* magazine about his employee policy, he had described it as "benevolent dictatorship. Easy on the benevolence, heavy on the dictator. In another era I would have made a great king."

The interviewer had concluded her article by agreeing that he probably would.

Retirement meant that Grey spent a lot less time at the office, but not that he had slowed down any. These days he split his time between the antigambling battle and his grandkids. Anything left over went to what he called his little hobby. This involved scouring the countryside for the beat-up wrecks of vintage cars, then working with a couple of local garages in restoring them to pristine condition. Once the cars were finished, he lost all interest in them except to sell them off for a tidy profit. His interest was not in the driving, but in the challenge of returning them to bygone glory.

When Chase arrived, Grey was out giving a final polish to his latest find, a 1951 Rolls convertible with cream exterior, ivory leather interior, and burl dash. Four months earlier, the car had been a sad, tired excuse for a machine, battered by several wrecks and almost buried under a decade of dust and neglect.

Chase climbed from his truck, commented, "Nice."

"The last of her kind, kiddo." Grey had really worked up a sweat, the thick pelt on his shoulders matted down. Even at sixty-eight he remained a bull of a man. "Hand built from start to finish."

"Yeah, well, remember me in your will."

"Everybody who's ever owned one has their favorite Rolls legend. That's part of what makes these cars special. Mine goes like this. There's this farmer over in England, you know, the gentleman kind, coupla thousand acres and a castle. He owns this company I used to do business with. Anyway, he's out driving his Rolls along the dirt paths on his land, checking out things after this really hard rain. Seeing if his prize sheep got their cashmere coats wet, stuff like that. So he dips down into this culvert the rain's dug, and wham! Hits this big rock and his front axle breaks in two. Back he goes, on foot this time, calls up the Rolls people, and orders a new axle. Two days later, get this, a helicopter comes buzzing over loaded with jacks, a new axle, tools, two mechanics, the works. They fix the car, drive it back, load themselves in the chopper, and off they go.

"The guy is understandably nervous at this point, wondering what Rolls is going to charge him for six or seven hours of a chopper's time. Six weeks go by, though, and no bill. The guy calls, says he's waiting and mind they don't charge for what he didn't order, like the flying chauffeur service.

"Another coupla months, nothing. He calls again, says, look, I'm closing out my books for the year, either you send me the bill now or it's quits. This snooty voice on the other end goes, bill for what, sir? He gets hotter, gives them the whole nine yards — chopper he's not paying for since he didn't order it, mechanics, axle, the works. The voice comes back, sir, a Rolls axle does not break." Grey stopped to grin and swipe his forehead with one burly forearm. "Can you believe it? What, maybe a twenty-thou outlay, they're gonna write it off to protect their reputation. Sir, a Rolls axle does not break. Only the Brits, Chase. I'm telling you. They're a class all their own."

Chase decided he had been patient long enough. "I've got a problem."

"Yeah, I sorta figured that, you standing there with a face all angled the wrong way. You wanna talk about it?"

"That's why I came."

"Go on in, make yourself comfortable out

193

on the porch. I'll clean up and join you. You know where everything is."

The house was built like the man — big and hearty and open and rich. Since his wife had died three years earlier, he had lived there all alone, much to the dismay of the blue-rinse crowd. Chase walked through the white marble foyer, crossed the paneled den, stopped in the vast kitchen for a Coke, passed through the double French doors, and took a seat on the shaded deck. The swimming pool sparkled a pristine blue in the sun. Palms lining the walled garden clattered a welcome.

Five minutes later Grey walked out toweling his hair. "So what's on your mind, kiddo?"

Chase pointed over to where a pair of tricycles lay upended by the pool. "Joy's kids are sure growing up."

"Yeah, three and four now. Apple of their granddaddy's eye, both of them." He plopped down in a neighboring chair. "Been seeing a lot of them recently. Something tells me there's been some problems on the home front. She won't tell me nothing, though. Just comes over with the kids, sits there watching us whale around with this sad look on her face." He looked over. "How come you two never got together?"

"I tried once. She wasn't interested."

Grey grunted. "Yeah, she never did have much of an eye when it came to men. That lame-brain she married is a perfect example." He tossed his towel aside. "You about done beating around the bush?"

Chase nodded. "Matter of fact, the lame-brain is part of why I'm here."

"Barry?" The astonishment was real. "I never figured that guy had enough fight in him to work his way out of a wet paper bag."

"He's into something bad."

"You think this or you know it?" Hard now. Showing the steel that had taken him from plumber's assistant to owner of one of the largest chains of plumbing and construction supply companies in the country.

"Ninety-nine percent certain. Maybe more."

"I'm listening."

So Chase told him. Trying to concentrate strictly on the property issue and ignore his worry over Carlotta's disappearance. Heavy with the sense of too much hitting him at once. Too much.

When he had finished, Grey sat in silence, staring out over the swimming pool, his face grim and angry and sad. "Gambling."

"That's what it looks like to me."

"It's the only thing that makes sense,"

Grey agreed, reluctant yet too practical to ignore the clearest answer. "Fifteen million dollars for her property is just plain ridiculous."

"I know."

"Three million, five mil tops. Fifteen million, they want this thing sewn up quiet and fast." He turned a bleak gaze toward Chase. "I get the feeling you're not telling me everything."

Chase sighed his way around the other worry. "Something on my mind. Nothing to do with this, though."

"You want to tell me about it?"

He was tempted but shook his head. "Maybe it'd be better not to mix the two up."

Grey nodded his acceptance. "You change your mind, let me know."

"Thanks. I really appreciate that."

"Barry and the lieutenant governor," Grey mused, suddenly looking his age. "Who would have thought?"

"That's not for sure," Chase said. "Well, to be honest, nothing about this is certain. But most especially that. All I know is, the lieutenant governor's office calls to invite me to a special meeting almost immediately after word of this land deal gets out. First time they've ever made contact. Then I hear that the lieutenant governor's office has gotten in touch with Barry and Linda to inform them how displeased they are with how I'm handling Marie's property. And you told me at church that Laroque was backing Sylvan Rochelle's casino project. It all just seemed like more than coincidence."

"It is," Grey agreed. Definite now. "Lamar Laroque sees himself as power broker to the insider superparty. He calls himself a Republican because that was the party that brought him to power. But in truth he owes allegiance only to himself. That man inhales power like other people inhale air."

"Sounds like you know him."

"We've crossed swords before. He knows what I think of him, and that makes me his enemy. But because I still might be useful, he's held off on coming after me. Until now." Grey hesitated, then asked, "Your old girlfriend used to work for the LG's office, didn't she? What was her name?"

"Sabine. She still does."

"She the one who contacted you?"

"Yes." Remembering the call. Feeling the onset of another bout of uncertainty. So much going on.

"Think you can handle working with her?"

"If I needed to. But I'd pretty much decided not to show up at tomorrow's powwow. I don't see what good it would do." Not to mention his reluctance to rock the boat he and Kaitlyn were on.

Grey was silent for a time, inspecting the sky beyond the pool, then said, "I think you should play along."

"What?"

"See where it takes you, find out what's underneath the rock." Grey glanced over. "You're a good question asker. Ask all you can."

"This is not exactly what I expected to hear from you."

"You know the old adage," Grey replied. "Keep your friends close and your enemies closer. Get in tight enough to find out who's involved. We need ammunition. Something we can use against them."

"I can tell you who's behind this," Chase said. "Sylvan Rochelle. And from the sounds of things, he's got Laroque in his pocket."

"Can you prove that?"

Chase thought it over. "No, I guess not."

"That should be your first aim. And second, find out if there's anything fishy going on. For example, who's behind Rochelle? Where does his money come from?"

"They say his family's rich."

" 'They' would say anything if it meant new money for a big project." Grey shook his head. "A deal of this size, especially one based on gambling, is going to bring in a different kind of player."

"Sure," Chase agreed. "Ones with power. Like Sylvan Rochelle. Not to mention his squid of a lawyer."

Spenser shook his head. "Don't focus just on the players they want you to see. Look behind this front. Search the shadows." His eyes were still on the horizon as he added, "I promise you one thing. You won't like what you find."

10

Chase drove directly to Marie's house after the meeting with Barry Tadlock and Linda Armacost. By that point, he was not in the best frame of mind to visit a critically ill friend. But he did not want to put off this visit any longer.

Yes, yes, he had told Barry and Linda, he knew he had made a mistake. He understood it perfectly now. Agreeing from the outset had thrown them off balance. How had he dared talk to Rochelle's lawyer in that way? Chase had searched, could only come up with, I hoped to get a better deal. Putting it forward almost as a question, wondering if it sounded as weak to them as it did to him. They had swallowed it, though. Clearly not knowing how high Rochelle's offer had been. Chase had offered the most abject apologies he could manage and gotten out as fast as he could.

He pulled into Marie's driveway still seething from the need to play the contrite employee, taking only minor satisfaction at Barry's and Linda's obvious disappointment that he had not put up more of a fight. He cut off the motor, took a couple of deep breaths, willed himself to calm down. Little success.

He stepped from the Camaro, but before he had crossed the lawn the front door opened. Out stepped a woman from church whose name Chase could not recall. In an exaggerated whisper she greeted him with, "She's resting."

Chase stopped on the bottom stair. He looked up at the woman who barred the door with her fake smile and her flower-print dress. "How is she?"

"Fine." The smile was firmly in place. Crossing her arms, letting him know he'd need a battering ram to get by her. "She just needs to be taking it easy, that's all."

A querulous voice from within demanded, "Who is it, Gladys?"

"Chase Bennett, Miss Hale," she said, still smiling down at him.

"Well, let him in."

"I can come back later, Miss Marie," Chase said, more for Gladys's benefit than the woman inside. Let her know he was on her side, pave the way for future visits.

Not turning around, Gladys raised her voice and said, "Now, Miss Hale, the doctor said —"

"I heard the doctor same as you. Being sick doesn't make me stupid, just trapped. Now move out of the way and let the boy inside. I want to talk to him."

Chase murmured his apology, hid his smile the best he could, and slid past the woman's disapproving gaze. He felt better than he had all day. "Hello, Marie."

"Come over here and sit down." Raising her eyes and her voice. "The boy and I have something private to discuss. Go back to the kitchen, why don't you, Gladys."

Marie watched him pull a chair up beside her daybed. "Don't see why these ladies have to insist on treating me like I was a nitwit."

"They're doing the best they can."

"Well that don't earn them a passing grade in my book." She inspected his face. "I detect some worries underneath that smile."

He felt the grin fade. "Never could hide anything from you."

"That bad?"

"Bad enough. How are you?"

"Hanging on. Barely." Her color was high and her breathing was rough. But her eyes were as alert as ever. "Pull your chair up closer. Now, do any of these worries have anything to do with our land?"

"It's your land, Marie. Not mine."

"You mix yourself up in my affairs, you share the whole shebang. Now tell me what's the matter."

"Nothing, really. I can handle it."

"Lesson one in dealing with the not-yet-deceased: Don't kid a kidder."

"I don't like it when you talk that way."

"Then don't give me reason to." She leaned forward a touch. "You think it's fun lying around here being waited on by people who think it's their Christian duty to smile all the time? Tell me what's going on out there, Chase. Give me an excuse to think I'm still in the land of the living."

So he told her. All of it. Starting with the missing friend and the disks, ending with his conversation that morning with Grey. Finding great comfort in sharing his burdens with a friend.

When he was finished, Marie lay watching his face with bright, burning eyes, then asked, "Have you ever thought they might all be connected?"

"There's no way. How could they be?"

"Probably aren't," she agreed. "You'd be surprised what this addled old brain comes up with these days."

"You're not addled."

"I *am* addled and I *am* dying." The gaze

much softer than her tone. "Best you get used to both, Chase."

"You can't," he said. Unable to say the last word. Die.

A glint of humor. "Now is that a fact?"

"I need you," he said hoarsely.

"How sweet." She reached up one hand. "Now give the old gal a kiss, then go back out there and join the real world. Live a full day for me."

He did as he was told, miserable with new hurt. "It couldn't be much fuller."

"That's the spirit." Her hand remained upraised toward him as he let go and walked away. "You're a good boy, Chase."

He was at the front door before the idea came to him. He turned back around and asked, "I have to go away for a couple of days. When I get back, could I bring someone by to meet you?"

The glimmer of a smile returned. "Someone special?"

"Maybe. I hope so."

"Then I'd be pleased to meet her. Afternoons are better for me. Call so the ladies can have me dressed proper."

When he had finished packing, Chase walked to the phone and hesitated one last time. Knowing that to pick it up meant he was committed. Knowing it had to be done. He dialed the number from the attorney's card, took a couple of deep breaths to still the tremors.

The guy came on fairly swiftly for a Miami lawyer, caution mixing with surprise in his voice. "Claude Sorrens, Mr. Bennett. What can I do for you?"

"I need to be down your way this weekend," he said, making it up as he went, playing it as casual as he could manage. "I was just wondering if maybe I could meet up with the man himself."

"Well, hey." Reluctant now. Uncertainty slowing the pace. "This weekend looks a little busy for me. I'm scheduled to be down in the Keys with some friends."

"I meant Sylvan Rochelle," Chase said, knowing he had been understood the first time. "Nothing official. Just a casual five minutes to get acquainted."

"Mr. Rochelle is booked solid for weeks in advance," the lawyer said, clearly disliking the idea of their meeting when he was not around. "Was there anything in particular I might be able to help you with?"

"Not at all." Firm now. Accustomed from his years with the chamber to playing the corporate chess game. "I'd just like to put a face to the name. It'd make me feel a lot better about doing business with him."

"Sylvan has a table booked every Saturday night at Portofino's." Offering a negative response while saying yes. Portofino's was virtually impossible to get into. "But otherwise —"

"Portofino's would do just fine," Chase replied. And it would.

"Well, hey." Alarmed that his ploy had not worked. "I could maybe shift things around, fit you in somewhere early next week."

"Just tell Mr. Rochelle that I'll try to stop by, have a brief chat sometime Saturday night. Thanks, Mr. Sorrens. Have a nice weekend."

Chase stopped by Kaitlyn's on his way out of town, wanting to see her before he left for Tallahassee, needing to ask for printouts of what was on the disks now that the files were no longer encoded. At the door he met her father, a gentle-voiced elder copy of the daughter. The man was on his way out, invited Chase to wait. When Chase was alone, he found his footsteps tracking down the long wooden back porch, past the padded sofa bed, along the line of well-tended houseplants to the final door. He hesitated, battered once again by the smell emitted from within, but willed himself forward. "Mr. Picard?"

"Who's that?" The head shifted just far enough for the now-alert eyes to fasten on him.

"Chase Bennett. I'm a friend of Kaitlyn's."

"Well, don't hang around there in the doorway, son. Come on in where I can see you."

Chase walked over and sat down, wondering why he was there. "How are you doing today?"

"Can't complain." Clearly this was not a topic of choice. "You say you're a friend of my little gal's?"

"That's right."

"She's been through a hard time, sure enough." The voice had the strength of a weak summer breeze passing through marsh islands, all rattles and rustles and bare breaths of sound. "Still waiting to see which way she's gonna turn."

"Kaitlyn's going to be all right," Chase assured him.

"Didn't say nothing about all right," the old man replied. He watched Chase pull up a chair and sit down beside the bed. "Kaitlyn's bearing the burden of a lot of believers, something trying to separate them from God. You understand what I'm saying?"

Chase had never seen eyes that color before, the white-blue of a morning sky before the sun rose over the horizon. "I'm not sure."

"Some folks, they got lots of trouble letting go when they've had their forty days in the desert. They hold on to the memories, keep 'em a constant temptation to turn in anger and frustration away from the one true strength. What they remember ain't just that God was silent. Naw, that they could stand. Far as these people can tell, God turned against them. For folks that've built their world upon the Word, that's the hardest blow of all."

He turned his head back toward the ceiling and paused to wipe spittle from his cheek. "Most folks, they stay Christian. The light of faith don't die. They do that and they count themselves well done. And it's true enough, far as it goes. But what they don't see is what they've lost."

Chase sat and watched the eyes close, the breathing ease. He was tempted to stand and leave, but felt there was something more there, something more he wanted to hear. Not for Kaitlyn. For himself. "What's that?"

The eyes of palest blue shot open. "Eh?"

"You said there was something they lost, the Christians you were talking about. What was it?"

The head swiveled far enough for the gaze to fasten upon him once again. "You said you were Kaitlyn's friend?"

"Yessir."

"You more than that?"

"I'd like to be." There was no room here for anything less than the truth.

The old man nodded once, as though satisfied that it was worth the effort. "Most folks draw in. They retreat. They stop growing. They don't reach out for opportunities. They've seen the risk, felt the pain."

Chase gazed into eyes flecked with the clouds of time and listened as the old man went on, "The Lord's waiting to heal them. He calls to them, says, come and drink and let me fill you with purpose. But they don't listen. They're afraid."

"I know the feeling," Chase murmured.

"They build up walls. Don't venture into the unknown, not ever again. It stops them from reaching out, from doing for the Master. It's like the helping hand of Jesus has been plumb cut off."

Chase looked down at his own hands, felt the fear, knew the beckoning call.

"Days get filled with what's safe," the old man went on, his voice a dry-throated whisper. "World just keeps on shrinking smaller and smaller. Folks fill their days with busy, never looking at what's outside the borders. Don't hear the calls of those in need. Got problems of my own, they say. Doing all I can. Truth is, they don't want to *reach* anymore. And whatever it is they should've been doing, it never gets done."

The eyelids tracked downward as though pulled by invisible strings. They reopened with an effort. "Been waiting to see if my little gal's gonna be strong enough to accept her healing, learn to reach out again. She's been trying to hide behind her old grandpa, but I ain't gonna let her. Nossir. Ain't got no business letting the world have its way with her, she's too good a gal."

Chase sat and watched the old man drift away. When he was sure the old man was asleep, Chase eased back and only then saw the shadow in the doorway. He turned, saw it was Kaitlyn. "How long have you been there?"

"Long enough."

He walked over, was met by an open-hearted gaze. They walked down to the other end of the porch holding hands, gazing out over the lawn. They knew a moment of that wonderful silence which comes to friends now and again. Full of peace and a sharing beyond words. And because it was new, both the peace and the sharing, they grew shy, both about themselves and what was growing between them.

When he thought it was safe to speak again, Chase asked, "Is this really happening?"

She turned and looked up at him with disarming frankness. "I've been hurt," she said.

"I know."

"I don't know how this is supposed to go anymore. How to trust, how to give, how to just be with someone."

"I'm not someone," he corrected, but without heat. "I am me. This is us."

She nodded slowly. "You're right. That's part of the problem."

"Is it?"

She raised those lucent eyes of hers, studied him, said in a voice stripped of defenses, "Maybe not."

He started to raise one hand, wanted to wrap his fingers around that graceful neck, draw her close, found he could not. For an instant his own ghosts closed in, whispering fears and worries from the time when his heart was not yet whole again.

He let his hand drop and asked, "Do you think we could be friends? I mean, I want to be more than that. But friends as well." He took a breath, afraid of sounding foolish, knowing it needed to be said. "Sharing things, talking about stuff that matters, trusting each other with more than just the relationship. Am I wrong to want something like that, to be friends with you as well as . . ." and there he stopped, unable to go on, too full of the sudden hunger to even say what he thought.

Her gaze had not moved. She had not even blinked while he spoke. Kaitlyn let out a long breath. "I don't know how you do that."

"Do what?"

"Say the absolute right thing at the time I need to hear it most."

What he felt in his heart approached pain. He swallowed the lump and confessed, "Maybe it comes from waiting so long to have someone to say it to."

The trip to Tallahassee took six hours of steady driving. Chase drove until fatigue began clogging his vision, then pulled off into a motel. A quiet dinner, then back to his room and several hours of reading Grey's antigambling brochures and staring up at the ceiling, reviewing all that was happening, trying to shape out what he wanted to do the next day. He fell asleep to a whirling kaleidoscope of thoughts and worries.

The next day dawned fresh and clear.

Chase started off after breakfast in a much brighter frame of mind, resolved and ready. He found himself truly happy to be back in the Panhandle, an area he had loved since his first visit the year he started with the chamber.

The Florida Panhandle was a land of endless pine forests and swamps and snow-white beaches and towns from a bygone era. One could stand along some stretches of the Gulf shoreline and not see another soul in any direction. Cities with names like Bagdad and Sumatra and Sopchoppy and Two Egg dotted the inland forests, modest islands of humanity in a sea of sweet-scented green. There was the redneck glitz of the Miracle Mile, the endless calm of windswept dunes, the seventy thousand acres of nothingness called Tate's Hell Swamp, the more than a thousand lakes and streams with the best bass fishing in the country. And at the heart of this lush, undeveloped landscape nestled the jewel known as Tallahassee. He approached the city limits with the anticipation of one returning to the welcome of an old friend.

Tallahassee was a jumble of graceful mansions and modern high-rises that lived and thrived for one purpose only, to govern the state. In the early 1800s, when the Florida

213

peninsula had been an impenetrable jungle, the capitol had been established at the mid-point between the state's two main cities, St. Augustine and Pensacola. Three log cabins had been erected on a hillside called Tallahassee or "old fields" in the Apalachee Indian tongue. Since then, the hill's shimmering waterfall had been replaced by a twenty-two-story skyscraper, a parking lot, and a collection of governmental add-ons. Yet somehow Tallahassee remained a lovely town. Driving most streets was a journey through a patchwork of lush gardens whose beauty kept speeds to an appreciative crawl. Even most downtown buildings were embraced by graceful dark arms of live oaks trailing shawls of gray moss.

Matthew's office was on Blairstone, a street lined with blooming azaleas and dogwoods and magnolias so large two grown men could not encircle their trunks. His building apologized for being modern by sitting well back from the road and holding itself to only four stories, well below the level of most trees.

Chase entered the AG's string of offices, greeted the receptionist, and asked if he could make his own way back. He found Matthew's office exactly as he had recalled. The man was seated behind a desk only slightly smaller than Chase's boat, its entire surface stacked with towering piles of folders. The in-basket was completely lost beneath urgent pink slips and letters and onionskin copies. The wall of diplomas and commendations behind Matthew's desk was covered with yellow sticky markers, all of them inundated with stars and exclamation points and double underlined words. A long line of more stacked folders crept out around the far wall.

Matthew himself was immaculate as ever, coat slung over the back of his chair, starched striped shirt, suspenders, muted silk tie — what Mildred, Matthew's wife, always called the GQ courtroom model. He was totally immersed in his work, a great frown creasing his forehead, chewing on one pen with another stuck behind his ear. Three half-empty coffee cups balanced on various folders.

"Better hope nobody ever opens a window in here," Chase said.

Matthew looked up and gaped. "Good grief, old son, what on earth you doing in Tallahassee?" Not satisfied with what his eyes were telling him, Matthew stormed around his desk, grabbed Chase by the arm, shook him back and forth. "Why didn't you call and let somebody know you were coming?"

"Didn't know myself until yesterday."

"Come on over here and sit down." He bent to divest the side chair of its load of folders. "How long's it been since you were up here?"

"Too long."

"You're right there. Shoot, must be all of a year, ever since the last time you and —" Matthew stopped himself. "Anyway, it's great to see you."

"You can say her name, Matt. Sabine. There, see, I didn't melt."

"Never did understand how that woman could've treated you like she did. Nice guy like you deserved better."

"Thanks."

" 'Course, from what I hear these days, you're good to be rid of her."

He asked because he needed to, not because he wanted to. "What do you hear?"

"Only that she's sidled herself up to Lamar Laroque close as a tick to a hound dog. You know what that means."

"Maybe you better tell me."

"Well, gambling for one thing. Also, loosening the state's regulations every whichaway, hands out to all the wrong folks. That plus all the old rumors. Lamar's got more smoke pouring outta him than a five-alarm house fire. Only reason nobody's pinned anything on him yet is because he's slicker than a greased hog and faster than a turpentined cat."

"You're mixing metaphors again."

"Yeah, well, that's what comes from talking to juries for a living."

"Matter of fact, that's why I'm up here today," Chase said. "Lamar's called some sort of meeting and wanted me to be there for it."

"Then you better watch your back. Politics in this town is so tough, the hit men don't even use guns. They insert the bullets manually."

Chase played at unconcern. "They don't seem all that smart to me."

"Did I say smart? No I did not. Most of these folks're so dumb they erect kiddie swings next to brick walls. But dumb don't make 'em any less dangerous. You watch your step out there." He glanced at his watch. "I got a full load the rest of today, but how about you coming by this evening, let's do the old barbecue routine. Mildred and the kids'd love to see you."

Chase shook his head. "I'd like that, but tonight's sort of taken."

Matthew inspected him. "You're gonna go over and see her, aren't you."

"I have to."

"Aim on burying that ghost once and for all?"

"If I can."

"Need some backup?"

Chase let his relief surface. He had been hoping for this, afraid to ask. "Maybe just to drive over there with me. Would you mind?"

"Shoot, old son. I'd be right there beside you with a shovel all my own if you'd let me." Matthew glanced at his watch again, lifted Chase with his impatience, started him toward the door. "Want to come back around five?"

"Sure." Chase dragged his heels a moment, decided it needed to be said. "I've been doing like you suggested on that other matter."

That stopped Matthew in his tracks. "Didn't waste any time, did you."

"I couldn't afford to."

The gaze probing, searching. "Find out anything?"

"Yes."

"Important?"

"Very." Swiftly Chase sketched out his trip to Miami and the hacker's discoveries.

A lightning-fast decision. "Maybe I can help you pass this on to the right authorities. Five o'clock, old son. Be on time."

★ ★ ★

He strode toward the main entrance to the government skyscraper, was astonished to find Linda Armacost come storming out to meet him. "You're late! The meeting started fifteen minutes ago!"

He could only stop and stare. "What are you doing here?"

"Barry suggested I come, make sure we were well represented." She glared up at him. "Now I see why he was so worried."

Chase mulled over how this was going to affect his plans, decided not at all. "Linda, I —"

"Don't make things worse than they already are," she snapped. "Another of your lame excuses is the last thing I need. Come on."

He followed her across the foyer and into the elevator, endured her glares and frigid silence, watched the light ping them up to the nineteenth floor. He was mildly pleased to find himself untouched by her anger. The lines were drawn, sides chosen. He would not be stopped.

He slipped into the room behind her, felt relief that the remaining two seats were widely separated from each other. Chase felt eyes track his progress around the room's wide oval conference table.

Lieutenant Governor Lamar Laroque held

sway at the podium, too caught up in his florid speech to do more than glance his way. "Florida is built on growth, more so than any other place on earth. Since the end of the Second World War, we've had almost constant growth. We don't know what it's like to have a decline. And now it's hit us. It's not something coming. It's already here. Our recession started before the rest of the country, and it has never ended. New construction starts are at their lowest level in modern history. Good jobs are drying up. And we, this great state of ours, remain standing with our heads buried in the sand."

Sabine was stationed just to the right of the podium, seated back and slightly apart from the gathering. Chase returned her slight smile, felt the faintest hint of nerves for the first time that day, forced himself to turn his attention elsewhere. She remained achingly beautiful, utterly appealing. Especially to him.

"We need something new to lift us out of this ongoing decline. Something big. Something that has the power to push us back to the forefront of the American dream." Laroque paused to sweep the room with his lofty gaze. "And that power is to be found, ladies and gentlemen, in legalized gambling."

There were perhaps thirty people at the

table. Chase glanced around, recognized most of them. Development specialists from many of the counties hard hit by the current recession. They were nodding in time to Laroque's message. Listening closely, but in truth hearing a litany of only one word repeated over and over in their minds. Jobs.

Laroque brought the crowd up to a crescendo of promise, then stopped to soak in applause fueled by the hopes of thirty competitors wanting to draw attention and business their way. Jobs. When the room was again silent, Laroque asked if there were any questions.

An eager young woman halfway around the table asked, "Do we have any idea just how much an impact gambling might have on a county's growth?"

"An excellent question." The honeyed voice oozed with pleasure. "Biloxi and the surrounding county over in Mississippi have had gambling now for just five years. This year their gambling revenue will approach one billion dollars in that county alone. Gambling, my dear, has ended a twenty-year recession and given Biloxi full employment for the first time since the Civil War. Just imagine, if you would, what effect such revenue and employment figures might have on your own counties." He cast another self-satisfied glance about the room. "Now are there any further questions."

Chase raised what he hoped was a timid hand. "Do your statistics contain any figures on what has happened to the local families?"

"Families?" Laroque appeared mildly amused. "Why, sir, the families are doing just fine. They've got jobs. They've got food on the table. They've got new schools, all paid for courtesy of the casinos."

"I was just wondering," Chase said, trying to keep his voice meek and soft, not a threat, just a goof with an unwanted question. "See, because I'd heard that gambling had a pretty devastating effect on local families, especially kids. Like how the divorce rate in Biloxi has doubled in this same five years. And I was just wondering if there were any statistics to either support or contradict this."

Laroque stared down at him with a new watchfulness. The people to either side of Chase sidled away as far as they could, separating themselves from the coming explosion. Most others avoided looking his way at all. Trying to grant the condemned man a little privacy.

"And what is your name, sir?" Laroque demanded quietly.

"Chase. Chase Bennett."

"Ah, yes. Mr. Bennett." A flicker of something deep beneath the surface. "A pleasure to make your acquaintance, I'm sure."

A deep sigh shivered the room, drawing the others back from the brink. The explosion had been delayed. "Likewise, Mr. Governor," Chase replied.

"Well, Mr. Bennett, the answer to your question is, a great number of knee-jerk reactionaries are grasping at straws, trying to weave themselves a basket strong enough to carry them against the tide. Are you understanding what I am saying to you, sir? Is the message getting through?"

"Loud and clear, Mr. Governor."

"I am delighted to hear it. Yes, Mr. Bennett, the time of reckoning is fast approaching for all who would rather hide behind such outdated arguments. The facts are plain as day for anyone willing to see them. The future is upon us. Either we adapt or we are left behind to dine on the dust of those willing and able to march ahead to the tune of progress." Again that flickering of something deep within the man's eyes, like a submerged beast rising upward through a murky swamp, skimming just beneath the water's surface. "Now, which do you think it will be for the great state of Florida?"

"Progress," Chase said, holding to his

meek tone, trying to keep the defiance and the anger from showing. "Definitely progress, Mister Governor."

"So glad to hear it, Mr. Bennett." He lifted his gaze to encompass the entire table. "Now perhaps I might invite you ladies and gentlemen to join me for lunch."

Once out in the hall, Chase's neighbor to his left murmured, "Nice knowing you, Bennett."

Before he could reply, Linda Armacost forced her way through the jostling throng and stomped up in front of him. "What was the meaning of that?" she said through clenched teeth.

"Hello, Linda. How did you enjoy the presentation?" Now that he was out and away and no longer facing the spotlight of that highly focused glare, holding to his mild-mannered attitude was a piece of cake. "What do you think we'll be having for lunch?"

"I asked you a question, mister," she snapped, losing the battle to keep her voice down. "Do you have any idea how disruptive you've been in there?"

He tried for round innocent eyes. "All I did was ask a question."

"A question!" Planting fists on hips. "Did it ever occur to you, mister, that we are *com-*

peting here for this business? That they could just as easily take this project to any of the other counties represented here? That your addlebrained attitude could have just sunk our chances?"

Chase did a slow sweep of the hall, took in the snickering throng pretending to ignore them, made for surprise. "Gee, I never thought of that."

"As far as I'm concerned, Bennett, you've just walked over the edge." She turned and stamped away.

One of the Miami developers gave him a little three-finger wave. Chase stood and waited as they moved toward the dining room's great open doors. Then he swallowed his smile and followed meekly in their wake.

Laroque barely waited for the doors to close behind the departing group before declaring, "That Bennett fellow has a positively loathsome attitude."

When Sabine made no comment he turned and looked down at where she remained seated. "How did that simple-minded old woman come to give him the rights to Rochelle's property?"

"It's not Rochelle's yet," Sabine replied quietly.

His secretary knocked on the door and poked her head around the doorway. "The governor is on line one for you, sir."

"Thank you, Doris. I won't be a moment." When the door had closed behind her, he went on, "You must speak with Bennett on our behalf, my dear."

"I understand." Sabine refused to meet his eyes.

"You must impress him with the great opportunity which he is threatening to miss out on, both for himself and for the county he purports to represent." The hand gripping the lectern tightened until the knuckles stood out white as bleached bones, but the voice did not alter. "You must."

11

"He trotted out all kinds of statistics," Chase told Matthew that afternoon. "Mostly talked about how Mississippi had found the golden goose by setting up casinos."

Matthew was not impressed. "Did he mention how the number of local businesses going bust had tripled in the last two years? Or how the number of personal bankruptcies have gone up five hundred percent and foreclosures on houses a thousand percent? Or how statistics in every state where gambling has been introduced points to casinos' being destructive to local economies?"

"I asked him something about it, but somehow he wasn't all that interested in answering."

"I bet he wasn't. I bet he also failed to mention how the feds think the mafia's involved at the highest level in Mississippi gambling. Or how New Jersey has twenty-one gambling agents monitoring only twelve casinos, while for some strange reason Mississippi thinks seven agents is enough for twenty-five casinos."

"Can't your people over there do something?"

"They're facing a state-run business, old son. There isn't a lot they can do unless we find evidence, and it's hard to find that when they're not allowed to investigate openly. The state's not interested in helping, to put it mildly. Mississippi's treating this like a big old money cow they aim to milk just as hard as they can. They act like any kind of sensible control is a noose that'll choke that old cow to death."

"Sounds like blind panic at work," Chase said.

"There's a special science a fellow's got to learn to understand what makes folks involved in politics act the way they do," Matthew replied. "I call it the science of political astrophysics."

"This sounds like the time you told me to write my book report saying that Moby Dick should have eaten the whole boatload, since it would have made for a better story."

"Hang on, Slim, this won't take but a minute. Now, first off is the Law of Quirks and Fields. It goes something like this. Take a normal, decent human being and put him in the political field, and soon enough he starts coming out in quirks. This leads us to the second law, the Law of Wave-Particle Credibility. That one says, you wave every particle of your credibility goodbye soon as you start preparing your next campaign. But if your equation of mass appeal is enough to push you up and through the final frontier, then you boldly go where no sane man would even dream of going. Your face gets stuck in newspapers, you start believing what they're saying about you in the campaign ads, and then the real craziness begins."

"I assume this is going to lead us toward Laroque sometime in the next couple of hours."

"Old son, Lamar Laroque is so far out he's looking at the next galaxy from the wrong side. That fellow was born to politics, which means he was born crazy. Certifiably corrupt. Man would sell his mother for a campaign contribution."

"Shame they don't just come to you for answers, isn't it."

"Shoot. If everybody was as smart as me, what would we do for fun?" He looked up as his secretary appeared in the doorway. "Visitors?"

"Singular." She smiled. "Hi, Chase. Nice to see you again."

"Humph." Matthew played at disgust. "Don't never see smiles like that for the guy that pays the salary."

"Maybe you would if you didn't show up for a year," she said, winking at Chase.

"Show the singular visitor on down here," Matthew said.

The man wore a dark suit which hung like a shiny sack on his wiry frame. His pale gray hair was cut so close the scalp showed through. Matthew rose, shook his hand, turned to Chase and said, "This is Josh McNair from Justice."

"Actually, I'm from the DOD, seconded to liaison with the FCC," he said, his voice irritatingly nasal.

Chase accepted a hand that brought to mind a dead catfish. "I don't deal with the federal government enough to understand all that alphabet soup."

Matthew waved them into seats, said to Chase, "What you found, old son, is the tip of a thirty-five-billion-dollar iceberg. They call it troll fraud, because the majority of guys actually doing the stealing are techno-freaks who live out their lives in garages and cellars, hardly ever seeing the light of day."

"Which doesn't mean they are not highly sophisticated," McNair said. "They have gone far beyond the planting of viruses on computer networks. This year the White House has joined Internet, and we learned that the big Christmas challenge for the underground cracker network is to get behind the Firewall series of protective barriers and enter the President's phone system."

Chase asked Matthew, "How do you know so much about this?"

"Let's just say," Matthew replied, "that we have a strong personal interest in this case."

"What case?"

"Could you tell us, Mr. Bennett," McNair demanded, "how you came upon this information?"

Matthew eased back beyond McNair's line of vision and gave his head a minute shake. Chase replied, "I can't say that."

"Why not?"

"I just can't."

"Mr. Bennett, it would be a very grave matter if you were seen to be obstructing a federal investigation."

"Why should I be seen as obstructing anything?" Chase said. "I was the one who contacted you guys." To Matthew, "Do I need a lawyer?"

"No you do not." Matthew looked at his associate. "Your call, McNair. Take it as it comes or go away empty handed."

The federal attorney looked pained. "Why do I have the distinct impression that you are siding with this gentleman?"

"He called me because I have known him

a long time. He told me he might have something we could use. He said he would come in on the condition that I not ask where he discovered this information."

"That's the only way," Chase agreed.

"Look," the FCC guy snapped back. "Work with me, or go to jail. How's that for a choice."

Chase looked at Matthew. "This is your idea of helping?"

Matthew raised a hand. "Can we call a time out here?"

"Tell your friend," Chase said, rising to his feet, "if he wants the time of day from me, he'll need to get himself a new attitude first."

"I'll tell you what I'm getting," McNair said. "There'll be a subpoena issued this afternoon."

"This guy needs restraining," Chase told Matthew.

"This is not exactly what I had in mind," Matthew replied wearily, rising as well. "We'll be in touch, McNair."

"I'm not through."

"Yes you are. Show yourself out, okay?"

McNair jumped to his feet and glowered at them both. "Your superiors will hear about this first thing Monday morning."

"Hey, look at me now, I'm shaking in my

boots." Matthew shrugged on his coat. "Come on, Chase. We've got a ghost to bury."

"Sorry about that."

"Not your fault."

"In a way it was." Matthew sighed his way into the car, started the engine, paused to watch McNair storm from the building. "Look at him go, the aging desk jockey who always dreamed of playing the spook."

"What are you talking about?"

"McNair was a major mistake. Even if he was the logical choice. Local rep with NCS, nexus with DOD, liaison with the INCT and the FCC. Shame about the attitude, though."

"Would you mind," Chase asked, "putting that in plain English?"

"National Communication Systems," Matthew recited, "Department of Defense. Bureau of International Narcotics, Crime, and Terrorism. Excuse me for forgetting how Tallahassee has scrambled my brain. Such as it is." He gestured through the windscreen. "McNair's like a lot of those Reston guys. That's as in Reston, Virginia. Want me to spell it?"

"This is leading somewhere," Chase said. "I can feel it."

"He's supposed to be one of our great

new communication spooks. Truth is, he's just another meeting junkie. Too many like that, unfortunately. Bumped from Defense because he's got a specialist engineering background, which unfortunately is fifteen years out of date. He and all the bozos like him are one hundred percent bureaucratic nerds."

"Not your favorite people, I take it."

"Professional time-wasters. They just love sending public information in top-secret mode. Anyway, McNair somehow got himself hooked in as our local liaison on an investigation we're cooking up, or trying to. Generates more paper than Weyerhauser, hasn't done anything for us except tie me up in meetings. Yammer, yammer, yammer." Matthew grinned at Chase. "Me telling him he actually had to make an executive decision, talk to you off the record, do something without a paper trail from here to Mars — I tell you, Slim, that must've pushed every panic button the guy had."

"Glad to know I'm keeping you entertained," Chase said.

Matthew reversed from the drive, asked, "Where to?"

"Sabine's moved since I was up here last." Chase read the slip of paper, said as calmly as he could, "1515 Tamiami."

"Nice address." Matthew started off. "Just wish I could do something to help. Really help."

Chase fought off jangling nerves by returning to business at hand. "For starters, could you maybe explain what's going on in words of less than fifteen syllables?"

"Doubtful, old son. Real doubtful."

"Try."

"Okay." Matthew mulled it over for a couple of blocks. "The first problem is, telephone fraud is nobody's problem. That's why we got stuck trying to work with a loon like McNair. The vendors of all this new telephone equipment, like the mobile phones and the corporate switchboards, they're masters at playing innocent. Whenever we come to them with this problem of fraud, they wave their hands in the air and say, hey, all we do is sell the stuff. We guarantee against faults in the equipment, not against somebody breaking in and running away with the annual payroll."

"Are we talking about that much money?"

"More than you would ever imagine," Matthew said. "A lot more. Not so long ago, Mitsubishi's America headquarters got zapped by phreakers — you know who they are?"

"Sort of."

"Ran up a weekend bill, are you ready for this? Four hundred and fifty thousand dollars."

"Over a weekend?"

"Three days. When a company's been defrauded they get handed a Big Brick. That's the name the FCC gives their telephone bill. Comes from the size of the printout, two or three hundred accordion pages." He cocked his head. "Now where was I headed with that?"

"You were saying nobody was to blame."

"Everybody's to blame, old son," Matthew corrected. "Just nobody's legally responsible. Not yet, anyway. But Justice is working on that. For the moment, these mobile phones and 800 access codes are a drug dealer's dream and an honest citizen's nightmare." He shook his head. "Right now blame's being passed around like a hot potato. The vendor's not responsible that his codes can be broken by anyone with the right software and a modem. The local companies who sell the 800 codes, their contract reads that they provide the service, you pay the bill. Period. The long-distance companies, they're just as bad. All they want is to make a buck."

"But all this is being changed?"

"Takes time. Divestiture — that's when

Bell's monopoly was broken up and the seven so-called Baby Bells, the local exchanges, were formed. It's helped when it comes to price competition, but it's created a mine field when it comes to problems like this. Everybody knows there's a problem, but they're all in a panic, fighting tooth and nail against any possible solution, because they don't want to be made responsible for plugging the loopholes."

"And all the while," Chase surmised, "drug dealers are getting away with murder."

"Yeah, they're having a field day." He turned down a side street lined by oaks so ancient they formed a green tunnel overhead. "That's Sabine's house up ahead on the right."

Number 1515 was styled after the old Victorian dwellings — an ornate wooden house with peaked corners, rimmed by a veranda and crowned by slate shingles. On this house, however, the walls were lavender, the doors and frames were fuchsia, and the windows were all one-way bronze.

"That house fits Sabine down to the ground," Chase declared. "Southern modern."

"It looks like somebody's granny designed it while on some serious drugs," Matthew replied.

"I'm sure Sabine would say it grows on you."

"Cancer grows on you. Bad hair grows on you. Ticks grow on you. I don't like them, and I don't like this." He looked at Chase. "You want me to come in with you?"

"No," he said slowly. "This is something I need to do on my own."

"Probably best. Sabine knows exactly what I think of her. Wouldn't get things off on the best footing if I was with you. I'll hang around out here, try to come up with some way to get Sabine and our friend McNair together. That'd be a marriage made in heaven. Or elsewhere."

Chase opened the car door. "Thanks for coming with me, Matt."

"Shoot. Couldn't let you face the swamp fiend alone."

"I'll tell her you said hello."

Matthew snorted. "Better yet, tell her the indictment's in the mail."

The car in the drive was a power-puff blue Porsche 968 convertible with navy leather interior and vanity plates bearing her name. Chase walked up the front stairs, remembering how her car had always been one of the few places where Sabine didn't smoke. She hated how the smell of old smoke gathered in a car — her car, at least. Otherwise, she smoked everywhere, except when a superior wanted it otherwise, but rarely inhaled. She couldn't have cared less what those lower than her thought of her smoking. If they didn't like it, they could leave. If they couldn't leave because they needed her or the power or the access she held, so much the better.

She smoked Dunhills because she liked the fancy flat packs, and she lit them with a gold and platinum Cartier lighter, a gift from a long-forgotten friend. The ritual of drawing a cigarette from the red and gold pack and lighting it with her lighter was all part of the pleasure.

The house appeared to be divided into four apartments. Chase pressed her buzzer, tried to sigh away the tension in his chest. So many memories. So many conflicting emotions.

She had been both hungry and poor. That much she had confessed in one of those brief instances of intimacy, come and gone so swiftly that he only believed it had happened because he had yearned for it and because he loved her so much.

One night he had asked her, aren't you afraid of growing old alone? She had shifted in his arms, replied softly, the only thing that scares me is the fear of not having. He had tried to look into her face, seen only the night shadows and hints of familiar lines, and said, that doesn't make sense, you have so much — power and looks and money and prospects. More, she had replied. More of everything. It's the only answer. Answer to what, he had demanded. But she had shut herself off then, and never opened up again. Not to him. The next time they had been together had been the day on the beach.

Now he heard her light tap-tapping step across the foyer, saw the kaleidoscope form appear behind the smoked glass, and suddenly he was busy trying to swallow his heart.

She opened the door, pushed back an abundance of dark hair, said, "Chase. It's really you."

"You asked me to come." His throatiness almost matched her own. For different reasons.

She unveiled her smile. "I hoped you would. But I wasn't sure. Come in. You've never seen my new home, have you? I've so wanted to share it with you."

He followed her down the hardwood hallway, unable to help himself, watching the walk that was meant for him. She had always dressed as provocatively as her position allowed, and then a bit more. Her suits were the required somber colors, yet the cut was far tighter, the skirts an inch or so higher, the stockings etched with an alluring design. Her blouses were sheer silk, her undergarments just dark enough to hint through the shimmering fabric.

She turned in the doorway to her apartment and rewarded him with another glistening smile. "I've really been looking forward to this."

He stepped in, gave an appreciative, "Very nice."

"I'm so glad you like it." Sabine stepped forward so that she was included in his view of the room. "I fell in love with this place the moment I saw it."

Burnished oak floors were accented with brilliant swatches of color in the form of Persian rugs. The lamps and chandeliers were brass, the living room's two outer walls adorned with great bay windows. The central portion of the ceiling was two stories high, with a second-story balustrade forming a wood-lined cupola. The furniture was either upholstered and pale and modern, or wooden and polished and antique.

Sabine watched him take it in. "You like it. I'm so glad, Chase." She led him over to a settee done in raw silk. "Sit down here so I can look at you up close."

The voice was richer than he remembered. Throatier. More practiced. She used it for effect, like her body and her clothes. He found himself slipping, being drawn back, and looked for something, anything to keep himself out of reach. He resisted her directions toward the sofa and stopped by laundry draped from a brass wall-hanger, the plastic wrapping flung up and aside in one of her typically impatient gestures. He knew she would eventually put the clothes away. In a week or so.

"Look at these clothes." He pulled up one item after another. "Biker shorts, perfect except you don't bike. Track suit, you haven't jogged in your entire life. Apron dress, you can't even boil water."

"I didn't ask you up to criticize my wardrobe."

"Who's criticizing, I think this is fantastic. I heard denial wear was the coming thing for the nineties. I'm just pleased as punch to see you've kept up with the changing times."

"Would you put down my clothes?" The edge returning to her voice, the one he had detected the other day on the phone. "Now would suit me just fine."

"Sure." He knew he was okay then. He moved to the sofa, content in the knowledge that her appeal was as false as the rest of her. And the knowledge gave him the power to reply in kind. He settled back, said, "It really is nice to see you again, Sabine."

"Oh, Chase." The eyes opened wide, the lips parted, the voice lowered and softened. The edge sheathed. "It's been so long."

He nodded as though giving that very serious thought. "Yes, it has."

She slid her chair up closer until their knees were almost touching. "I had to speak with you, Chase. I had to. You're taking such a dangerous course, going up against Lamar. He's powerful. Really powerful."

Chase made for surprise. "I don't plan to go up against anybody, most especially him."

It was her turn to pull back. "You're not?"

"Good grief, no. What do you think I am, crazy?" He was pleased with the way his laugh sounded in his own ears. "I mean, how many times does a guy get a chance to accept an offer of fifteen million dollars for a piece of undeveloped property?"

"Not often," she agreed, watching him.

"You're right there. This is the chance of a lifetime. No, what Miss Marie said was that I had to weigh all the pros and cons, look at every side." He hoped he sounded sincere. "That's all I was trying to do today. Find out some answers to some questions."

As he spoke he recognized the power of her total attention. That had been one of the things that attracted him to her and held him for so long. When she switched her attention on to something, she had the ability to focus with a laser intensity. A focus born of insatiable hunger, so strong it had fooled him into thinking it was born of love. Now as he sat and watched and talked, he wondered with an aching heart how many other men had felt that awesome focused passion, and how many at the same time as he.

"So that's all you were doing," Sabine pressed quietly. "Trying to get some answers to the old lady's questions?"

"Sabine, you know me. If I take on a job, I try to do it all the way. Miss Marie's not been well, otherwise she'd probably be on this herself." Chase dredged up another smile. "You think you've got troubles with me, I'm nothing compared to how she can be."

She answered with a smile of her own. And relief. "Feisty?"

"Like a full-blown hurricane." He shook his head. "Totally out of control."

Sabine reached over and took his hand. "I'm so glad it's you, then."

"Me too." Looking down at the hand. Aching with all the past, all that he had hoped for and worked for and dreamed about. All that could have been.

He took a breath, tried to focus on the here and now. "What's Laroque getting out of all this?"

The hand was swiftly withdrawn. "What do you mean?"

Chase shrugged, still looking at where the hand had rested, sorrow making the casual tone easier. "Just wondering. I mean, he's pushing Rochelle's plan, right?"

"Lamar feels that gaming is the only way for our state to maintain its rightful position at the forefront of America's growth." A hesitation, then moving away from the party line. "And he thinks that Rochelle's plan for a larger, controllable gaming casino is the best way to show the state that this opposition is unwarranted."

"Yeah, but what's in it for him?" He kept his eyes down, holding to the soft tone. "A guy like that, he's not dumb. Something this big, he's going to want a piece of the action." Probing now. "You too, if you're as smart as I've always thought."

A longer silence, then, "Is that what you're after, Chase? You want in on the deal?"

A casual shrug. Eyes locked on his knees. "I don't know. Sure. I guess. But that doesn't answer my question."

"I think I see."

Something in her tone caused him to raise his eyes. He searched her face, saw a calculating certainty. Here was familiar terrain. Chase took her expression as his cue. "I mean, if you were planning on doing business with someone, you'd want to know where they stood, right?"

The calculating gaze was rock hard. "This is strictly confidential."

"Hey." Chase spread open palms. "What could I get from letting the cat out of the bag?"

She nodded slowly, avarice glinting from her eyes. "Do you have any idea how much a gubernatorial race costs these days?"

"A lot, huh?"

"Try twenty, maybe even thirty million dollars. Not many places where that kind of money can be found. Especially when it has to come from a lot of small sources."

"And then," Chase went forward another step, "newly elected Governor Laroque would back Florida's being completely open to casino gambling. Done so that it most benefits his major backer, Sylvan Rochelle."

"It's the wave of the future, Chase." She reached for her briefcase, which she had open and ready on the side table. "Look, I've gathered some information you might want to pass on to Miss Hale."

She opened a bound document and started leafing the pages, pointing out various details, so familiar with the data she could read it upside down. Up close to him again, using her fragrant presence with casual ease. But now it was no longer a distraction. He nodded and tried for polite attention, but found himself caught up in an awareness of seeing *beyond* her looks and actions. And then he was unable to hold it inside any longer. "Who are you really?"

The sudden change jerked her back. "What?"

"I've been sitting here wondering who you really are. The only problem is, I don't know who I should be looking for. Before, you played the exciting coed. Now it's the competent but alluring executive. But who are you really?"

There was an instant of fear, then a flash of irritation, both coming and going so fast that he saw them only because he had studied that lovely face for so long. "Are you going to go off on another one of your tangents?"

"No." This he knew for sure. No more tangents. No more desperate appeals for shared love. Not with her. Not ever.

He rose to his feet. She was instantly up and close to him. "This is important, Chase.

Absolutely vital. To the state and to you personally. It would do you a lot of good to have us on your side."

"I am very, very glad I have you to count on," he said and extended his hand. "Goodbye, Sabine."

She took his hand in both of hers. "But you can't go so soon, Chase. You haven't even had something to drink."

"I need to be getting back to Cocoa tonight. Next time, all right?"

A look of open invitation. "Sure you can't stay? I had all sorts of plans for tonight."

He smiled, glad it came easy, knowing for the very first time that he was really and truly free. "You don't know how much that means. But I can't."

"Your next trip up, then," she said, her voice returning to the throaty burr.

"Absolutely. And in the meantime." He hefted the documents. "I'll give these my number one attention."

Chase walked across the front porch, stopped, and inhaled the sultry breeze. Then he walked down the stairs, filled with the sensation that he was departing from a cemetery.

He was leaving behind the remains of a love which only he had given life to. And time. Almost two years of his time. She had given nothing. He knew that now. Even when they had been together, she had given nothing.

He felt sorrow, but not overwhelming sorrow. Instead he found himself looking forward to tomorrow. Another day at Cocoa Beach. A day spent with someone who seemed to value laughter. Someone who might enjoy a sunset watched from his boat. Picnics on windswept dunes, the gulls singing a raucous chorus overhead. Talks which could go on forever, and might do just that.

"Sure I can't tempt you with a night at our place? Backyard barbecue, play with the kids, remember old times, have a few laughs?"

"Next time I'm up, I promise. Right now, I really need to get on the road."

Matthew pulled up in front of Chase's truck and stopped. He turned and inspected his friend's face. "Something to do with that lady we had dinner with?"

"Kaitlyn." He loved the sound of her name. "Sort of."

"Sort of, the man says. Sitting over there grinning like a teenage goof back from his first date." Returning to serious. "Speaking of goofs, sorry about McNair. Give me another chance?"

"I don't know, Matt. Maybe."

"Hang on a second, old buddy. You're not thinking of getting involved in actually investigating this stuff, are you?"

"I already am involved." Chase started to slide out.

"You know what I'm saying." He reached out and gripped Chase's sleeve. "If you really have something, you've gotta hand it over to the proper authorities."

"I already tried that," Chase replied. "Twice."

"Yeah, well, I can't help it that some of our public servants are a little thick on paranoia."

"Let go of my arm, Matt."

"I don't like the look on your face, Slim. I don't like it one bit. You're up to something, and it just might wind up getting you killed, you hear what I'm saying? These are bad people, Chase. This is not the time to play gunslinger at high noon."

"I'm not going to ask you again," Chase replied.

Matt dropped his hand. "I don't have enough friends to lose any, Chase. Stop with the foolishness while you still can."

"I'll see you around, Matt. Thanks for the help."

12

All of Saturday they sailed along the Banana River, which was not a river at all, but rather a broad sound separating Cocoa Beach from Merritt Island. Which in truth was not an island either. Merritt Island started as an afterthought of land at the end of the Kennedy Space Station, broad and verdant and only partly recovered from its original jungle state. It gradually tapered off to a thin sliver that connected to the real coastal island by a narrow-gauge bridge at Dragon Point.

Just south of that, the Banana River joined the Indian River and was no more. But to the north, up where Merritt Island was hefty enough to be a town of its own, the Banana River waters were six miles wide. Here and there the sparkling blue was dotted with green islands not fifty yards across, some of them ringed by untouched white-sand beaches. One of them, George Island, was home that time of year to several flocks of migrating egrets.

Chase and Kaitlyn stopped there for lunch, anchoring where the boat's bottom scraped on sand and walking ashore, carrying lunch high up over their heads. They sat and shared their meal with the gulls, watching long-limbed birds whose necks and wings seemed impossibly delicate for their size, like adolescent ballerinas who showed grace only in the flight of dance.

She sat with her back resting against an ancient loblolly pine, her feet stretched out over sand so clean it looked like a field of miniature pearls. "Why did you go in and talk with Grandpa the other day?"

"I liked doing it." He struggled to explain. "He reminded me of stuff."

She drew long legs up closer to her body and wrapped her arms around them. "Like what?"

"All the things my cleverness would like me to forget." A white crane rose from the neighboring marsh island, riding wings so fragile they appeared painted upon the sky. "Sometimes I think my heart might someday grow cold if I don't hold on to the simple things. I left him feeling like I'd been shaken awake."

"That's something I like about you, Chase Bennett," she said. "You're not afraid to examine your own heart."

"Yes I am."

She shook her head without lifting her

chin from her knees. "You know fear, sure. But you're not afraid. It doesn't hold you back." She examined him a moment, then asked, "What happens if you find something you don't like?"

"As long as I am able to sort of know it's coming," Chase slowly replied, "I guess I can handle most things. The big problem for me is when I get hit by something I don't expect."

"I know what you mean." Quiet. Words burdened by memories and more.

There in the peace and the calm, with the birds and the warm southerly wind for friends, he asked. Knowing it would hurt him to hear and hurt her more to tell, knowing he needed to know just the same. "Why did you wait so long to go to college?"

"I wanted to go before." A pause, a settling down, a resigned tone entering her voice. "But I got married."

Chase gave a slow nod. This one would take a while to digest.

She gave him one of her deeply measuring gazes, the sorrow still there, clouding the otherwise clear light. "If I had not had my faith to see me through, I don't know how I could have survived."

"If it helped you through the rough spots, then I'm glad," he said, and he was.

"It's more than that to me," she said, her voice softer still.

"I'm glad," he said again. He waited a moment to let her know he both understood and accepted, then asked, "What happened?"

"I was in my second year of college when I got married. My husband asked me . . ." She stopped. Accepted the truth, possibly for the first time. "He told me, but he made it sound like question. He did that a lot. He said we needed to save money and work for a house and a future together. So I gave up school and found work as a teller at a local bank."

"You didn't like it."

"I hated it. The people were wonderful, but the job was a real dead end. Once I learned the ins and outs, there was nothing else I was allowed to learn or do. I was hired to be a teller, and that was that. There was no chance for advancement without a college degree." Her face took on the pinched look of remembered pain. "I started putting on weight. I told myself it was the job, sitting at the counter all day long, exercising nothing but my smile. Now when I think back, I know it was also unhappiness. Nothing I could put my finger on then, but it was there."

"Unfulfilled," he ventured.

She nodded. "At work and at home. Somebody came in with a box of doughnuts, I didn't even think about it, suddenly I was eating one. Or two. Or three. And it added up."

He watched her sitting there curled up around herself, hiding all she could from him. Dressed as always in an oversized top, today it was a man's sweatshirt which hung almost to her knees. Her face, her beautiful face, showing nothing but shame.

"My father tried to understand when the divorce happened, he really did. But it was hard on them both. A daughter married less than two years, and suddenly her husband just doesn't come home. Daddy kept all his questions to himself, just tried to be there for me, but I could see the questions there in his eyes."

"You don't have to tell me this."

"Yes I do." Struggling to hold on to her control now. Only the tremble in her voice and the ragged breaths showed what it cost her. "Mom was awful. Just awful. She kept pestering me. Surely I had some idea why he had gone, or where, or what I had done wrong. Me. Always me. I was the one at fault. Jeff was such a nice guy. Always so polite around my folks. It had to be something I did. At least partly."

Jeff. Hearing the name was like a lance in his side. Still he reached over, took her hand. Her fingers were limp and cold as ice.

"Then I started hearing things. Stuff nobody had bothered to tell me before. How Jeff had been seeing this girl, nobody knew for how long, at least six months, maybe longer. She was two years younger than me, he was eight years older. Then, after he'd been gone for almost two weeks, I saw them together. He came by to collect his things, she waited in the car, I went out to see her. She was so slim. She had on one of those slinky latex leotards. Not an ounce of fat on her. And there I was, I had gone from a size eight when we got married to a size twelve. Standing there bloated and heartsick."

"I think you have a lovely figure," he said, and put every ounce of feeling he could behind it.

"More of me to love, right?" Tension etched her voice like a drill on glass.

"I mean it," he said. "I think you're gorgeous."

She looked at him for a long while, the watchfulness there alongside the pain. He understood her need for it then, the cautious observation, the watching without confidence left to draw decisions from what she saw. No longer able to trust her own judgments. Chase sat and waited and wanted nothing more but to answer her with honesty.

She took her fingers back, swiped her face with the back of her hand. "All I could think was, am I really that dumb? Am I so blind that this man could fool me so completely even while we were married?"

"You're not dumb," he said quietly.

She did not hear him. "And my mom. Finding out about this other girl, I hoped it would turn things around, make it all better between us. I needed her. When I went by to tell her, all she said was, look at how cool you are. You can handle a crisis, but you sure can't handle a man."

She broke down then. He reached over to hold her, draw her close, but she stopped him with what force she had. She took as deep a breath as she could manage, swallowed hard. "It's been harder forgiving my mom than it has been forgiving Jeff."

He stroked his hands through her silky hair, held the trembling body. "It's amazing to hear you talk about forgiving them at all."

"I had to. Don't you see? I had to forgive them. If I didn't, how was I ever going to be able to love anybody ever again?"

She raised her head, let him see through the hurt and the pain to the tender wounded heart within. "And I want to love someone. I really do. I'm so lonely, Chase. I feel like I've been lonely all my life. I want a man. I want a family. I want to be good for somebody. Is that so much to ask?"

The time of confession left her bruised and exhausted. Chase sailed back to the marina, Kaitlyn quiet and withdrawn and seated alone on the bow. Once the sails were stowed he drove her back in silence. Chase stopped outside her house and waited. She continued to stare through the windshield for a time before finally stirring. "Do you want to come in?"

He hated the defeated sound in her voice. "I have to go to Miami."

She glanced at her watch. "But it's already late."

"What I have to do couldn't be done any earlier."

She nodded, not understanding, not strong enough just then to ask more from him. As she slid from the truck he reached across, grasped her hand, halted her progress. "Can I call you tomorrow?"

"If you like." Not even able to look his way.

"Kaitlyn," he said, then stopped. Somehow knowing that no words would make it better. Only time. Only showing over time that he really did care. So all he said was, "Thank you for talking with me."

She nodded, still looking down, then turned and walked into the house without a backward glance. Chase watched the empty front porch for a while, wanting to go in after her, knowing that nothing could come of it. Not then. He started the truck and drove home.

For the trip to Miami he dug out clothes he had let Sabine pick out for him, clothes he had not touched for over a year. Now he saw them as futile attempts to show he could change, could be whoever he needed to be, so long as she loved him. Chase went from drawer to drawer, feeling the foolishness of one who had given his best to a relationship that had deserved so little.

His catchall was an antique steamer trunk that stood upright and almost as tall as him, occupying the back corner of his bedroom. He had found it half buried under books in Marie's upper room and paid for it by building her floor-to-ceiling bookshelves. The trunk was the better part of a century old and bore the grace of years with pride. The thick leather was cracked, the brass handles and catches worn to the quick, but the hand-varnished walnut drawers and fittings shone with burnished luster. The stickers from faraway lands and long-forgotten ships were a treasure in themselves.

He selected what Sabine had called her favorite outfit and what he had always thought of as his Night Rider rig. Midnight blue gabardine slacks, studded belt with silver buckle, dark silk shirt buttoned to a tight little collar never meant to hold a tie. Dark smoky gray linen jacket. Slip-on boots. He looked at himself in the mirror, could not help but grin. Fairly conservative for the places he planned to roam.

Driving to Miami did not constitute one of his top hundred things to do on a Saturday night. That went double for spending the evening in the trendy parts of South Beach. But three hours later Chase was walking through the capacity crowds jamming the lanes around SoFi, which was the hot way to describe the area south of Fifth Street. He looked into some of the most beautiful faces on the planet, saw great smiles and excited chatter and the sincerity level of extras on a movie set. He passed bars and cafes and late-night malls, all packed and overflowing. Each place proclaimed its own identity — upscale, youthquake, rave, raw, disco czar, fully gay. Just another choose-your-vice night in wonderful South Miami.

The crowds thickened, slowed, coalesced around a garish door and a brilliant neon sign flashing the name *Amnesia*. He squirmed through the crowd to the velvet rope, waited until the massive bouncer, Chase's friend from the boatyard, turned his way. Chase gave the guy a little wave. The bouncer stuck his head in the door, shouted, waited until another man joined him, then sauntered over. "Don't tell me you actually want to go in there."

"Is that any way to greet the guy who found you your boat? Not to mention taught you how to sail."

Conrad Sanders was tanned to a deep mahogany and built like the proverbial brick wall. He shifted the bulk under his T-shirt, said, "Speaking of which, know where I can buy a decent set of used sails?"

"What happened to the ones you have now?"

"Got caught offshore by a little wind. Sort of blew them apart."

"Sort of?" Chase grinned. "Must have been some wind."

"Yeah, had me fair worried there for a while." He looked down at Chase. "How you been, anyway?"

"Can't complain. You?"

"They pay me ten bills a week to stand out

here and keep this herd from stampeding. Plus tips. Most I've made since my knee gave out and took me out of football. Nice scenery, too, if you don't mind girls who prefer their meat still on the bone."

"A thousand dollars a week?" Chase was impressed. "You need a hand?"

That brought a genuine smile, and the years melted away. "Skinny dude like you wouldn't last a night."

The girl next to Chase, a bleached blonde in a skintight body stocking, squirmed up close and made a face of lecherous promise. Bartering her way into the discussion, seeing Chase as her ticket inside. He eased himself as far away as the crowd would permit, said to his friend, "I could think of worse ways to go."

"Right. So what are you doing here, anyway? I never figured you for disco sleaze."

"I'm supposed to meet somebody in the restaurant."

"Better hope he's picking up the check."

"Expensive?"

"Hundred to sit down, hundred for the menu, another for the water. Then it starts getting costly."

"Thought I could make an impression," Chase explained. "Stroll in like I own the place."

"Then you need a hand," he said, un-hooked the rope, and motioned him through while doing a body block on the surge that tried to follow. "Stay close, old buddy. I lose you in there, you're gone for good."

Amnesia called itself a disco mall and was large enough to dry-dock the QEII. Chase decided the place held all the charm of a jet engine test plant. Conrad led him through the crush, up a flight of stairs, into the relative calm of an overpacked, overchic restaurant. Huge bay windows opened down into the pit, where thousands of bodies writhed in weekend ecstasy.

"I belong here about as much as my pet hog," Chase declared.

"You don't own a hog and never did," Conrad replied, scanning the crowded room. "And you're not near as country as you'd like people to think."

"I hate places like this," Chase went on. "The waiters treat you like you got seated by mistake, the menus are written in some script readable only by a professor at Harvard, and the prices are high enough to fund a shuttle launch."

"Heads up," Conrad said. "Here comes the help."

"Why, Constance." The head waiter glided over, inspected them both, spoke in arch disapproval, "How nice of you to join us."

"This is Mr. Chase Bennett, sir. He's one of the top movers and shakers from the Space Coast."

"How utterly charming. Welcome to our little establishment, I'm sure."

"Thanks. Is Sylvan Rochelle around?"

Eyebrows lifted. "Is he expecting you?"

"I think so. His lawyer suggested I meet him here."

"Did he? Well, then you certainly are starting at the top. Thank you, Constance, I'm sure the front door is experiencing pandemonium without you."

Chase started to offer his hand, stopped when Conrad rolled his eyes and hid the look by going into a deep bow. With his height and bulk the move was noticed by every table in the room. "Pleasure to see you again, sir."

"I owe you," Chase murmured and turned away.

"This way," the waiter said, weaving smoothly through the room. Chase followed, paying no mind to the glances cast his way, his attention already focused on the man watching his approach. The table sat on a slightly elevated platform, commanding pride of place, looking out both over the restaurant and the dance floor below.

"This gentleman says you are expecting him," the head waiter announced and waited.

Sylvan Rochelle moved smoothly to his feet. "Mr. Bennett?"

"That's me." Chase extended his hand across the table. "Sure is nice to finally meet you, Mr. Rochelle."

"Call me Sylvan, please." He gave the waiter a casual wave. "Find us another chair."

"Certainly, Mr. Rochelle. Right away."

A fraction of space was made for him, a chair brought and held as he sat, a glass of something put into his hand. Chase sipped, tasted nothing, smiled at his neighbor, shook another hand, spoke words neither heard. All the time aware of Sylvan Rochelle's watchful gaze.

He judged it time to turn back, playing it as casual as he could. "Nice of you to see me like this."

"A pleasure, I assure you." Rochelle's voice carried the faintest of accents, his words as polished as the rest of him. He was the only conservatively dressed person at the table, a king holding dominion over his subjects, so comfortable in his power that such things as trendiness meant little or nothing. He took in the table with a regal sweep of his hand. "Now that you are here, I do hope you enjoy yourself."

Chase smiled and nodded his thanks, understanding that he had been politely put in his place. Relegated to the rank of courtier. There to await the bidding of his king. He turned to the person on his left, a stunningly beautiful girl who paid as little attention to what she was saying as he did. Out of the corner of his eye he caught a fleeting glimpse of muscle seated at the next table. Watching everyone and everything with the poised calm of attack dogs in human form. Their presence gave him a foreboding chill.

He waited through the proscribed time, trading inanities with whoever turned his way, laughing at all the right places, feeling Rochelle's gaze rake over him from time to time. When he had endured all he could, he rose to his feet and offered his hand a second time. "This has been great, Mr. Rochelle. Truly."

The man's grip was smooth as silk. "Not the place for a genuine conversation, I'm afraid."

Chase gave an easy shrug. "Like your lawyer said, you're a busy man."

"Yes." A probing look, then the polished smile. "Monday I have a luncheon meeting up the coast at the Bath and Tennis Club. Do you know it, by any chance?"

"In Palm Beach. Sure."

"Meet me there at four, why don't you?" A moment's calculation. "That is, if you are truly interested in doing business."

Chase tried to appear eager. "That's why I'm here."

"You had a curious way of demonstrating it to Lamar Laroque." At the sound of the lieutenant governor's name, further glances were cast his way from around the table. Anyone who dealt with that level of power was worth noting.

Chase felt a little surging thrill, saw in Rochelle's satisfied reaction that it showed, knew he had been misunderstood, was content to let it go. There he was, sitting in the doldrums, restless and uncomfortable with his own skin, when the first whiff of wind rustled the water. Not touching him yet, but strong enough to feather across the water's surface, hinting of things to come. They had thought him important enough to warrant discussion, Rochelle and Laroque. "I have," Chase replied, "some conflicting responsibilities."

The calculating gaze became as keen as an ice-bladed knife. "I shall look forward to seeing you on Monday, Mr. Bennett. Perhaps I can assist you in resolving this conflict."

"I'd like that," Chase said, hiding his satisfaction by nodding and turning away. Chase pretended to ignore the bodyguards' bulk and watchful menace as he stepped off the table's dais and walked from the room.

He passed back through the disco's deafening din, strafed by lasers and the sticky-sweet smell of good-time drugs. Chase pushed through the front doors, took his first full breath since walking inside.

Conrad walked over. "How did it go?"

"All right." He looked up, saw the strain and the tightness he had missed before, said, "You need to find yourself another job, Conrad. Do it before it's too late."

The big man understood him perfectly. "They couldn't pay me enough to get me inside. Long as I'm out here, I'm safe. Safe as anybody can be in Miami."

13

Monday morning Chase walked into the office and handed Troy half the sheets Kaitlyn had printed out from the disk's file of 800 numbers. "Call these numbers. Find out where the companies they belong to are located."

Troy scanned the two pages. "All of them?"

"I've got the other half, so don't complain. Get their full mailing address."

"I'll need some valid reason for asking."

"Tell them who you are. Say we're planning to conduct a campaign to attract leading-edge companies."

"And if they're not? Leading edge, I mean."

"Have you ever heard of a company that doesn't consider itself one?" Chase headed for his office. "Try and finish this up quickly. It's on the urgent side."

Chase rounded his desk, tossed through the weekend mail, scribbled a couple of notes on what could not wait, glanced out through the window, found himself worrying about Marie Hale.

He had taken Kaitlyn by yesterday. He had sat and listened to them talk, immensely glad to see the two women get along so well, very troubled by Marie's continued decline. The woman had not looked good and sounded worse. She had been as alert as ever, though, and toward the end of their visit had returned to her feeling that the two problems of his, the casino interests and the telecommunication fraud, were somehow connected. Chase had found her suspicions harder to shrug off.

Especially when yesterday afternoon Grey Spenser had almost agreed with her. Chase had stopped by to give a quick summary, looking as much for a chance to sort through his own thoughts as for guidance. Grey had heard him out and shrugged. "Hard to tell what's hidden under the rug when you're dealing with people like this."

"What's that supposed to mean?"

"A moral vacuum breeds moral extremes. That is what we are struggling against, make no mistake about it. These are people who feed off the vacuum. They're appealing to our basest nature, dressing up this evil called gambling and passing it off as something we can't do without."

Chase looked at his old friend, saw the fatigue and the frustration which was aging him beyond his years. "Why do you do this, Grey?"

"Because I am convinced that gambling is a curse and lottery is a plague." Not tainting his words with unnecessary heat. "The poor schmoe who stops by the Seven-Eleven every night on his way home from work is putting his faith in chance instead of in God. This state-backed gambling hurts everybody and helps nobody. People play to feel the thrill of risk, ignoring the documented fact that gambling is addictive and destructive. Yet the state entices them to keep at it with their slick advertising campaigns. Why? Because this is a lazy way of collecting taxes. They call the lottery voluntary, because they don't force anybody to put their money down. That makes about as much sense as saying a heroin addict isn't being forced by anybody to buy his next fix."

His tone was bitter as he rose to his feet. "You think I don't see the smirks, hear the snide remarks? I hear it, all right. Boy, do I ever. Especially when it's coming from my own son-in-law. You wouldn't believe the pressure Barry's been putting me under. Even has my daughter arguing with me, trying to change my mind."

Chase stood and followed him from the room. "Then why —"

"Because a few years back I found out

something about myself that I didn't like. I discovered that I was using my actions and my words and my thoughts to better my own position, and not my faith. I realized I needed to accept this cause which I felt God was thrusting at me, a cause that had nothing to do with me and everything to do with what I felt the Father was calling me to do for Him."

When Grey saw him out to the truck, he leaned against the running board and said through Chase's open window, "There's a basic tenet that goes like this: Crime follows money. I'll take that one step farther. Where gambling goes, scandal and corruption and organized crime are bound to follow. Why? Because what we're talking about here is pure, liquid cash, and there's more of it in a casino than anywhere outside a bank vault." His expression was ancient. "Now what does that tell you? That the gambling interests will spend anything, do anything, to make gambling in Florida a reality."

"So what's the answer?"

He patted the door, stepped away, replied, "Do exactly what you're doing, son. Go out there and fight the good fight."

Troy entered his office and set down the first page of numbers. "Got some funny over-the-phone looks from some of the companies."

Chase accepted the sheet. "Why's that?"

"Those with the stars beside their names are Florida firms. They didn't see why we would be trying to pull them away from somewhere else in the same state."

Chase scanned the sheet, counted eleven starred names. "I've got another eight so far myself. Thought maybe it was just my first page."

Troy shook his head. "It's working out the same on my second sheet. Six so far in Brevard County. With them, I just said I wanted to check our records, make sure we had the correct address." Troy looked at him. "What's going on here?"

Chase let the page drop, ran his finger down his own sheet to the next name, reached for the phone. "I wish I knew."

The night before he had stopped by Kaitlyn's house, tired and drained both from emotional strain and the confusion. He had thought to stay only a moment or two but had found himself guided into the front porch's slatted glider. With little urging she had pressed him into sharing it all, what had happened, what had not happened, what he feared, what he hoped.

When he had finally talked himself out, she rocked in silence for a while, then asked, "Do you have a plan for tomorrow?"

He stared out at the night. "Kind of."

"*Kind of* a plan? You're meeting the serious players down in Palm Beach, and that's the best you can do?"

"Things have been a little busy. But I'm working on it."

"Don't you think maybe it's time to have a little something stronger to rely on?"

He turned toward her. "Like what?"

"You're supposed to be doing this for a higher purpose. At least you say Grey is, and in a way you're in this with him. So maybe it's time you prayed about it." She lifted her chin. "Or do you do that?"

Quietly. "I do it."

"I think we should ask for guidance now. Together."

Quieter still, but comforted, and happy with the idea. "You say the words, okay?"

She bowed her head and spoke, and nobody ever came close to being as surprised as Chase when the peace settled in on him. Just like that. A comforting knowledge that he was neither alone nor wandering. Potent, certain, complete. Perfect.

"Amen," he said. "And thanks."

"I wasn't finished," she protested.

"I wasn't talking to you." He draped one arm around her. "Would you come with me tomorrow?"

"Down to Palm Beach? Why?"

He explained what he had in mind. She listened to him in silence, and when he was finished said softly, "Grandpa would call you a guardian of the distance."

"What's that?"

"Someone who holds the long-term view," she replied. "Somebody able to see beyond their own self-interests."

"Ever since that trip to Washington," he said, "I've been caught up in things I haven't been able to really see at all. I catch little glimpses now and then, but only the tiniest portion."

She kept looking at him. "Like me?"

"Totally different." He reached for her hand. "You're a natural person from the heart out. Just being around you, I'm learning to see myself better."

Chase was halfway through his final page and growing increasingly bored with the entire address-gathering process when Troy's bulk again filled the doorway. "Phone call for you. John Dearfield. Line two."

"Didn't I say to hold all calls until we were done?" Chase finished dialing, pressed the receiver to his ear. "If I didn't I should have."

"You may want to take this one," Troy said.

Something in his tone caused Chase to look up. "Why's that?"

"Because," Troy replied, "Dearfield Industries has one of the 800 numbers I just called."

Chase hit the button for the second line, kept his eye on Troy, said, "Long time no hear, John. How's tricks?"

"Bad," he spat. "We've been the victims of toll fraud."

"Sorry to hear that," Chase said, his eyes still on where Troy stood. He punched the speaker-phone button for them both to hear. "Just exactly what happened?"

"Somebody weaseled their way into my company's 800 number. We have an outside coding system so our salesmen can call in, punch the code, and dial out at company rates. Saves a bundle when they're on the road, trying to do business from hotels." There was the sound of papers rustling. "Took us for seventy-five thousand dollars in calls. Over one weekend."

Chase let out a low whistle. "What will you do?"

"Pay." The word punched at the air. "Don't have any choice. The phone companies say it's our own fault for not having proper safeguards. Doesn't matter that they didn't warn us about this risk."

"I'm really sorry, John."

"You and me both. Well, just wanted to let you know. Maybe you ought to send out a circular, let the other chamber members know there are crooks operating in the area."

Chase made waving motions at Troy. "It so happens," he said, "that we've just been working on a list that targets some companies as possible toll-fraud victims."

"Am I on it?"

"Afraid so." He waited while Troy slid the page down on his desk and thumped a sunburned finger on the number. "That is, if your 800 number is 555-2100 and your access code is, let's see, 2828. Sound familiar?"

Heavy breathing, then, "How long have you known about this?"

"Only picked up the sheets this morning, and that's the honest truth," Chase said. "Nothing we could have done about yours. Sorry."

"How many companies are there?"

"We're not sure," Chase hedged.

"Ballpark." Not willing to take less than all he had to give.

"In this area, close to two dozen."

"Cripes."

"We're calling them right now," Chase said.

"Any idea who's behind it?"

"Not yet."

"You find out, you tell me. Understand? I want to be the first to know."

John Dearfield was a former Marine who had boxed light-heavyweight in the nationals. "Second, maybe," Chase said. "After the police."

"Anything you need tracking them down, you get back to me," John said. "Still have my private number?"

"Yes. Thanks, John."

"Somebody doesn't believe how serious this is, have them give me a call." A moment's hesitation, then, "And if you could let me know before the police, I'd be in your debt."

The peace of his visit with Kaitlyn the night before had scarcely lasted until he had arrived back home. Chase had walked in and punched the answering machine's playback button as he headed down the hall. He had been brought to a jolting halt by the sound of a tired but too-familiar voice. Carlotta.

"Chase. Had to risk this. I'm okay. Really. With a friend. It's safe here, safe as any place is. Don't worry. About me, anyway. Wanted to hear that you're all right. Jack tells me there's still a big stink down Washington way. Remember, if somebody shows up, I didn't send them." A couple of seconds of heavy breathing, then, "Sorry you're not there. Gotta go."

Chase had spent hours afterward lying in bed and staring up into nothingness, his mind tracing dark patterns across the night.

"This is Chase Bennett down at the chamber of commerce. We have reason to believe your PBX network has been compromised."

"What?"

"Your telephone system." By the twenty-third time he weaseled his way into a senior exec's office that morning, Chase's supply of courteous bonhomie was dwindling. "Someone has managed to obtain your secret 800 code."

A silence, then bluster. "That's absurd."

Chase ran his finger down the sheet and read, "555-3768, PBX code 8899. That ring any bells?"

Another silence, longer this time. "They said that was impossible."

By then Chase could have written the script for the conversation. "Who's they?"

"The jokers who sold us the system. Seventy thousand dollars for the switchboard alone."

"All I know is," Chase said, "your secret code has become public knowledge. Have you received any monster bills yet?"

"Not that I know of." A note of panic creeping in.

"Well, maybe I got to you in time. I would suggest you cut the whole system off until this has been cleared up and another code has been installed. Let your salesmen pay hotel phone rates for a few days."

"Right." A tense breath, then, "We're just getting into the busiest part of our season. Why us, why now?"

"If it's any consolation," Chase said, "you're one of twenty-three local companies that were marked down for a hit."

"Yeah, well, at least you got to us before they did. Who are 'they,' by the way?"

"No idea," Chase replied. "I wish I did."

"You and me both. Okay, time to run. Thanks, Bennett. I won't be forgetting this."

Chase left the office just before noon, drove across the causeway and down the interior highway to where a rutted drive suddenly opened through an ancient stand of loblolly pines. Two signs flanked Colin's driveway, nailed to a pair of live oaks that predated the nation's Constitution. The neater sign sported professional lettering and scrolled edges and announced, "Colin Poyner, Carpentry, Joining, Handcrafted Furniture, Interior Finishing." The other sign had been hand-painted on a rough pine board in dribbled letters and read, "C. Poyner, Bass Fishing Guide. Half price special for anybody that hates talk in boats as much as I do."

Chase climbed the swaybacked stairs to the porch, pressed his face to the screen, and called, "You folks in to visitors?"

"Since when have you ever been a visitor to this house?" Samantha Poyner unlocked the screen and pulled the door wide. "You want some fresh-made lemonade?"

"Suddenly I've gone all dry."

"Come on in. Colin's out back, as usual. Working himself to death, as usual." Samantha wore cutoffs and a bright cotton shirt knotted below her ribs. At forty she remained as compact and energetic and tanned as she had been at seventeen. She crossed the living room floor toward the kitchen with a dancer's bouncy step. "You can take him out some too."

He accepted the sweating glass, sipped, asked, "How is he?"

"Busy. Got two jobs should be finished up

next week and a head full of ideas that won't let him sleep."

Colin Poyner had long since graduated from the carpentry job Chase had found for him. Nowadays he was considered to be one of the finest woodworkers in central Florida. Interior decorators from Palm Beach to Gainesville were after him to do cabinets, specialty shelves, floors, molding, anything and everything he would agree to. He spent all his free time designing and building furniture, which was usually bought before he hammered in the first nail.

Chase sipped again. "How is he really?"

She looked out the back window in the general direction of the hammering. "About the same. Hasn't been fishing in I don't know how long."

"He sleeping?"

"Now and then." She turned from the window, auburn hair fringing a strong brown face and gray eyes full of concern. "He's been having those dreams again."

"He gone to the doctor?"

"No. He says talking about it only makes it worse." She reached for his glass, took a swallow. "How long have you known Colin?"

"I think my first Florida memory is of him. You remember how they had all the grades in that one building for a while. I was just another third-grade punk and Colin was the big varsity football star. Then one day there was this group of guys, what passed for a gang back then, they started picking on me. Colin just popped up out of nowhere and took on four or five of them by himself. We've been friends ever since."

"Yeah, he's always going on about what a runt you were." She tried hard at a smile, almost made it. "You think maybe you could talk to him?"

"About the doctor?" He shrugged. "I can try. But I'm not sure he's wrong to stay away. How long did he go for therapy, three years? And it never seemed to do any good. Maybe talking about it more isn't the answer for him."

She turned her face back to the window. "I had a dream the other night. About how it used to be. You know, before."

"I know," he said quietly.

"I'd give anything to see him get better."

He mulled it over, decided there wasn't any reason not to say it. "Last night I had this idea."

She looked up at him. "For Colin?"

"Just an idea. But I thought maybe it might help."

"Well don't just stand there." She jammed a second glass into his free hand and shooed him toward the door. "And tell that man of mine if he faints out there in this heat, he might as well ask the mosquitoes to cart him off. I'm not wasting any sympathy on a fool that won't get out of the sun."

Colin was where he usually was when he wasn't off on some job, out by his open-ended carpenter's shed surrounded by wood and dust and noise. He looked up and cut off the band saw. "Hey, boy, you're a sight for sore eyes."

"You don't have to shout, I'm not deaf."

"Yeah, but I am." He slipped off his protective goggles, accepted the glass of lemonade, drained it in one long pull, shuddered, and declared, "Think I might make it after all."

Colin Poyner was dressed in ancient shorts, cap, and sawdust. The only part of his body that showed clean was the strip of tan around his eyes where the goggles had rested. His Vietnam Vet and Proud of It cap bore the brass badge of a master sergeant and another of crossed rifles. Colin wore it pulled down far enough to hide most of his graying hair and all of his bald spot.

The only time Colin's sadness showed through was when he stopped, which was seldom. When he was working he just looked tense and tired. When he stopped, like now, the hollow point in his eyes opened to reveal that empty space at the center of his being. He seldom looked at anybody when he was still. His gaze remained locked on something only he could see. The longer he remained quiet and still, the lower his body slumped, as though bearing the weight of the world and the mistakes of the human race.

"Sam tells me the dreams have started back."

He handed back his glass. "That woman talks too dang much."

"That woman is the finest lady I've ever met and ten times the woman you deserve," Chase replied, but without rancor.

Colin squinted through the heat. "You looking to get yourself whupped again?"

"She talks about you because she's worried about you."

The defiance slipped away. "There ain't nothing nobody can do about what's the matter with me," he said, matter of fact now. "Especially me."

"So the dreams are back."

He reached to his bench, picked up the hammer, started tossing it from one hand to the other. "Just when I think maybe I got them ghosts licked once and for all, there they pop up again. I just don't understand, Slim. Ain't no logic to it."

Chase let the silence hang between them for a moment, then said quietly, "I've got a problem, Colin. A big one. Sure use your help."

Colin grunted. "The only help I've been giving anybody lately is nailing down wood for swishy fellas in tight pants and little gold earrings."

Chase set down his glass. "I think maybe I'm getting involved in something dangerous. Risky enough that somebody might decide to take a swipe at me."

Muscles tightened beneath Colin's second skin of sweat and sawdust. "You serious, Slim?"

He nodded. "Maybe more than one somebody."

Colin reached for a towel as grimy as his shorts and made a pretense of cleaning his hands. "Well, then, why don't we get outta this heat and you can tell me all about it."

"I don't have time right now. Got to get down to Palm Beach for a meeting. I was just wondering if maybe you could stop by my place tonight, let me lay everything out." He took a breath. "Basically I think maybe I could use a little security."

Eyes glimmered with a new sort of light. "Play hunter-seeker, you mean."

"It may be nothing at all, Colin. I'm just

running on hunches." Feeling more foolish than ever, but going on both because he had started, and because of this strange new light in his buddy's eyes. "I just thought maybe it'd be a good idea if you could see your way to give me a hand."

"You've never been one to cry wolf unless the pack was on your heels." Colin nodded once. "I'll stop by tonight, we can chew on this a little more."

Kaitlyn's father was there to greet him before he knocked. "Chase, hello, good to see you."

"Morning, Mr. Picard."

"Call me Joe, why don't you?" The graying man had the same kind of a grip as Chase's father, broad and flattened by years of outdoor life. "Kaitlyn's been talking about you nonstop."

The news brought a flush of pleasure. "She has?"

"Sure enough. Come on in. Kaitlyn's class ran a little over, she's in the back dressing. Shouldn't be too much longer." He held the door for Chase. "She mentioned you stopped by the other day, said you had a talk with Pop."

"He's an interesting guy."

Joe Picard was tall and slightly stooped,

but he bore his age with the calm of having tapped his inner strength and found it sufficient to weather life's storms. "Wish you could have met him back when. Want something to drink?"

"No thanks." He chose a stool by the counter that separated the kitchen alcove from the dining room and served as breakfast nook, work station, and a place for visitors to sit and chat with the cook. Comfortable and casual and practical, a familiar feature in many older Florida homes.

The house bore other signs of a Florida lifestyle that was quickly being lost as developers frantically tore down older places in their haste to plug up the shoreline with concrete condos. Cedar-slat walls stained the color of sourwood honey rose to a big timbered ceiling. There were floors of pegged oak, a big stone fireplace to ward off winter chills, and louvered windows to direct whatever wind might drift through. "I sure do love this house."

"Yeah, it's a fine old place. Looks like it'll go to Kaitlyn, what with my wife not liking Florida so much." He laughed without mirth at his own joke. "Boy, is that the understatement of the year."

Chase watched Joe Picard and understood on some instinctive level what was happening. The father had shared his daughter's pain so deeply that he found it hard to welcome any new man into her life. He still felt protective, worrying that more pain might be in store. Yet he recognized that she was grown, that he had no place to speak or warn or worry out loud. And seeing what an effect Chase was having on his daughter, he was warming to the idea of this young man hanging around. It was the nicest compliment Chase had received in a very long time. He tried to repay it with, "You have a wonderful daughter, sir."

The grin was genuine. "Yeah, she's something special. Been through a tough time."

"I know."

"Hard on my wife, too. Didn't handle it too well, I'm sorry to say. Tough to say how much of it was due to Kaitlyn's troubles and how much to me stopping work early and then coming right down here to see after Pop. Lot of changes all at once, none of them welcome." The smile was thinner now, tainted with old worries. "Just have to wait and hope, I guess."

A light tread down the side hall turned them both around. Kaitlyn appeared wearing a full-length knit dress which managed to be both conservative and very alluring. Her short hair was brushed to a burnished sheen. A single strand of pearls hung from her neck.

Chase looked at her for a long moment, taking in the glow to her cheeks, the care with which she had dressed for this trip. "You look fantastic."

She dimpled and spun on high heels, exposing shapely calves. "It's been a long time since I had an excuse to play dress-up." She walked over, placed a cool hand on his arm, gave him a full-wattage look from those gorgeous eyes. "Has anyone told you how handsome you look in a suit?"

"Not that I recall."

Joe Picard cleared his throat, held up a pocket camera. "Mind if I get a shot of you two for the old album?"

He had them pose by the fireplace. As they stood in place, Chase glimpsed the two of them in the tall side mirror. In heels Kaitlyn stood almost exactly his height, calm and poised and keeping a proprietary hold on his arm. He wore a navy double-breasted gabardine suit, his finest, with a striped shirt and matching club tie. His power rig. Barely able to keep pace with Kaitlyn's beauty. His chest so swelled with pride that he worried he might pop a couple of buttons.

With a few minor exceptions, Miami's rule extended all the way north to Palm Beach.

The final ninety-mile stretch of coastline before Florida surrendered to the Keys, the Bahamas, and the Gulf was an almost continual wall of high-rise condos and monumental villas for the super-rich. Behind that wall of fairyland, however, stretched mile after mile of cheap bars and malls and housing estates and locked-in poverty and anger.

And traffic. I-95 and US-1 and the Florida Turnpike were all eight-lane madness. Souped-up Mustangs with dingo balls bouncing crazily from rearview mirrors played suicide tag with terrified tourists wanting only to find their hotel, their airport, their exit ramp, their way home. The only drivers spared this frenetic aggression sat behind wheels of late-model Jags and Mercs and Lexuses and Ferraris bearing Dade County plates. The risk of going mano a mano with a Miami drug king forced even the most foolhardy to keep a safe distance.

Chase stopped to fill up the truck at the final service island before his turnoff. The air conditioning on his Camaro had chosen that morning to start acting up, and the day threatened to be a scorcher. When he climbed back into the cab, he turned to her and said quietly, "It means more than I can say to have you here."

Kaitlyn gave him dimples and affection. "So I'm more than just a pretty face?"

"Rochelle is going to expect me to come with backup. His kind always do. A lawyer, usually, but if not, somebody else to check that all the i's are crossed and t's dotted."

"Or something like that," she agreed. They shared a comfortable silence for a time down the road, until their exit sign came into view and Kaitlyn confessed, "I've never been to Palm Beach before."

"The town claims to be different, but it's just a myth," Chase told her. Relishing the role of know-all tourist guide. "All Palm Beach did was push its high-rise complexes back across the causeway. The Miami virus is still alive and growing, just on the other side of the Inland Waterway. Then they made the beachfront area a Disneyland for millionaires."

Chase fought for right of place on the exit with a black-on-black Trans Am, held his own because he was driving the truck. "West Palm Beach is also the world's largest user of wheelchair ramps."

She rewarded him with a smile. "You're saying the people here are old."

"I'm saying that this is the place old people come to visit their parents. So many, and so old, all the street signs wear bifocals." He cruised along the lake, turned by a pair of faceless high-rise office buildings, and went on, "I like to think of it as Camp Palm Beach. Most of the people living here have three things in common besides age. They're rich, they're more than willing to stand back and watch the world go to hell in a handbasket, and they've got skin like cured crocodile hides."

"I think I may have served a few of them, strays who made it up as far as my restaurant."

He crossed the causeway and took Coconut Row down to the A1A. The area took on the contrived air of a movie set. "People here, their calendars are filled with tennis and golf and horseback riding and cocktail parties. Their friends are all safe, all too rich to need help, and all ferocious Republicans. They share a determination not to let anything ever rock their private little boat."

He pointed down a side street, as well manicured and made up as a shopwindow mannequin. "Worth Avenue, the East Coast's answer to Rodeo Drive."

"Ferragamo, Gucci, Ungaro, Cartier," she read from storefront signs. "All the common household names."

They passed by a Greco-Roman-Tudor villa identified by a little sign as "Sandcastle."

Pink pillars rose to support a chartreuse arch overlooked by a clay-tile roof of palest lavender. Kaitlyn declared, "This place is too chi-chi for words."

"The whole town is a monument to ego." He took the A1A's curve, then turned again through the massive Bath and Tennis Club gates. "Heads up. We're on."

The parking attendants were all tanned and fit and wore tux shirts with dark shorts and running shoes. None appeared overly eager to approach the dusty pickup. They clustered by the shaded station, glancing their way, snickering and tossing around audibly snide remarks. Chase climbed down, slid his coat out from behind the seat, checked his tie in the side mirror, played at patience.

Kaitlyn stepped from the truck, straightened her jacket, said across to him, "Looks like a convention for juveniles with an attitude problem."

A young kid sauntered over, tossed sunbleached hair from his face, asked, "Help you?"

"We're here to see Sylvan Rochelle."

The kid took him and the truck in with one glance. Another flip of the hair, then doubtfully, "Mr. Rochelle's expecting you?"

Kaitlyn leaned across the hood. "Tell you

what, why don't you just park the truck, how's that for an idea? And stop trying to find out how short a fuse my boy has." She clip-clipped across the pavement, her high heels and irritation making the act worth watching. Then turning back said, "You can stay out here and play with the help. I'm getting hot."

Chase watched her climb the steps and disappear, then turned to the valet. The attendant took a cautious step backward. Chase hid his grin and said, "Keys are in the ignition."

He found her standing to one side of the front foyer, ignoring the pair of muscled bodyguards in matching gray suits who eyed her with undisguised interest. When Chase appeared in the doorway, she demanded, "Did you see the way that juvenile acted?"

He took her arm, steered her down the main hall. "Your boy," he repeated. "Pretty cute."

As they appeared in the restaurant anteroom, a polished, slender gray-haired man in a tuxedo walked over and asked, "Can I help you?"

Chase worked at seriousness, said, "We're here to see Sylvan Rochelle."

"I see. And your name is?"

"Bennett."

"Of course, Mr. Bennett. Mr. Rochelle is expecting you. Right this way, please."

The main dining hall had grand high windows overlooking lawns, a pool, rocks, and the sea. The interior was plush carpet and chandeliers and discreet murmurs and acres of starched tablecloth. The head waiter led them through an archway and into a screened alcove where Sylvan Rochelle stood, his back to the room, smoking a Panatella and staring out over the vista. "Your guests have arrived, Mr. Rochelle."

He spun around. "Excellent. And right on time. I like that. Thank you, Carlos."

"Very good, sir."

"Have you seen Claude?"

"I believe Mr. Sorrens is visiting with other guests in the bar."

"Just like a lawyer, to leave one client hanging while he goes off hunting others." He smiled at his attempt at humor, walked around the table, extended his hand to Kaitlyn. "Sylvan Rochelle, at your service."

"This is Kaitlyn Picard," Chase said. "She is both a friend and a business adviser."

"And such an attractive one at that." Rochelle made a semblance of bowing over her hand, not quite bringing it to his lips. On a less polished man the gesture would have appeared foppish. On him it fit perfectly. "A pleasure, Miss Picard. Won't you sit down."

The table held chairs for twelve, and the tablecloth still had imprints of a heavy meal. Now only one wine glass, a crystal ashtray, and a silver centerpiece of flowers remained. The lawyer, Claude Sorrens, hustled in just as coffee arrived and was being poured. "Why didn't somebody tell me they were here?"

"Why didn't you bother to stay put and attend to matters at hand," Rochelle replied. He ignored the flush of irritation that sprang to Sorrens' face, said, "This is Miss Picard, Mr. Bennett's adviser."

Sorrens rounded on her, demanded, "Attorney?"

"Miss Picard comes from a career in banking," Chase replied for her. "I was wondering if you could sort of walk her through the draft contract you've drawn up for the land. You brought a copy, didn't you?"

"Sure, but —"

"An excellent idea," Rochelle interrupted smoothly. "Take Miss Picard to one of the other tables. We'll be with you shortly."

When they were alone, Rochelle lowered himself into a chair, picked up his cigar from the ashtray, puffed on it several times, said through the smoke, "We have only met briefly, Mr. Bennett, but I believe I am coming to understand you. Better than Laroque. Better even than his beautiful assistant. Certainly better than my lawyer."

"Is that a fact?"

"Indeed it is. You have convinced them that you are a buffoon. A foolish boy who clouds the issue with oafish questions." Rochelle shook his head. "My business requires me to see beneath the surface, and to do so quickly. I am coming to realize that this is not true."

When Chase said nothing, Rochelle dipped his cigar to the ashtray, rolled the tip into a cone of burning cinders. "Tell me, what is it exactly that you want to get out of this transaction?"

"Exactly." Chase sighed the word, willing the band of tension to ease around his chest. "Exactly, I want to use this opportunity to start playing with the big league."

A thoughtful puff. "You are not seeking money from me, then."

Chase shook his head. "Money isn't much of an issue. A *lot* of money is. And information."

The eyes narrowed. "What sort of information?"

"I want to know what you intend," Chase said. "I want to know why this property is so important. I want to be a part of what-

298

ever it is you're building."

Rochelle examined him a moment longer. "I was right, wasn't I? It takes a very intelligent man to play the fool so well that people believe it. And you, my friend, have fooled the best." Rochelle rose smoothly to his feet, circled the table, said, "Now you and your associate really must accept my invitation and come to the gala launching of my new casino liner on Thursday evening."

Chase let himself be guided back through the restaurant toward where Kaitlyn and Sorrens sat confiding. "No offense, but I'm not much on crowds and galas of any kind."

"Ah, but this one you simply cannot afford to miss. It will be a gathering of movers and shakers from all over the state. It is a charity event costing a thousand dollars a head. Except, that is, for a select few local leaders whose support I need for this new project. It is destined to draw an immense crowd of people you need to know."

"All right, then. Thanks."

"Excellent." A tightening of the pressure on his arm drew Chase to a halt. "Tell me, Mr. Bennett. What do you think I have planned for your property?"

"Whatever it is, for the price you've offered it has to be big."

"In my business, Mr. Bennett, we say that

three things determine a property's value — location, location, and location. That land you hold happens to rest alongside the Cocoa port. The very same port which I intend to use as my primary base for an expanding line of luxury cruise vessels."

"A perfect setup for a hotel-casino," Chase said admiringly.

"A supercasino," Rochelle corrected. "The largest casino in the world."

"Then you've decided," Chase said, and knew it was now all confirmed. "You're definitely going for this location. The rest was all a smokescreen."

"Quite necessary, I assure you. We must leave all communities feeling that they have an equal chance, if not for this one, then the next." Rochelle led Chase forward, vastly satisfied with the internal vista he beheld. "Cocoa Beach Harbor Resort. Catering both to tourists and to all the central Florida population. The twenty million people expected to live between Jacksonville and Palm Beach by the end of this century. All these people who live too far from the delights of Miami, but who would gladly travel several hours for the chance to visit such a place. A perfect home market, Mr. Bennett, with a guaranteed monopoly for the services I intend to provide."

"Granted by your friend and mine," Chase added, "Lamar Laroque."

"Once he has become Governor Laroque," Sylvan agreed, "our fortunes are assured. The plans are already structured and ready to be implemented. Four, perhaps five supercasinos, strategically set around the state. Sold to the welcoming public as the easiest means to control gambling while granting the state this needed income."

"But in the meantime," Chase asked, "how do you intend to get around the ban on casino gambling in Florida?"

Sylvan Rochelle rewarded him with a grand smile. "An excellent question. One which you must for the moment leave with me. Rest assured, however, that this will not remain a problem for much longer. Of that you can be absolutely certain."

14

Chase pulled into his drive, slid from the truck, eased his back, smiled across at an equally tired Kaitlyn. "How about a nice quiet dinner for two, maybe eat out on the deck and watch —"

Colin came stomping over. "How's it going, old buddy?"

Chase groaned. "I forgot about him."

"About who?" She looked from one to the other. "Do you know everybody in this town?"

"Everybody in the whole state, more like." Colin gave her an admiring up and down. "Nice. Are you attached, or can I make an end run here?"

Kaitlyn looked at Chase, showed vast disappointment that their evening had been disturbed. "Has there ever been a single girl in the entire history of mankind who has fallen for a line like that?"

"I guess that answers my question," Colin said. "Nice girl, Chase. Shame about the lip."

"Oddballs and misfits," Chase said. "I collect them."

"Draws 'em like flies," he agreed. "Name's Colin."

"How nice for you." To Chase, "Are we ready to go inside?"

"Colin is a friend," Chase said gently. "And rendered harmless by a very wonderful wife."

"Keeps me on a mighty short leash," Colin agreed.

"Peel the touristy wrapping off Florida," Chase explained, wanting for her to understand, to accept, to like, "and you've got a state of good old boys split by their allegiances to football teams."

She crossed her arms, declared, "I hate football."

"I'll pretend I didn't hear that," Colin said.

"I mean, I don't hate-hate it. But it's just a *game*."

Colin plugged up his ears and started humming a single note. Chase slapped at his arm. Colin stopped, unplugged one ear a half-inch, asked her, "You done?"

"All my life I've sort of been the odd one out around here," Chase said to her. "I don't hunt or fish. I hate golf. I'm not all that much on watching somebody else go out and play a sport. I'd rather be *doing*."

"Your boat," Colin said, shaking his head.

"You missed the big game on Saturday to be out on your boat. I oughtta sink that thing, save you a passel of misery."

"I love Florida," Chase went on. "It's friends like Colin who've made it home for me, accepting me for what I am, letting me go my own way. Watching out for me when I get in a pinch. Which is why I asked him over tonight."

She softened a fraction. "You're saying I've got to take you as you come."

"I've heard about relationships where all the friends slowly vanish. I'm just saying I really don't want this to happen with me. My friends are too important. Too much a part of my life."

"Relationship," she said softly.

Colin looked from one to the other, asked, "Is this going someplace?"

"All my life I've collected people like Colin. Don't ask me why. I don't know. And they're friends. Not just good-time buddies or business colleagues. Friends."

"True enough," Colin agreed. "Old Chase here has more friends than a dog has fleas."

She turned to face him square on. "Why?"

Colin met her gaze calmly. "Chase cares. That just about sums it all up. That boy cares more than anybody I've ever met. Shame he cared so much for so long for the wrong gal. You ever meet Sabine?"

"No."

"Sabine Duprie is a monster in high heels," he went on, relishing the genuine interest she was now showing. "Hides out in those fancy outfits of hers, looking for prey." Colin stopped, listened, said, "Phone's ringing."

Chase took the steps with a single bound, left Colin playing gossip hound for Kaitlyn, reached the phone in three strides. "Hello?"

As soon as he heard the weeping on the other end, he knew. Even before the woman could bring herself under control and shakily give out the news, he knew.

The funeral itself was filled with old friends and shared remembrances and smiles, just as Marie would have wanted. Chase drifted through it all. He responded when people spoke, went through the motions, let the familiarity and habit and custom hold him in place, despite the sensation that all ties to his past were being severed one by one.

It was at the cemetery that it all threatened to unravel.

The path leading through the trees and up to the gravesite was ten thousand miles long. And it was lined with memories all the way.

Chase stood in the brilliant green and remembered his parents' funeral. He remembered the loneliness that had loomed like an open grave. He remembered the way he had strained and strained to hear the pastor's voice, wanting desperately to hear something that he could take away with him. Anything to fill the emptiness, make the loss easier to bear, keep the loneliness at bay. But his mind had made no sense of it. None at all. The people who surrounded him and shook his hand and hugged him after the service, who held him up at the gravesite and kept him from falling in himself, they and their love and their concern had all been held at bay by the vacuum which had consumed him on that day.

But not now.

A warm and gentle hand slipped around his upper arm. When that was not enough, a second hand slid up his shoulder, across his shirt collar, to trace a feather-touch up and down his neck. A fragrance as sweet and fresh as the surrounding spring filled his nostrils. A soft body pressed gently to his side, and a voice filled with concern for him said, "I'm here, Chase."

He took a ragged breath, pushed himself erect, turned and looked into those wide, caring eyes. They imparted the strength of her concern, filling the emptiness, soothing the ache. He raised one hand, touched her cheek, then let her steer him around to where the other pallbearers waited for him to come and take his place. He let her separate herself from his side, knowing it was all right, that she was with him still. That he was not alone.

The next morning he shut his office door on the world and told Troy to hold all calls, use whatever force necessary to keep him from being disturbed. Then he spread all the pages from the disks' files out on his desk, and he thought.

One by one the pages were stacked and put to the side until he was left with a single sheet. Here was what had set his mind racing around dawn. What he knew held the answer he had been searching for. The question now was, how to obtain the necessary key without giving himself away.

To most, the sheet would have appeared still to be encoded. A scattering of maybe thirty names, brief comments, a single number followed by a letter. Chase would have willingly tossed it aside had it not been for two names which had leapt off the page and electrified his gut. The first was TADLOCK, the second LAROQUE.

He picked up the phone, dialed the

number to Grey Spenser's home. When the older gentleman came on the line, Chase said, "I'm going to read off some names to you. Tell me if anything comes to mind."

When he was finished, Grey replied, "Most of them are familiar. Those I recognize are currently either in the state House or Senate. Plus the lieutenant governor."

"Bingo."

"What's that?"

"Nothing." Chase leaned back, staring at the sheet. "Anything else?"

"You mean, other than the fact that I don't like any of the ones I recognize?"

His chair slammed back down flat. "You don't?"

"The best of them are what I'd call passing honest. The worst I wouldn't bother giving the time of day to. I'd say they were all susceptibles. Lobbyists are pouring money into our state and government in support of gambling. The faucets are open, and the legislators like those on your list are running for buckets."

Chase stared at the sheet in his hand. "You're sure about this?"

"Absolutely. In the months running up to the last Indiana election, the gaming companies spent over two million dollars on advertising alone. The pressure got so bad, the state legislature decided to make it a local issue, where each county could decide to hold a referendum. That's when things really got crazy. In one county with only twenty thousand voters, the casino groups spent over five hundred thousand dollars. That we know of, anyway."

"That's crazy."

"Not if you're playing for the stakes they're after. Counties that organized church groups to fight the invasion were overwhelmed. The gambling companies brought in professional pollsters, paid them ten cents a signature to get names for a public ballot. Then they used professional PR men to redesign the casino proposal, attaching all tax revenue to education. They figured it would draw the maybe voters over to their side. It was a ploy, pure and simple."

"Let's go back to the legislators for a minute," Chase said. "How would you go about bribing somebody like that? I mean, you can't just walk up to a politician and stuff money in his pocket."

"Is that what this list is about?"

"I don't know, Grey. Really."

"Well, it's simpler than you think. First off, I'd locate somebody with a fistful of power, a bellyful of greed, and more ambition than morals."

Chase thought of Laroque. "Then what?"

"Then I'd make him my number one guy. My people and his people would sit down and draw up a list of possibles, officials open to a little persuasion. Might be money, might be horse trading, might be a position in the private sector they could step into once they've left politics. Lame-duck politicians are especially susceptible."

Lame duck. The word appeared up and down the page. "I thought stuff like that went out with pork-barrel politics."

"Wish that was the case. In 1990, eighteen South Carolina state legislators were caught in an FBI sting, selling their votes to gambling interests. Same year, six Arizona state legislators were convicted of the same thing. Not to mention a governor, the president pro tem of a state senate, and the leader of another state's House of Representatives." Grey sighed. "What you have is a small group of totally amoral people controlling access to a monumental amount of money."

Chase decided he had what he needed. "Thanks, Grey. This has been a big help."

"No problem. What's going on over there?"

"I'm not sure," Chase said slowly. "I'll get back to you, though."

"You do that. Say, that was a nice-looking

lady I saw you with at the funeral."

Chase felt the dark flower of sorrow bloom in his chest. "Were you there?"

" 'Course I was. Waved to you twice." The tone gentled. "You miss her, don't you, son."

"Yes."

"Miss Marie was a fine lady. Thought the world of you."

"She taught me." The words were hard to come by. "All my life long."

"There's no greater compliment you could have given the lady than that. Well, give me a call if I can do anything more for you. And let me hear what you find out."

When Chase hung up the phone, he found himself still captured by the feelings and the loss. And the memories. He sat and stared at nothing until his mind gradually centered down on the last few visits with Marie. Her weakness, her courage. Her labored breathing, her determined smiles.

Her insistence that somehow everything was tied together.

Chase looked again at the sheet in his hand. He scanned down the page, came to Barry's name, read: "TADLOCK. Lame duck. Hndl CB rl est. 300K. OK. Corbett."

Chase leaned his head on the back of his seat, stared at the ceiling, unwound the abbreviations. Barry Tadlock was a lame-duck senator, meaning he was not going to run again. Meaning he was going to be interested in padding his civilian nest while he still had a vote with which to barter. That much was clear. The following notations were what sent Chase's heart rate zinging. Handle Cocoa Beach real estate dealings. Three hundred thousand dollars. Agreed. Chase glanced at the page, tried to remember ever hearing of a Corbett, could not. Wondered if he was the one giving approval. Or something else?

The lieutenant governor's notation read: "LAROQUE. Gub cmpgn. 2M. OK. Dunlevy."

Chase found himself returning to Marie's gentle insistence, wondered who else might have both an interest both in Cocoa Beach real estate and in seeing Laroque become the next governor of Florida.

He stood and rounded his desk, poked his head outside the door. "Troy, do you have a number for the Omega Corporation?"

"Should do." His fingers typed keys. "Miami head office?"

"Great."

He wrote down a number, said, "Linda Armacost called. Repeatedly. I stopped counting somewhere around number sixteen. Said you were ordered to attend the chamber's monthly dinner tonight. Repeat, ordered. Didn't seem all that pleased when I claimed not to know where you were or what you were doing. At least half of which was the truth."

Chase accepted the slip of paper with the number and glanced at his watch. Almost two. He had missed lunch entirely. "Not sure I'm going to be up for it."

Troy grinned. "I personally can't see why she shouldn't accept that for an excuse."

"Run down to the diner, grab me a couple of sandwiches, will you?" Chase shut his door, returned to his desk, dialed the number.

"Good afternoon. Omega Development Corporation. How may I direct your call?"

"Mr. . . ." Chase ran his eye down the sheet of names. "Mr. Corbett, please."

"Mr. Corbett works out of our Tallahassee office."

Chase was on his feet again without realizing he had moved. He played like a goldfish, gasping silently.

"Hello?"

"What about," he scrambled down the list, "Mr. Dunlevy. Is he in?"

"Also Tallahassee. Do you want that number?"

"Yes, no, wait." He searched the sheet for another name. "Mr. Bendix?"

"I believe he's down here today. Whom may I say is calling?"

Who, indeed. A wild sweep of the mental reaches, then, "This is Tony, Sabine Duprie's assistant."

"Why, I believe Miss Duprie is scheduled to be in the same meeting as Mr. Bendix. Do you want her or him? Hello? Are you still there?"

Chase gently set the phone back in place, raised clenched fists toward the ceiling, cried, "Thank you, Marie!"

After recovering from the thrill of discovery, Chase did his best to track down Matthew, but the man was at a three-day conference in New York and had left orders with both wife and secretary not to be disturbed by anyone. No exceptions allowed. Apologetic, understanding Chase was in a bind, but firm. Both promised to pass on his urgent request for a telephone contact as soon as Matthew was in touch. There being nothing more he could do for the moment, Chase tried his best to return to the more mundane matters of work. When that proved futile, he went home.

For as long as Chase could remember, home had been his protection from an unfriendly world. The great willows had lifted up their roots and walked with him into whatever adventure he and Carlotta and Matthew could imagine, three misfits shunned by the enclosed little town — one because his skin was the wrong color for so intelligent a boy, one because her body grew too large, and one because he had made the fatal mistake of being born somewhere else. Sometimes joined by an older boy too big to easily refuse, one made lonely by the angry ghosts who whispered to him even then.

They had gathered at Chase's yard almost every day until sports and the enlarged world of high school began breaking down the outside barriers. Back then, waterfront property had not been such a big deal. There had been so much water and only so many people. They had gathered there because having the water on his property meant their games and their toys and all their imaginary friends would be created in a world wed with the sea and all its mysteries.

That afternoon, Chase took his thoughts and his worries out on the back porch, sat and gazed over the river. As usual, he found that while the answers were no easier to come by, a measure of peace was certainly to be found.

The knock brought Chase out of his reverie and off the back porch and through the house before his brain was fully alert. Which was probably why he looked at the two guys in sport jackets and ties and grim expressions and said through the screen, "Simmers, right?"

The guy standing closest to the screen door stiffened. "What?"

"You guys are lawyers for Tom Simmers, aren't you? He wants to make another bid for my house and this land. Happens every year about this time."

"Are you Chase Bennett?"

"Tell Tom I admire his persistence, but he's going to have to build his condos someplace else." Chase scratched his head and started to turn away. "Bye."

"We are with the police, Mr. Bennett."

He stopped in mid-yawn. "Say that again?"

"Are you Chase Bennett?"

"Yes."

"I'm Detective Peters and this is Detective Costas. We'd like to ask you a few questions."

Chase pushed the screen door open and struggled to gear up his brain. "Could I see some identification, please?"

Both flashed leather-clad badges, open and shut and back in the pockets. "Do you know a Carlotta Krepps?"

He was fully awake now. Zinging into high gear. "Could we run through that ID thing a little slower?"

Their faces were as blank as their voices. "Miss Krepps stole some very valuable evidence, Mr. Chase. We have reason to believe that she passed it to you. If you have it, we want it back."

Back? Chase reversed a step, let the screen shut. "You guys hang on there just a second, I want to make a call."

The second agent's suit did not hide his welterweight build. He took a step forward and pulled the door back open before Chase could latch it. "You're not going anywhere, bud."

Then another voice glided up. "Kinda far from home, aincha boys?"

Chase turned with the pair, was too relieved to be surprised when Colin stepped into view. The first detective, a solid six-footer with a bruiser's flat eyes, asked, "Who're you?"

"Name's Poyner." Colin wore cutoffs and a grimy T-shirt and lace-up boots. Smaller than either of the detectives, but with a fierceness that neither could match, and a strength his quiet half-smile did not begin to dim. "Sort of a roving Neighborhood Watch."

"Yeah, well, we've got business with the

boy here." The second detective had a nasal voice and the air of one permanently irritated with life. "So buzz off."

"I don't think so," Colin replied, all reasonableness. Turning to Chase, asking, "You want me to leave?"

"You're always welcome here, Colin." Glad to hear his voice did not hold the same tremor that rocked his belly. "You know that."

Colin turned back to the pair, crossed his arms, said conversationally, "I know most of the detectives around these parts. Never seen either of you before. Where you guys from?"

The first one bulled forward, his stance fueled by sullen anger. "Get outta here. Now."

Colin did not move. "I was just wondering, see. Thought it had to be pretty far, you know, like out of what you might call your normal jurisdiction." Colin cocked his head, squinted up. "Guess you guys must have some sort of court papers for showing up here, bothering a prominent local citizen."

"Am I hearing this?" The first detective gave Colin an incredulous up and down, turned to his partner, said, "Do you believe this guy?"

"Get rid of the creep."

"My pleasure."

Chase started to offer a warning, something about who Colin was and what he'd done to earn the medals his wife kept framed in the living room. But before the first word was fully formed, the bulky detective made what the manuals probably called a "threatening gesture." Or started to. Before the swing turned into a punch, he was already flying. Tossed like a sack of rumpled clothes. Landing hard. Lying there unmoving,

"What the —" The second guy started to reach in his jacket. But Colin was already there, one powerful fist wrapped around the unseen hand, the other reaching under his T-shirt to the small of his back, coming out with an old army-issue forty-five. From where Chase stood, the gun looked as big as a cannon.

"You don't want to experience some massive life-threatening changes," Colin said, his voice holding to the soft conversational calm, "you're gonna bring that hand out slow and easy. Empty too. You hear what I'm saying?"

The guy took one look into Colin's eyes, gave a single nervous nod.

"Okay, Chase. Move on out here." When Chase joined him on the porch, he said, "Relieve this gentleman of his gun and badge, why don't you?"

Chase did as he was told, heart in his throat.

"Have a look-see, find out where these guys call home."

Chase opened the heavy leather case, breathed, "Washington, D.C."

"What do you know." Colin motioned with his head. "Go liberate the other guy while you're at it."

When he had done so and returned to the porch, Colin twitched the gun and said, "Time to be heading home, officer. Pick up the trash on your way out."

The detective lowered his hands a fraction. "What about our guns and badges?"

"We'll hold on to this hardware a week or two, or however long we like," Colin said. "If nothing else troubles my neighbor here, I mean covering all the bases too, right on down to lightning and freak storms. If nothing like that happens, why, we'll toss it all into the water out back."

The detective started a curse, was cut off by Colin raising the gun. "Wait, it gets better. If my good buddy here experiences the first little bit of bother, even a bad tummyache, why, a lawyer friend of ours is gonna mail this little bundle back to the D.C. chief of police with an explanation as to how we happened to have this stuff in our possession."

Colin planted the gun back on the man's forehead, showed him the blaze in his eyes, spoke two more words very softly. "Move. Now."

"Thanks," Chase said for the tenth time that afternoon. But it sounded better this time, because his knees weren't so weak anymore and his heart had stopped hammering the air from his chest. "Thanks a lot."

Colin just stood there beside him, surveying the quiet street in both directions. "Was that all of them?"

Chase remained too close to his recent fear to manage bravado. "Probably not."

"Will you have any warning next time?"

"I don't know." He squeezed the empty Coke can in his hand, swallowing on a throat so dry the drink hadn't made a dent. "To tell the truth, that pair was sort of from an unexpected direction."

Colin shrugged his unconcern. "You start turning over rocks, you can't always name every slimy thing that starts crawling out. You've just got to be prepared."

"Prepared like how?"

"If I was you," Colin replied, "I'd try to throw the next lot a curve. Put an unexpected spin on their little job."

"That's how you see this, a job?"

Colin looked at him with a gaze still bright from what had just taken place. "That's how *they* see it, Slim. For them, this is just taking care of little chores. These guys, you have to do something pretty radical to make them take you serious enough to back off."

Chase turned his gaze back to the house. Quiet, calm, solid, orderly. He knew a sudden anger that his peace had been threatened. "Tell me what I need to do."

"Hard to say. Times like these, man's gotta grab whatever opportunity pops up. Even when his head is telling him to dive for cover. That's what courage is all about."

"So give me an example. How I should grab for my opportunity."

Colin thought a moment. "You remember me telling you about my friend Ferris?"

"The guy who saved your life over in Vietnam. Sure." Chase sorted through an adrenaline-jumbled memory. "He runs an airboat business, right?"

"That area around Rutland where Ferris lives would be a pretty fair place to throw somebody off balance."

"And just how do you expect me to get them out there?"

With his grin, the years and the worries just melted away. Colin replied, "You're the one looking for prey, Slim. All I can tell you is, it's downright amazing what you can catch with the right bait."

"Government should stay out of business," intoned the Brevard County chamber's unexpected dinner speaker, Lieutenant Governor Lamar Laroque. "The unfettered marketplace is the only means of maintaining the consumer's freedom of choice. Grant them the rights they were promised in our own great Constitution, I say. They are adults. They have the power to vote. If they want to gamble, then let them."

He was flanked on his right by Senator Barry Tadlock and chamber president Linda Armacost. To his left sat Sylvan Rochelle. An empty seat beside Rochelle awaited Chase Bennett. Laroque could not look in that direction without feeling a lance of irritation. No matter what Rochelle might think, he did not like that Bennett. Not at all.

He gestured to the politely attentive Rochelle and continued, "I asked Mr. Rochelle to join us today so that you might meet the man who could, under the proper circumstances, bring to your community the largest commercial development in the history of the Space Coast."

He turned back to the group and solemnly concluded, "Away with this parody of prohibition. The best thing any government at any level can do for business is to keep a hands-off attitude. Government has never done anything for business and never will."

"I don't know," said one gentleman halfway around the tables once the applause had died down and the meeting had broken up to gather around Laroque. "Speaking for myself, I think we receive very good support from our local government and chamber."

"Local chamber," Laroque sniffed. "With the exception of a few rising stars such as our Miss Armacost, the only thing a local chamber is good for is handing out brochures and maps to the tourists. It most certainly has no place in overseeing the activities of local companies."

"No, really," the businessman persisted. "One example. A fellow from the chamber called me the other day, you all know him, Chase Bennett."

Barry Tadlock snorted. "Chase Bennett is exactly the type of irritant busybody Governor Laroque is referring to."

But the company executive did not back down. "He warned us that our 800 number had gotten in the hands of criminals, along with our secret PBX code. Gave us the code himself. Scared the daylights out of us, I can tell you that."

"He did *what?*" Rochelle exclaimed.

"He contacted us as well," a woman executive agreed. "Had our code too. Refused to say how he got it, just said he was passing on a warning from friends."

"Ours too," another added. "Had the phone company in the next day, gave them what-for, I can tell you."

"Chase Bennett," Laroque murmured, his eyes on Rochelle. The developer's face had blanched and tightened with icy fury. "How remarkable."

"He's a real up and comer," the first man said. "If that boy ever decides to go into politics, my prediction is he'll take off like a rocket."

"Indeed?" Laroque said dryly, eyes flickering back and forth between Rochelle and the executive. "No doubt I should make a point of congratulating this young gentleman personally."

Through the casual glad-handing Laroque kept glancing back to where Sylvan Rochelle stood. Rochelle was making an effort to respond to the enthusiastic welcome most people were showing, but the effect was marred by the man's barely suppressed wrath. Laroque hid his smile, satisfied that at last the man understood what this Bennett represented. Yes. Seeing the mask stripped from Rochelle's face, observing clearly what lay beneath, was almost enough to make him feel sorry for this Bennett character.

Almost. But not quite.

15

It was a fairly typical big-spender political do, full of lights and sound and hoopla. The rich, the famous, and the hangers-on decamped from their long stream of gleaming automobiles at the grandest of the Cocoa Harbor buildings. They handed their keys to the hustling attendants, walked up the gangplank, and stepped onto one of the fanciest liners money could buy.

The ship was an oceangoing three-hundred footer, not overly large for a liner, but big enough for one never meant to travel far. Its primary purpose, at least until casinos opened on the Florida mainland, was to cart passengers beyond the twenty-mile limit into international waters and give them a chance to gamble.

The boat gleamed from stem to stern with polished teak and stacked crystal and brilliantly lit ice sculptures. Starched waiters glided back and forth along long tables groaning under their loads of food. The well-heeled guests mingled and smiled for the cameras and kissed the air alongside numerous cheeks. A few were excited, many were smug, some were hungry for the connections the night might bring, the richest were merely bored.

Eventually the last limousine pulled up, and the lieutenant governor alighted. He was cheered on board even by the richest and smuggest, his intentions to run for governor known by all, his presence assuring them that this was an event worth attending. Then all but the paying guests, the local VIPs, and the tame press were ushered off the boat. The lines were cast, the whistle sounded, and the boat pulled away.

Chase saw how Kaitlyn observed the crowd, her poise unruffled by all the foppery and superior attitudes, and felt another crushing internal pressure, a pleasure so strong it bordered on pain. He moved in close enough to be surrounded by her fragrance and kissed her neck. "You are the most beautiful girl on board."

She batted long lashes. "La, sir, how you do go on."

"Chase! Great, great, just the man I wanted to see." John Dearfield, president of the company hit by toll fraud, his solid bulk plowing through the throng.

"John, I'd like to introduce Kaitlyn Picard," Chase said, pride turning him formal.

"Hi, nicetameecha, great, come on over here."

Chase allowed the man to drag him away, cast an exasperated glance back toward Kaitlyn, was rewarded with a smile. "What's up, John?"

"Listen, you got something going with that Rochelle guy?"

The world sobered and tightened and focused down to this one moment, etching itself with sudden, chilling clarity. The fresh sea breeze, the musical laughing talking swirling crowd, the setting sun, the lights of Cocoa Beach dimming on the horizon, all held in freeze-frame lucidity. "Not really," Chase said, his voice sounding distant and remote even to himself. "Why do you ask?"

"I was at the chamber dinner last night. Rochelle showed up with the lieutenant governor — am I saying it right, Rochelle?"

"Far as I know."

"Lamar was giving us his usual spiel, you know, how government needs to back off, let gambling and goodness knows what else move in. Supply and demand rule supreme, you know what he's like."

"I know." Heart fluttering like a captured bird.

"Right. So somebody pipes up, hey, there's this guy over at the chamber, Chase

Bennett, he's great for business. Like just this week, he saved us a bundle, let us know about trouble going down on the PBX exchange."

Fear banded his torso and squeezed out a sigh that took every last bit of breath. "Oh my."

"Yeah, so here I was, about ready to stick in my nickel's worth, when this Rochelle guy does his nut. Right there in the middle of the crowd, with your empty chair right beside where he'd been sitting."

Chase turned to the railing, searched the open sea, struggled to settle his frantic brain.

Dearfield moved in closer. "Is that the guy who's behind it all? The one who took us for seventy-five grand?"

"Maybe."

"Maybe nothing. I want the truth, Chase."

"The truth." Chase turned back to him. "The truth is, I don't know, but I think maybe yes, maybe somehow he or his organization is involved."

"Well, if you'd seen his face at the dinner when these jokers started popping off all over the room, how you'd been on to them, let them know their secret code was public knowledge, you'd have the answer you were looking for." Dearfield's eyes scanned the crowd. "Now's as good a time as any to get to the bottom of this."

"No it's not," Chase said, Dearfield's explosive nature forcing him to steady down. "There's more to this than you think."

"Yeah?" Dearfield standing there like a cocked gun. "Like what?"

"I told you, I'm not sure. Not yet. But I feel like finally, finally I'm moving toward getting a handle on it."

Dearfield searched his face, finding something there to pull him back a notch. "You ask me, there always was something fishy about how fast Omega rose over the horizon."

"A couple of days," Chase urged him quietly. "Just give me a couple more days, until I can work through a couple more things and talk to a friend in the attorney general's office. He's scheduled back day after tomorrow."

Dearfield thought it over and edged off another notch. "Yeah, probably wouldn't be the best place to take a swipe at somebody, on the deck of his new boat with half the state's movers and shakers watching."

"Not to mention the muscle," Chase said, motioning with his head toward the pair of minders stationed by the main cabin's entrance.

Dearfield tossed a glance over his shoulder. "You in danger?"

"I don't think they'd try anything here."

The somber tone tightened Dearfield's face. "This is big, isn't it."

Chase nodded slowly. "I think maybe so."

"Well, any time you need to call in the cavalry, you let me know." The gaze was fiercely protective. "You got friends all over this boat, not to mention the town. No need for you to face this alone."

"Thanks, John. I really appreciate that."

"Come to think of it, probably wouldn't hurt to pass the word around, let people know to keep an eye on you and the lady." He turned away. "I'm making it a point to be within hailing distance all night."

Chase walked back over to where Kaitlyn stood waiting, her smile fading as she caught sight of his face. "What's wrong?"

Chase turned his back to the crowd, said softly, "They know."

She blanched, fought for calm. "What? Who?"

"Lamar and Rochelle. Everything."

"I don't —"

"Ah, Mr. Bennett, how nice to see you again." Sylvan Rochelle's faint Continental accent was as finely turned out as his clothes, a sparkling accessory to match his smile and his looks and his carefully disheveled hair. He stepped over, bowed to Kaitlyn. "Miss Picard. So glad you could join us. I do hope you are enjoying yourselves."

As soon as Chase turned, he knew. There was a prescient sense of an answer there waiting for him. Chase looked into Rochelle's eyes and instantly knew what he was going to do.

"I don't have such a head for heights as you do," Chase replied. "This gathering is a little rich for my blood."

"Perhaps so." The polish masking all but the faintest glint of what lay beneath the surface. "Which brings us, of course, to the matter of the land. It is yours now, I take it, to do with as you wish."

Chase shook his head, showing a reserve equal to Rochelle's at the man's casual dismissal of Miss Marie Hale. "No, she left explicit instructions as to what I should do both with the land and the money from the sale."

"And what is that, may I ask?"

Chase met the flat gaze, felt he was watching a coiled snake. "It's going into a trust to help several of her favorite causes."

"How remarkable." A nod toward someone who patted his arm, a measured sip from his drink, all collected ease. "The same trust who no doubt would take up her instructions were you to leave off."

Chase played at confusion. "I guess so. But I promised to finish this for her."

"Of course you did." Another polished smile. "Oh, by the way. I am having a small gathering of movers and shakers tomorrow at my Miami headquarters. Just the sort of people you wanted to meet. Perhaps you should join us."

"Hey, what an honor." Striving for disappointment. Finding the opening he had been seeking, saying what he had planned. "Unfortunately I can't. A buddy and I have been planning this trip for quite a while now. We're going out into the wilds of central Florida, cruising by airboat."

Again the faint glimmer showed through. "How fascinating. Where might your trip be taking place?"

"We're going down the Withlacoochee River from Rutland, that's about eighty miles northwest of here. Some of the loneliest, most isolated landscape in all America." Keeping it as casual as he could muster. Scanning the crowd, as though not really caring what he said. Then looking back toward Rochelle, playing at politeness. "Maybe you've heard of him, Ferris Campbell of

Campbell Boats? Biggest airboat company in Florida."

"I fear I have never even seen an airboat except on television."

"Ought to try it sometime," Chase suggested politely. "Running an airboat is one of Florida's forgotten thrills."

"Perhaps I should at that," Rochelle replied. "Well, nice chatting with you, Mr. Bennett. Miss Picard. Enjoy your evening."

When he had turned away, Kaitlyn asked, "What was that all about?"

"Just baiting a hook," Chase replied, watching him move on through the crowd. "Come on, let's mingle."

They entered the wood-lined main saloon, stood behind the high-roller table, watched the players. Chase found himself trying to see them as Grey Spenser would, looking beyond the glamour, trying to observe the whole scene.

Most of the seats were occupied by big men whose dress shirts strained at massive bellies and whose remaining hair was carefully groomed. The three women were made up like old lacquered dolls. Gold watches and rings glittered on the tanned arms. All of them shared the same single-minded stare.

"Watermelon, watermelon," droned the

dealer. "Twenty-dollar ante."

Two blue chips were casually tossed by each player. Each received two cards, face down. Then another two chips, another card face up, the first open bet, forty minimum, another card, another bet, another card, eighty minimum last bet, an even dozen people playing, and suddenly the table sported a four-thousand-dollar pot.

Over and over, two minutes tops per hand.

There were twenty poker tables, stakes starting at five-dollar ante. Twenty blackjack stations. Roulette. Craps. Hallways lined with electronic poker and blackjack, not to mention hundreds and hundreds of banging clattering flashing one-arm bandits.

Bandits. Chase scanned the floor, watched the watchers.

"Watermelon, watermelon," droned the dealer. "Twenty-dollar ante."

A heavy better's game. Five cards to each player, toss back three, five played face up by the dealer, make the best hand of five cards. Bonus chips for full house, four of a kind, all sorts of trick hands. All sorts of energy coursing the room, most of it bad.

Flat-eyed dealers taught to jerk the flow along, pressure the players' adrenaline glands by playing at a faster than comfortable speed. Pushing people to stop thinking.

Not giving them time to pause and realize what was happening. Thrusting them forward into the next bet, the last bill. Give them no time. Lift them further into the crackling, *demanding* high.

Until it was all gone.

Faces were tired, drawn, lined, intent. Smiles were rare and fleeting as winners. Pushed beyond their limits, that was the mask most wore. Pushed by the adrenaline high, a drug as demanding and addictive as anything on earth.

He was not at all sorry when Kaitlyn tugged on his hand and said, "Can we go back outside? I can't breathe in here."

"Absolutely," he agreed, turning away. "Now is as good a time as any to tell you what I hope is going down."

Much of Florida's Atlantic coastline was a paradise gone gray, hemmed in by high-rise condos and flooded with tourists. But for those who knew where to look or were willing to search, the paradise was still there. Still open and beckoning and lovely to behold.

They started early the next morning, Kaitlyn with him partly to return with the truck, partly because she had adamantly refused to let him go off alone. They took the Bee Line to Orlando, then the Florida Turnpike north a ways, finally veering off into a land as far from modern Florida as the last century. Chase rolled down his window, breathed air filtered by a billion trees, reveled in the prospect of returning to a truly primitive place. Stripping away the veneer. Traveling to the perfect land from which to really look and finally see what lay beneath his suppositions and his fears.

"Central Florida is a flat world filled with vacant spaces," Chase told her. "The plains aren't plains at all, but rather lakes and stunted pines and high grass and shallow swamps. People in these parts are either rooted deep in the rich earth or perpetually restless, hating the heat and the insects and the stillness."

She had swiveled in her seat so she could face him full on. "I wish you could hear yourself."

"What's that?"

"Never mind. Tell me more."

"This land is deceptive," he continued. Something in the power of her attention granted newfound grace to his tongue. "At sixty-five miles an hour, with the driver's mind set on the coast, it's easy to see nothing but the beaches and the brand-new cities. People come to think of Florida as all the same, blank and bland, full of tourist glitz from start to finish. Nothing could be further from the truth. Go twenty miles in four different directions from this point, and you'll enter four different worlds."

The map lay spread out between them. When Chase stopped the third time in fifteen minutes to squint at dirt-stained road signs, she pointed at a blue line on the page and asked, "Why don't we take this little road here and cut straight across?"

He had to laugh. "You don't want to get onto a Florida backroad. Not if you plan on going anywhere for a week or so."

"Why not?"

"Florida backroads defy all description. They begin in places that make no sense, run off in directions nobody could explain in a million years, and take you places nobody in their right mind would ever want to go. Florida backroads are the answer to every crooked politician's dream."

Kaitlyn had a great pose for listening. She sort of folded up on herself. A knee would rise, the arms cross and settle, the chin drop, the mouth pucker a little as though waiting for a punchline she already knew she was going to love. He sat watching her, grinning at the simple pleasure of just being near. She picked up her head and asked, "What's so funny?"

"You. Nothing."

"You don't seem very worried about what might be up ahead."

"It either happens or it doesn't," he replied. "For the moment I'm just happy to be here with you."

She shared a look, waited until he had turned back and started off, said, "Florida backroads."

"Right. A lot of our blacktops were laid just because some federal works program offered a county a whole hatload of money for a development project. The problem was, no Washington bureaucrat had ever bothered to come down for a visit. If they had, they would have seen straight off that the county's land was so swampy that the only way it could support a two-story factory was to build it on a boat. So the county commissioners would say, we sure could use us a road. And Washington would say, great, send us the bill. I've been down roads not more than twenty miles from the coast that're so barren folks still stop and wave at every passing car. A lot of these roads stop at the next county's border. They also cost a fortune to build, because they first had to build a dike for it to stand on."

Chase spotted another road sign, squinted and read as they passed, then slowed down and declared, "We're lost."

Kaitlyn pointed up ahead. "There's somebody walking."

"Great." Chase was already rolling to a halt before he saw who it was standing beside the road. "Uh-oh."

"What's the matter?"

"This ought to make your day," Chase said to Kaitlyn, then stuck his head out the window and said to the old man, "Afternoon, sir."

"Howdy." The man was tall as a reed and dressed in overalls made for someone twice his size. He bent over and revealed eyes as washed out as his hair, peering with no curiosity whatsoever from a face burned the color of the clay under his feet. "Help you folks?"

"We seem to be lost," Chase said, giving it his best northern slant. "Could you possibly help us with directions?"

"Mebbe. Where you aim on heading?"

"We were hoping to arrive in Rutland before nightfall." Rutland being no more than fifteen miles away and it being just after eight in the morning.

The man took careful aim and spit a long brown stream at the nearest orange tree.

"Shoot, boy. I wouldn't never dream of starting off for there from here."

Chase made wide eyes. "Oh my goodness gracious me. Well, does it make any difference which road I take?"

The man shrugged bony shoulders. "Not to me, it don't."

Chase grabbed the map, held it upside down, said helplessly, "Then whichever way should I go?"

"Shoot, that ain't no nevermind." The cracker pointed with his chin. "Mosey up thataways and you'll hit big water 'fore too long. Turn around, same thing."

"Well, you have been most kind, sir. Thank you ever so much." Chase gave a cheery little wave and rolled up his window.

When they were underway, Kaitlyn said, "I get the distinct impression there was something going on there I didn't understand."

"That guy wasn't going to give us usable directions," Chase replied. "Not in a kazillion years. I thought maybe I oughtta just play along, brighten up his day."

A half hour later Chase spotted Colin's battered rig thundering toward them. He blew his horn and made a frantic U-turn and was vastly relieved when Colin pulled over. He stopped on the shoulder and waited as Colin trotted over. The gleam in his friend's eye was still there, strong as the other day. "What was that all about?"

"Nothing," Chase replied. "I've just been waiting for you."

"Naw you haven't." He gave Kaitlyn a cheery nod. "Got you lost, didn't he."

"Sure looked that way to me," Kaitlyn agreed.

"We're not but five miles from Campbell's." Colin pushed back his ever-present cap. "I checked all the other camps like you said. Tardent's had a couple of gorillas in sport coats come by first thing this morning, hire a boat, ask for directions over to Ferris's place."

Chase felt his heart rate surge. "Looks like I was right."

"Yeah, done hooked yourself a couple of big ones." Colin straightened and patted the door. "Stay close now."

Kaitlyn grew quiet as they rolled forward. Chase felt her worry, reached over, grasped her hand. "It'll be all right."

"Promise me you'll be careful." All joking aside now.

"I promise." Trying to let her know he meant it. "I have every reason to come back in one piece."

They pulled up in front of a tall hurricane

fence surrounding a vast acreage of half-finished boats and sheds and mobile cranes and noise and activity. Chase motioned for Colin to go on without him and turned to Kaitlyn, found her waiting to be held, comforted, assured. "I'll call you as soon as this is over."

She nodded to his shoulder, said something his shirt muffled. He drew her back, asked, "What?"

She refused to lift her gaze to his. A gentle whisper, "I love you."

Not many tourists ever traveled by airboat. Those who did rarely sat in one more than once, and usually spent the entire ride wondering what would happen to their flat-bottomed craft if it hit a submerged log or stump or an alligator while going seventy miles an hour. That is, if they were able to think at all, what with the wind and the noise and the world whipping by.

The closest most snowbirds ever came to the world of airboats was talking to their painter or garbage collector or plumber. The man who sold them tires or fixed their car could tell them about a totally different Florida, one occupied by slow-talking people whose reverence for nature was masked by beer bellies and tractor hats and pickup trucks and heavy drawls. And guns. Most airboat owners hunted or fished or both, some even with licenses. They came about as close to America's first frontiersmen as possible in modern times, people who passed easily through a world so wild most outsiders would prefer to see it paved over. Airboat owners were generally people who shared their land in communal ownership, tough enough and wily enough to survive beyond the reach of air conditioning and city lights.

It was a world of forgotten names: Chassahowitzka Refuge, Tiger Tail Island, Mosquito Cove, Coffin Point, Hellgate, Shivers Bay, Pirates Cove, Forgotten Branch. All of it was enclosed by green — water, walls, and ceiling — for as often as not there was nothing overhead save trees. To either side of the narrow slipways undergrowth choked the earth, creating impenetrable barriers. The airboat was the only way to traverse such swampland, a modern adaptation to a primitive world. So long as the passengers could handle the noise and the speed and the barely harnessed power.

Chase walked across the yard, his heart still flying from the send-off. The area was littered with the skeletal hulks of what at first glance looked like half-finished modern art. Great flat surfaces sprouting nets of piping and cables and blades.

And motors. Colossal motors in various stages of assembly. Chase walked over to a completed airboat, saw how the motor assembly was bolted onto a steel frame which ran the boat's entire twenty-five-foot length. The boat itself was a rectangular fiberglass shell, flat-bottomed save for long ribs where the steel frame was attached. It looked too fragile to hold the huge motor even when it wasn't running.

And the motor certainly did look ready to run. A gleaming four-foot behemoth attached to two stubby exhaust pipes, a mammoth plastic fuel tank, and a five-bladed carbon-fiber propeller. The engine was enclosed within a ten-foot-high steel cage, open ended at the back, with broad steel fins fitted behind the prop for steering. In front of the cage were two bucket seats fitted to staggered towers. The higher seat rose a good five feet off the boat and had a gas pedal and steering column connected to the fins. The lower seat was wide enough to fit two if they didn't mind being a little snug. Chase took another look at the burnished motor and decided he would probably be a little too busy to worry about how close Colin sat.

"Colin, that you, boy?"

Chase turned at the voice, saw a man coming toward them in great bounding strides. The arms protruding from the workshirt were as dark as his face, taut and knotted and deeply veined. A graying Abe Lincoln beard covered a jaw that jutted out and met the world long before the rest of him ever arrived. He extended a work-hardened hand which remained slightly curled, as though fitted permanently for the tools he normally held. "Man, if you ain't a sight for sore eyes."

"How you been keeping, Ferris?"

"Can't complain. When I do, the missus is after me with a stick." Bright eyes the color of old smoke turned Chase's way. "Who we got here?"

"This is the friend I was telling you about. Chase Bennett."

"Colin has been talking about you for as long as I can remember, Mr. Campbell," Chase said.

"Friends call me Ferris." The hand extended his way. "Hear you got yourself in a whole passel of trouble."

"Looks that way," Chase said, trying to keep the wince from his face and voice as his hand was ground in a leather-covered vise.

"Well, you were right to send 'em down here. Them boys're about ready to bite themselves off more'n they can chew." He inspected Chase. "You know anything about airboats?"

"Enough to hang on," Chase replied.

"That there's lesson one. Lesson two is keep your mouth closed when we're pushing it, 'less you want to be feasting on flies."

Colin said, "Couple city fellers rented themselves a boat over at Tardent's. Refused his offer of a guide."

"You'll do that?" Chase demanded. "Rent strangers a boat like this without knowing if they can handle it?"

"Son, if I was to worry about all the blame fool things folks did, why, I'd long since gone blind and crazy both." He winked at Colin. "If they're long in the wallet, ain't none of my business if they're short in the head."

Chase looked back at the boat behind them. "Something like that could be dangerous."

"Shoot. All they got to do is take their foot off the pedal, that baby'll stop on a dime." His eyes glimmered with backwoods humor. "Ain't the boats that're dangerous, son. Just the loons that drive 'em."

"Speaking of danger," Colin broke in, "these guys are probably armed and loaded for heavy game."

"Then I'd say they came to the right place." He spun about on his work boots and stomped back toward the office. "We'll gas my boat and go see if these city boys mean business."

Chase watched him disappear into the cavernous hold. "He doesn't sound very worried."

"Ferris has his own way of handling the world," Colin said, not the least concerned. "Especially the world out here."

The rawboned man emerged from the warehouse carrying two great sacks. "Y'all aiming on hanging around here all day jawing? Thought we had us some snakes to skin."

The wind did not blow at him. It battered his body as hard as the noise pounded his ears. The boat skimmed over a broad ribbon of sparkling blue, scarcely seeming to hold to earth, the motor's roar matched by the rotors' blatant scream. The wind was a solid wall in his face. Great rooster tails of white water shot up behind them. Green walls blurred to solid flying masses on either side.

They passed under a bridge, and Ferris did a quick slow-down-spin-around, drawing them up behind one of the concrete supports. He stared off behind and declared in the sudden relative quiet, "Them boys are too cautious by a country mile."

"Maybe they're still working on how to drive it," Chase ventured.

"Ain't nothing to it. You step on the gas, the boat goes forward. Push on the tiller and the thing turns. Even a snake in a city suit oughtta be able to figure that out." He watched the other boat move across the water, a dark speck in the glistening distance. "Naw, I'll tell you what it is. Them boys, they're waiting and watching. Seeing how things are, figuring out the best place to take us out."

"I can't believe how calm you are about all this," Chase said.

"This whole doggone world is filled with skunks and snakes," Ferris replied calmly. "Man's gotta deal with them one way or the other." He looked at Colin. "You still remember how to drive one of these things?"

"Should do. Why, you got an idea?"

"Working on one." He leaned down to the side of the boat, dug up one of the sacks he had brought, opened the neck. He pulled out a few empty beer cans, tossed them high into the air, let off a rebel yell.

When the cry had echoed its way up and down the bayou, Chase asked, "Mind telling me what's going on?"

"Let them boys think we're having ourselves a good old time." He handed a pair of
cans to Chase. "See how high you can toss
them suckers. Colin, why don't you climb
on up here, give us a show."

"It's been a coupla years. I'll probably be
a little rusty."

"More's the better." He stepped down
from the high seat and stood by the transom,
tossed another can, gave another yell, said,
"Just mosey on toward that float down
yonder."

Chase said, "Float?"

"What we call that patch of green, looks
like an island there in the middle of the
river. Sometimes they're anchored, mostly
not. Water's so rich round these parts the
roots just suck up what they need. All sorts
of fish live there, and bigger fish living off
them. And other things."

Chase sat up straight. "Like what kinds of
other things?"

"Steady now," Ferris said. "Take us in
gentle like." When they were coasting over the
top of the green, he said, "Okay, hold it right
there for a minute." He craned, searched,
said, "See over there, them reeds rustling?"

Chase raised his feet off the deck. "That's
the wind."

"Slow and easy now," Ferris crooned, his

face concentrating hard on the thick growth sliding by to either side of the boat. "How're our buddies doing?"

Chase looked back. "Just through the bridge. Taking their time. Inspecting the cans we tossed out."

"Toss out a couple more, why don't you? Try to throw 'em out beyond the float. Don't want to disturb what's down there watching us."

Chase dug out a pair, threw them in high soaring arches, asked, "What is watching us?"

Ferris tensed, hissed quietly, "Cut the motor."

Colin did as he was ordered. The sudden silence was aching.

Chase watched in disbelief as the raw-boned man started sifting through the reed bed with one hand, swirling the water with his fingers. He gave a series of half-squeaking, half-grunting noises from somewhere far back in his throat. Waited. Made the noises a second time. Chase thought he heard the reed bed call back the same way, decided he was hallucinating.

Then suddenly Ferris lurched and grabbed, and the water around them exploded.

And suddenly their cries weren't fake anymore.

"Gotcha!" Arms raised high, lifting a greenish-brown writhing five-foot monster clear of the water. "Ain't she a beaut!"

It was only then that Chase realized Ferris was holding a live alligator out toward him. He started to do a backward flip off the other side of the boat, realized what might still be down there waiting for him, made do by scrambling back as far as he could, yelled, "Get that thing away from me!"

"Fire this sucker up, Colin!" Ferris slammed the gator down on the bow, locking his elbows and shoulders taut, holding the struggling animal fast. "We got us a package to deliver!"

Colin gunned the motor, wheeled the boat around, gave off a blood-curdling yell of his own, and roared back downriver.

Chase found himself too caught up in the manic scene to worry about what they were doing. He traded grins with Colin, reached into the sack, sent another couple of cans soaring overhead. Turned back to the bow, saw the gator was big enough to be lying all the way across the transom with its tail dragging in the water. Opening and closing its soft, cottony-white mouth, revealing rows of gleaming teeth. Ferris stood wild-eyed and grinning, muscles bulging from the effort of holding the gator, one hand just behind the jaw, the other halfway down the tail.

Ferris lifted his head and shouted back to Colin, "Aim for the other fellers, why don't you?"

Colin's driving took their boat all over the place. A gentle tap on the tiller and the boat skewed like a crazy thing, spinning wind and a fan-tail of water out in great curving arches. "What do you think I'm trying to do?"

"Close in now," Ferris called. "That's it."

Chase realized what was happening and shouted a laugh of his own.

Then their boat was speeding up toward the other, so close he could see the startled faces, the bulky muscles beneath brightly colored knit shirts, the sports coats settled on one seat, the indecision as to what to do.

The guns.

He had opened his mouth to call a warning when Ferris gave a loud cry of his own, lifted and hefted and tossed. Suddenly the gator was up and writhing through the air, tail and head arched and spinning, over and down and into the other boat.

Then they were past. Shouting and screaming great heaves of laughter, pounding fists and feet on the transom, deck, seats, whatever was closest. Trying to watch the other boat, having trouble what with their eyes all smeared and tightened down, not to mention Colin driving their own boat all over the river. Still Chase could see the two men do a fairly good imitation of Fred Astaire on a very bad day. Hands waving, mouths working, feet trying hard not to touch anywhere, a gun firing, the gator slipping over the side and into oblivion. Then guns going off in fury, shooting the water, the air, trying to get a bead on their boat, Colin making it difficult with his manic driving, finally slipping down a side creek and out of sight.

Ferris wiped his eyes and looked at Chase. "Think maybe we got their attention?"

Colin cut the motor. "They're gonna be after us like a hive of angry bees."

"Do you think they'll make it out?"

They were back in the slip leading toward the Campbell boatyard, traversing a water-lined tunnel after hours of speeding down swampy lanes scarcely as wide as the boat. Stopping and listening, shouting festive cries, hearing the angry yells and other boat's replying roar. Leading them farther and farther back into a land of endless, twisting swamp with no borders, no signs, no currents, no wind.

No way out for a pair of city snakes without a guide.

Ferris shrugged his unconcern, pulled the

boat in close to his dock, cut the motor. "Might. Might not. Rangers go through them parts every now and then. Maybe the law'll cut off their motor at the right moment, hear somebody shouting for help. Same for fishermen. Not the gator poachers, though. They hear somebody, they just slide on out of town."

"And if nobody comes by?"

"Don't you go getting queasy on me, now. They wasn't waving no popguns in our faces." Campbell turned a strong face to search back behind them, stretching the lizard skin of his neck out taut, squinting into the sun. "They might find their way on out to a settled patch. Then again, they might not. We had us a plane went down back there a while back. Took us two years to find the wreck."

16

After a sumptuous breakfast at the restaurant where Kaitlyn was working early shift, Chase glided through Cocoa traffic, tapping the wheel in time to the radio. The morning was bright and full of the salty chill brought by a fresh sea breeze. His head and his heart were filled with the glory of knowing Kaitlyn's special smile was meant for him, only him.

Matthew had called once and left an impatient message on his machine, to the effect that Chase was supposed to just sit tight until Matthew returned the next day. He didn't leave a number. Chase had stared at the machine, knowing the flow of events was building up, pressing forward, too strong now to wait for anyone.

Chase took the road leading to Grey Spenser's house. He found his old friend surveying a pair of bulldozers that appeared to be turning his front garden into a construction site.

Chase climbed from the truck. "What are you doing?"

Grey surveyed what was left of his yard.

"This is something, ain't it?"

"Looks like you're excavating a new canal."

Grey watched the machine plowing a ten-foot furrow parallel to the drive. "Shame you didn't get here an hour ago, you could have stood and watched him dig up all the azaleas."

"But why?"

"Heard they're gonna try and do me in." Rage mottled the strong face. "Look at this. Got me walling myself into a mink-lined cage."

Not really needing to ask, doing so anyway. "Who is they?"

Grey shrugged. "I have a buddy on the local force, he and his wife help out battling this gambling disease. Called to say he'd heard it passed around places that I'd been marked for extermination."

A second machine started gouging great holes from the earth. A pile of fifteen-foot steel girders rested beside four bales of hurricane fencing. "Can't the police do something?"

"Not much. No crime's been committed yet. They've been alerted. But they don't have enough manpower to do more than pass by every now and then." Abruptly he wheeled about, stalked off toward the house. "Let's go inside."

Chase followed him up the drive past two men stringing cable and another pair hammering three-foot steel rods into the earth at regular intervals. Grey waved in their general direction, said, "Motion detectors."

The house was quieter only by degree. Grey pointed to the pounding overhead. "I've hired me live-in security. They're building a second apartment, separate kitchen, entrance, the works."

"Somebody really got to you," Chase observed.

"Come on down here. The den's about the only place you can hear yourself think around here."

The den was Grey's at-home office, located at the far end of the house and connected by a glassed-in passage. With the door closed behind them there was a semblance of peace. "Sit yourself down. You like anything?"

"I'm fine, thanks."

"Wish I could say the same." The spacious room was fitted with tall French doors looking out over the pines and the palms and the flowers. And the bulldozers. "Part of me knew something like this could happen. The other part sort of felt like if I didn't worry about it, maybe it wouldn't come."

"What are you going to do?"

359

"Stand and fight." The older man's features were haggard but determined. "They're after me, Chase. They want my soul. And if I won't be their slave, they want to scare me so bad I'll run. Well, I'm sure scared. But I'm sure not running. This is still my country. Last time I looked, anyway."

Chase reached into his pocket, pulled out and unfolded the sheaf of computer printouts. He leaned forward and set them on Grey's desk. "Little something to help you out."

"What's this?"

"What you told me to find us," Chase replied. "Ammunition."

Chase pulled into a downtown Miami lot and paid the surly attendant an outrageous sum for the privilege of keeping radio, doors, seats, and all four wheels on his truck. He then walked two blocks over to a tall brick-and-glass structure. Chase stopped outside the main doors, fitted his tie up snug, and ran his hand through his hair before pushing through the tall glass doors and entering the air-conditioned bedlam of a major news operation.

Three operators fielded calls over a telephone network with maybe a hundred blinking lights. Two news machines chattered in corners. A half-dozen couriers danced in place, waving packets stamped urgent and talking into hand-held mikes and vying for the attention of somebody, anybody who would sign for the thing and let them get back out because there's another one due now on the other side of town, okay? People huddled in tight little clusters, struggling to hold their talk down to whispers. People hurrying for the elevators, running for the door, scrambling after somebody else, all moving faster than speeding bullets. Life on a deadline.

He walked over to the bank of pay phones and acted on the hunch he had had during the trip down.

"Poyner's."

"Samantha, this is Chase. Is Colin around?"

"Just got in from a look-see around your house. Where are you?"

Chase turned as far around as the phone's short cord allowed, surveyed the manic scene. "About as deep into Miami as I ever want to get."

"Poor you. Hang on, here he is."

Chase listened to murmured voices, then heard Colin say, "You lost your mind?"

"I will if I stay down here long." He turned back around and hunched his shoulders for a semblance of privacy. "Listen, you know Grey Spenser?"

"Sure, guy at church who tried to straighten me out way back when." A voice in the background, then, "Sam says, shame it didn't take."

Chase gave a skeleton outline of what Grey had told him. "Think maybe you could hang around the next few days, just see him safe until everything's in place?"

"All the electronics in the world won't stop a pro." Colin was all seriousness now. Focused down so tight Chase could catch the change even standing there in the center of the maelstrom.

"Maybe you could help him make sure the live-in security are up to snuff," Chase suggested. "Right now, I'd just breathe a little easier knowing he's not sitting up in that big house all by his lonesome."

"On my way, Slim. You take care, you hear? Sam says to watch out for those big-city women."

"I've had enough of those to last a life-time," Chase assured him. "And thanks."

The operator-receptionist station was still five deep in urgently impatient people, so Chase approached the only stationary person in the lobby, a uniformed security guard surveying the manic scene with bored calm. "Could you please save me a major battle and tell me where I'd find the radio department?"

Heavy-lidded eyes flicked his way and an indifferent voice asked, "You got an appointment?"

"With Toby Larrson."

The eyes went back to their perpetual scan. "Elevator to the seventh floor. Don't tell nobody I sent you."

"Time you went public with all this," was how Grey had put it that morning.

"You mean the press?" Chase shook his head. "That's your bailiwick, not mine."

"Not this time. This is your story. Besides, with the legislative vote on gambling only a week off, I've now got a thousand other things to do." He waved toward the print-outs. "Mind if I keep these?"

"They're your copies." Chase squirmed in his seat. "I've never felt comfortable around the press, Grey."

"Who does?" Grey reached for the phone. "I've got a friend over at UPI in Miami. They maintain a big operation there, handle all their Spanish-language broadcasts. Guy I know's named Toby Larrson. Happens to be extremely honest and a very good reporter. Let me see if he'll talk to you."

"Miami," Chase groaned. "You're not going to give me any choice about this, are you?"

"Absolutely," Grey replied, punching in the number. "You want to make it for this afternoon or this evening?"

"What'd you say your name was?"

"Bennett. For the third time."

"Bennett. Yeah, Bennett." Scribbling on a scrap of teletype which was instantly discarded and forgotten. "Okay, Bennett, what you got for me today?"

"Will I have to repeat all that three times too?"

"Depends. When I was eighteen, I worked in a radio station that got hit by lightning. Since then I only hear what I want to." A glance at his watch. "Grey said you had something important."

"Maybe."

Another glance. "Okay, so I've got about seven minutes until I make the next feed, and then after that I've only got another zillion things to do. So I guess it's talk or walk. What's your choice?"

The radio division of United Press International was a chaotic scramble of tape, papers, voices, and clattering teletypes. Spanish and English announcers worked microphones in neighboring cubicles. Soundproofing deadened all but a faint murmur of professionally tuned voices.

Toby Larrson had that same kind of voice, resonant and practiced and somehow artificial when not coming over the airwaves. Which was only partly the reason for Chase's reluctance. The other part was the guy himself. Nothing about his appearance bore any resemblance whatsoever to his voice. The shirt had probably once been white, the pants brown or black or dark blue, hard to tell. The shirt pocket so crammed with wires and pens and notes and portable tape machine that the seams were giving. Hair a rat's nest. Glasses skewed to port. Eyes spinning around the room like pinballs.

"Talk." Chase sighed. "I think I've got evidence that the lieutenant governor is tied to both telecommunications fraud and drug money. And the drug money is tied to casino gambling."

A stillness settled over the form like that of a bird dog pointing out a breaking quarry. "You don't say?"

"Tied in a big way," Chase said.

"And just who are you, Bennett? I mean, excuse me for asking, but information like this isn't handed out on street corners, right?"

Chase told him.

A grudging nod. "Somebody who maybe doesn't travel in the highest circles, but who stays plugged in to what's going on. Do I have that right?"

"Pretty much."

Another grab brought up a longer sheet of teletype. He folded it into a bulky ribbon and set it on his knee. "So let's have some details."

Chase gave him those too.

There was a long silence when Chase had finished. Larrson checked his watch, bolted from his chair, went over and banged open a cubicle door. "Come take this feed for me, will you?"

"Sure." An overweight woman in mismatched skirt and top came out and gave Chase a quick once-over. "Who's the cutie?"

"Nobody, and you didn't see him. The feed's supposed to have gone out ninety seconds ago."

"So I'm running, I'm running." She gave Chase a little two-finger wave. "Nice not meeting you, nobody. Come again sometime."

"In here," Larrson said, motioning Chase into the cubicle. Inside Chase found a pair of swivel chairs fronting microphones and a wall of taping and transmitting equipment.

Larrson plopped into one chair and pulled off his glasses, one lanky finger wrapping around the frame between the lenses and sliding them down his nose. "Okay, so what we got here is maybe a dozen stories, three big ones for starters. First there's the casino legislation being backed by the drug nasties, and then there's the phone fraud tied in with the drugs, and the lieutenant governor's got his hand in the whole thing."

"Right up to his shoulder," Chase agreed.

"Evidence," Larrson replied. "An important word in this business. I'm a real touchy-feely guy when it comes to evidence. Need to hold it in my hand, squeeze it, fondle it, make sure it's really, really real."

"Especially with something this big. I understand." Chase spread his hands. "But that's all I've got."

Larrson sighed and rubbed the red spot where his glasses had rested. "Everybody thinks a reporter's just sitting around waiting for the big scoop. Well, it's true and not true, like too much in this world. Digging up an exclusive is what makes the daily treadmill worth running. But you're asking me to put my professional life on the line here. Something this big, I'm going to have to run right up the chain of command, stick it on the flagpole for everybody to shoot at. Me included. I don't want to go down in history as the guy who got the big one wrong, you understand what I'm saying?"

"I'm not lying," Chase said quietly.

"There are a lot of pathological liars out there. But I have to admit you don't strike me as one. That's not enough, though, not for something like this. I have to be dead-solid certain. I'm going to need corroborating evidence. A lot of it."

"But you are going to check this out?"

"Sure. Between you and me and this console, Lamar Laroque would give a toxic waste dump a bad name. I'd love to see him pulled off his little pedestal."

"So would I."

"Then you're gonna have to help me. I need a second source. I need to make sure we can take all this public and stay out of jail. And," he said, feeding a tape through the spools and spindles, "I need you to walk me through this one more time."

"The whole thing?"

"Bells and whistles included. From the top. Okay, ready? And we're rolling."

Rico loved the games. It was what he did best, playing the tough guy, scaring the patsies into next week. People almost always backed down when he started his routine.

Just one look in his eyes, they'd see that here was a guy living out on the edge. The only time they'd ever seen it before was in the movies, sitting there with the popcorn in their lap, now here it was live. If that wasn't enough, if they tried to show a little backbone, all it usually took was a couple of slaps and a hint of what might happen if he stopped by in the middle of the night, gave the little family a chance to share the fun.

But every once in a while he'd be called in on the real thing. It came with the territory. He saw it as part of keeping the routine juiced, not to mention being a truly mean thrill all its own. Too powerful to take on all the time, though. He knew some that did that, gave it the thought he did brushing his teeth. But not Rico. He loved the games too much to let the thrill go numb. Still, when it came his way, he was ready.

Being his own man meant Rico could dress the part. Head shaved up three inches above the ears, then long brown hair greased back into a ponytail. Moustache. Three-day growth. Three earrings. Brass wristbands like some comic-book sword fighter. Leather vest, no shirt, leather laces strung through silver catches, shoulders of a serious body builder. Dark eyes, blank stare. A girl once told him it was hard to tell whether he was building up to a rage or just climbing down from one. He liked that enough to stand in front of a mirror, practice the heavy-lidded effect, showing them just a trace of what was there below the surface, barely under control.

He walked over the front lawn, no need for caution, the place looking like a war zone, with great gashes torn through turf as green as a golf course. All the machinery quiet, all the workers through for the day. He stepped up to a set of windows so big he could step inside without bending, glanced through, there in front of him was the guy himself.

Rico slipped out his gun, pushed on the window, perfect, unlatched like the guy was there just waiting for him. He tapped on the glass with the muzzle, getting the guy's attention, letting him see it coming, yeah, watching the surprise register and turn into alarm, then gliding in gun first, listening carefully, tasting the air, knowing without needing to explain how this guy lived here all alone.

Only something wasn't the way he wanted. Rico took another step toward the desk, let the guy stare down into the barrel, the biggest, blackest hole he would ever see. And the last one.

But still there was no fear.

"You know who sent me, don't you? They told me to make sure that was clear."

"I know," the old man said quietly. "I've spent the better part of my life struggling against who you're working for."

Rico looked the old man over, knew a moment's doubt. This guy was calmer than any hit he'd ever come up against. Not defeated. Peaceful, yeah, that was it. Crazy. Old fool was trying to play with his head.

"What're you talking about, old man? You never seen me before. You don't have any idea what you've got yourself mixed up in."

"That's where you're wrong." Still quiet, still calm, now not even looking his way. "I've known about you and your kind all my life."

His kind. Rico felt his hackles rise. Watched the old guy staring out the window, up at the sky, not even there.

"Might as well stop looking, old man. There's no cavalry comin' and there's no way out."

"Wrong again." Softer now.

"What, you think I'm just here to give you a little scare?"

"No, I know what you're here for."

"Man said to tell you this comes compliments of Rochelle and Omega. A little gift."

He raised the gun, waiting still, wishing he could figure where the old guy's head was at.

"On the outside, maybe you work for them." Still that voice, still that distance, still those strange eyes, seeing what wasn't there. "On the inside you've sold out to the one whose name I won't say."

Dropping the gun an inch. "I'm my own boss, old man. That's all —"

Down the hallway the front door creaked, and a solid man came bouncing through. "Door was open, Grey. Chase told me to come —" He saw the gun swiveled his way, stopped in midstride.

"Bad timing, man." Cool. Stay cool. All the while shifting back and forth between the old man and this newcomer, cursing himself for getting off guard, letting the old guy spook him. "Another minute and you could have spared yourself a load of grief."

This second guy wasn't acting right either. Looked at the gun like he knew everything about it, standing there all relaxed and easy. "I could come back."

"Let him go."

Hearing the old man speak with such strength almost spun him around, but he checked himself in time, saw the second guy slip slow and easy into a spring, caught him before he could get started, raised his gun, shook his head. "Don't try it, man. Now shut the door, easy now, just reach over and —"

Then the day was split asunder. Bells clanging. Sirens whooping. All the lights in the house blinking on and off. A voice shouting through some unseen megaphone, *"Intruder! Intruder! Security alert!"*

And before he had recovered, the second guy tightened and leapt and was out the door and gone.

Rico raced down the hall, searched the front lawn. Nothing. Spun about, saw the old man making for the open window. Shot too fast and from too far away, the old man taking a hit but still making it through the window and out into the cover of bushes. Rico shouted a curse, raced back, no sign of the old man. He spotted the alarm button on the side table beside the telephone, blinking now. He raised the gun again and blasted it, shot the phone, the desk, the windows and the rug, turned and raced back and out the open door.

And suddenly a wild animal erupted from the shrubs. Looking like the second guy, but only a little, this one wearing a mask with blazing eyes and teeth bared like fangs. Rico managed one quick unaimed shot, knowing he had hit, but not even slowing this guy down. Then slamming into something so sudden and so solid his feet kept going a step or two, not even realizing that his body had already stopped and his brain had totally shut down.

Chase's second time around was interrupted by a call to the state editor, who came in and perched on the side of a desk and listened deadpan as Chase answered question after question. Finally Larrson was satisfied. He turned to his editor, asked, "You got anything else?"

The man tucked hands under his armpits, shook his head once, said, "Get corroboration and we'll take it to upstairs."

Larrson showed his first sign of nerves. "How far upstairs?"

"Something like this," the editor shrugged, "all the way to Washington."

Chase demanded, "You believe me, then?"

"Lamar Laroque and Sylvan Rochelle are two worms of the same species. Wouldn't surprise me to hear they're working the same bit of fertilizer," the editor replied. "Got copies of those lists for us?"

"Right here."

He passed them on to Larrson. "Call Danielle in Tallahassee. Have her drop everything, start checking out these names." The editor stuck out his hand toward Chase.

"The greatest thrill in journalism is going after big game. This is as big as I've come across in quite a while. Thanks for bringing it to us." To Larrson, "Get on this. Full time."

Chase stepped from the truck, walked toward the house, knew it was Kaitlyn's mother even before he climbed the front stairs.

Her mouth was screwed down tight. Little cross lines strung out from her lips like primitive etchings. Eyes narrowed by semipermanent discontent scanned him quickly. "Are you the young man Kaitlyn has been going on about?"

"My name is Chase Bennett," he replied. Struggling not to accept the open invitation and dislike her instantly.

"I don't know where she's gotten to. She ought to be out here greeting you herself, of course. But there you go."

"She had no idea when I would be getting back from Miami," Chase replied calmly. "And wherever she is, I'm sure she's doing something that couldn't wait."

She inspected him carefully. Chase met her gaze head-on, let her see that here stood someone who would give her politeness, but never allow that to stop him from defending his lady.

His lady.

The eyes narrowed. "And what is it you do, Mr. . . ."

"Bennett. I work for the chamber of commerce."

"Oh yes. I believe I recall Kaitlyn mentioning something like that. It sounds most interesting." Draining the words with a totally flat tone.

"It is."

"Come in, won't you, please." Leading him into a house which now was as chilled as a meat locker. "I must apologize for not having been here to meet you earlier. I have been up at our home in Chicago. The Florida climate does not agree with me. To be perfectly frank, I don't see how my husband and daughter can abide it."

"Your father-in-law is certainly fortunate that they can," Chase replied.

Again the uncertain look. Not expecting these replies. "Won't you take a seat?"

"Thank you." Choosing the high-backed chair over the sofa, keeping himself erect. Wary. Pressing on. "And it certainly has been wonderful for me that Kaitlyn has decided to make Florida her home."

"Yes. Well." She finally seemed to have hold of something she could handle. "I suppose Florida is as good as any place to be picking up the pieces."

"Oh, Kaitlyn has done remarkably well," Chase said, refusing to give in to the anger, banking it up carefully, fueling his own quiet intensity. "As a matter of fact, she is the most beautiful woman I have ever met. Inside and out, Mrs. Picard."

Chase leaned slightly forward, as much as manners would allow, determined to drive this one all the way home. "She has not only managed to survive what must have been a horrible and extremely painful experience. She has also grown from it."

In the silence which followed, a quiet voice said, "Hello, Chase."

And there she was. Standing in the corner by the hallway, looking at him with those big, questioning eyes. Only this time there was a calmness there as well, a certainty, as though the watchfulness had finally been rewarded.

Chase walked over to her and slipped his hand into hers, turned back and said, "You must be so incredibly proud of your daughter."

Sabine slipped on a robe of cream Shantung silk and padded into the living room. Sighs she kept trapped inside filled her chest, left her with scarcely room enough to breathe.

She glanced back toward the bedroom. It was not like her to bring a relative stranger to her apartment. She usually preferred to go to theirs so she could leave easily, return to her own place, have more control over her movements. But he had brought her home because she had told him to, then stayed because she had changed her mind at the last minute, deciding that tonight she needed what she called one of her forgetfulness pills.

Sabine had a *lot* of men, all different. Old and young, rich and poor, married and unmarried, different races and professions, she had them all. The rich took her to ritzy places and gave her incredible gifts, the poor she treated to all-night raves. She liked the poor guys best. With them she was more in control. Next in line came the married ones. They understood the need for barriers and borders and rigid restrictions almost as well as she did.

She thrived on competition. She sought it out. It made her heart beat faster. Men, politics, it was the same. That was another part of the thrill with married men.

She loved playing men off against each other. The juggling was one of her greatest thrills. Some weeks she had as many as sixteen dates. It was a challenge, keeping them apart, scheduling it all, watching them get jealous and angry and confused, knowing she was the only one in control.

Sabine released one of the sighs and grabbed for her cigarettes and lighter. The problem was, she needed those forgetfulness pills more and more often these days. Even then, sometimes they didn't work like they should. They left her pacing the floor, chased back and forth by half-formed shadows, the night an endless aching emptiness.

Finally she stabbed out the cigarette, did the only thing which she knew would end the ceaseless silent voices. She picked up the phone.

His voice was blurred with sleep when he answered. "Hello."

Sabine opened her mouth and found the air trapped, locked in place by all the arguments that should have kept her from calling in the first place.

"Hello?" More awake this time.

"Chase." The name unlocking her chest, allowing her to breathe. "This is Sabine."

"What time is it?" Fully alert now.

She glanced at the wall clock's illuminated dial. "Almost three."

She heard the shifting of sheets, the sigh of him rising to his feet. Clearing his throat. "What's going on?"

"I heard them talking about you this afternoon." Struggling to force out the words. "I wasn't supposed to, but I did."

"Laroque and Rochelle." It was not a question.

"They were incredibly angry. Something about you stepping so far out of bounds they have to . . ." She stopped, asked, "Are you alone?"

"Yes."

"Chase, you have to stop whatever it is you're doing."

"It's too late for that."

Her anger flared. "Do you think this is a joke? If Lamar knew I was talking with you I'd be finished."

"Sabine —"

"Do you know what they're calling you?" Her voice shook with the fury of his not understanding. "A menace. You don't get classed as a menace by people like that and stay healthy."

"I believe you."

His tone drained away her anger. As fast as it had appeared, it vanished. It and all the tension she had been battling in making this call. "Aren't you afraid?"

"Of course I am." Still that same quiet tone, accepting what she had to say, believing her, laying it all out. "But it doesn't change what I have to do."

"Have to do? Chase Bennett, this is no time for any of your airy-fairy notions." Trying to retake control, but knowing she was failing. Even though he believed her, knew the threat was real, he held on to his calm. Quiet and steady and rock-solid certain.

"I cannot tell you how much it means," Chase replied, "that you would call me like this, Sabine."

For some reason she felt a sudden burning behind her eyes. "You were always so stupid about those things," she said, her ironclad control melting away. "A strong man with so much potential, made silly by caring so much about so many stupid things. Your boat, your friends, your high-minded principles, your little world. And now it's going to get you killed."

There was a long silence on the other end, then, "Have you ever been back to church since the last time I took you?"

That was just like him, changing the subject to something utterly meaningless. "I don't know. Probably not."

"Maybe you should."

Accepting that she had failed. That he was too weak to see what was right, what needed to be done. Wanting nothing more than to get off the phone. "I have to go, Chase." Hanging up. Feeling the emptiness of having struggled so hard against herself, losing control, angry with Chase and with Laroque and with the whole world.

Especially with herself.

Chase pulled the phone out onto the back porch, dialed the now-familiar number, held his finger ready to disconnect if anybody but Kaitlyn answered.

But the first ring had barely begun before her sleepy voice breathed a hello.

"I know I shouldn't be doing this," he said. "But it's a lonely moonlit night and I needed a friend."

"Then you did exactly right." A comfortable stirring. "What happened?"

"Not much. Just some night ghosts over the telephone wires."

"Tell me about her," she said softly.

"Who?"

"Don't give me that. You know perfectly well who."

"Oh." A sigh more than a word. "Do you want the then or the now?"

"I want whatever you want to tell me."

"Sabine," he said, and had to stop. Saying the name was like expelling a breath he had not even known he was holding. Leaving him lighter, buoyant, ready to rid himself of even more. "Sabine was an only-girl-on-the-planet kind of person. You know the type. Walks slow across the street. Cuts ahead of everybody in a line. Interrupts a waiter at another table to get service. Always speeds."

"Honesty," Kaitlyn said. "Good. This time of night I was hoping for honesty."

"Gives orders down to where the parsley is supposed to be on the plate," Chase went on, cleansing himself on some deep level. "Loves to send stuff back. Drank nothing but Dom Perignon from the year she was born. Her animals are all ornamental, a fish tank that she has serviced once a week and ceramic cats."

"And she's pretty," Kaitlyn offered quietly.

"Yes."

"Was that why you stayed with her?"

"It would be too easy to say that," he replied, knowing this talk was as much for him as for her. Seeing the truth in crystal clarity now, when he was openly confessing it. "I loved her," he started, and had to stop again. Loved her. Past tense. Felt the freedom of knowing it was true.

"You loved her," Kaitlyn repeated, the sadness clear in her voice.

He let it hang there, then finished, "I loved her for what I wanted her to be, thought I could make her into, felt that only I could find in her. I thought if I only loved her enough, she would change. That she would leave behind whatever it was that made her the way she was. That way, when she didn't change, when she did something that hurt me, I felt like it was my fault. Like I just hadn't loved her enough."

Chase paused, searched the star-flecked heavens, felt the soaring gift of truth's healing. "But I forgot that people only change if they want to change. And love is only fulfilled when it's returned."

Chase set down the phone, slipped off the porch, walked lightly across the lawn. Not wanting to disturb the quiet. He squatted down so his back rested against the willow's trunk and looked out over the water, drank in the many-toned night sounds.

He heard a car pass. Wind through a tree. Leaves chiming like silver cymbals. Crickets and nighthawks making sounds so constant he had to concentrate to hear them at all. Waves chuckling as they lapped against the bulkhead. Gentle wafts of outdoor fragrances. Chase held it all close to his heart, filled with a passion for life he did not even know he had. Until now.

A jukebox from somewhere across the river started on a gentle love song. He could tell the singer was a woman. The wind and the pines and the crickets and the water washed out most of the rest. Chase decided the music fit his mood perfectly, just as it was. Mysterious. He was filled with the sudden mystery of a life lived for more than just himself.

A divine presence resounded in Chase's heart like the deep bass pedal of a mighty church organ, more felt than heard. A note of meaning and determination, something to build the melody of his own life around. Chase breathed in the night, realized he had missed Him mightily. Especially in such uncertain times as these.

Then the blast hit him, threw him the ten feet to the bulkhead. Only the piling stopped him from going in the water. The same piling that knocked him cold.

17

It was nothing like the movies.

For one thing, there was no explosion at all. One minute he was squatting there in his minuscule backyard, his back supported by the willow. The next, the air behind him had solidified and came rushing at him like a giant metal fist. A hot fist. Scalding hot.

The next thing he knew, an alien dressed in shades of black was staring down at him, a corrugated trunk sprouting below two bulbous eyes. Then Chase's own eyes cleared and the fireman took off his mask. Chase croaked, "Am I dead?"

The fireman grinned at that. "I was just about ready to ask you the same thing."

He tried to raise his head, found he could not, moved his eyes enough to see that his house was no more. In its place, great hungry flames flung fiery cinders toward the silver stars overhead.

The fireman asked, "Anybody else in there?"

"No." Then Chase realized his body was not communicating as before. It did not really feel like his own. Instead of limbs and a trunk and feet and hands, all he had to tell him he was alive was a too-tight suit of pain.

The fireman shifted, revealing more men and equipment and water spouts and flames, all surrounding where his house should have been. He squatted down beside Chase and asked, "How do you feel?"

"Like —" But before the next word could be formed, Chase found himself deciding the world would be a much better place after he had himself a little nap.

Consciousness came and went in little freeze-frames of unfocused thought and vision and movement. Being lifted onto the stretcher, awake and away again so fast he did not even have time to cry at the pain. Another lifting, this one gentler, onto a bed that smelled of incredible cleanness.

A few overswift images of light strengthening in the window, revealing a strange white room with unknown smells and quietly beeping electronic sounds. An illusion of opening his eyes and speaking with Carlotta, of all people, suddenly materialized there beside him, her face all crumpled up, trying to tell him how sorry she was to have gotten him involved with all this. He replying that she needed to get to Kaitlyn, tell her what had happened, warn her to be careful, they knew about her as well. Returning to sleep like pulling comforting covers up and over his head.

Waking up again. This time knowing it was different. Really awake. Opening his eyes. Finding Samantha seated there beside him. Opening lips dried to gummy numbness, accepting the straw she put in his mouth, drinking, sighing, drinking again. His first word was a hoarsely whispered, "Kaitlyn."

"She's just stepped out to get a bite," Samantha said, brushing the hair from his brow. "She's fine. Carlotta's camped outside her house."

Then it was real. He had seen her. Chase settled back, realized he had not actually spoken the thought out loud.

Samantha graced him with one of her hundred-watt smiles. "Between playing your sidekick and talking to the police," she told him, "my man has had himself a genuine field day."

Before he could ask what that meant, the door opened to admit a bright-eyed Colin, upper arm swathed in bandages. "Leave you for a couple of hours and look what happens."

"Speak for yourself," Chase replied weakly.

Colin looked down at himself. "Thought

he'd emptied the chamber or I would've taken it a little easier."

"Come again?"

"Don't matter none. Just winged me, is all." A swift sobering. "Sorry about the house."

Chase felt the ballooning sorrow, pushed it down. Not yet. He wasn't ready to think about that just then. First see to the business at hand. Chase gave a rigid little nod, careful to hold on to control.

Colin read him correctly, returned to brisk. "Grey's gonna be fine too, by the way." A big grin. "The perpetrator is currently downtown singing like a canary. Lots of names keep popping up. Rochelle. Omega. Even some dude, calls himself Laroque."

Chase found himself still struggling through the fog. "Grey's been hurt?"

"That's why I didn't get back to you last night," Samantha said. "I was caught up with these two fellows in surgery. Not to mention the police."

Chase realized that she was apologizing, could not for the life of him understand why. "Would somebody mind giving this to me in bite-size bits?"

It was then, as they took turns explaining what had happened when Colin had stopped by Grey's the afternoon before, that the idea came to him. Just before there was a knock on the door and John Dearfield stuck his head in the door. "You in to visitors?"

"I am to you," Chase said.

A tousled dark head shoved its way in before Dearfield could shut the door. The reporter from UPI, Toby Larrson, greeted him with, "When I said evidence, this wasn't exactly what I had in mind."

Chase waved him in. "How'd you get here?"

"You're big news, fella."

"Police say there isn't any question," Dearfield agreed. "Definitely a bomb. Almost as though they wanted it to be known."

The door opened once more, this time with a blur of motion spilling through and Kaitlyn rushing over and half sitting, half lying there alongside and on him.

"This place is busier than the Inland Waterway over Labor Day weekend," Colin observed.

The feel of her arms sliding under and around him was worth the sudden pain. Lips pressed to his cheek and ear and hair, both of them totally ignoring the people, until she raised up a fraction and asked, "Are you all right?"

"Fine," he replied, and saw all the smiles. And suddenly knew that he really and truly was. "Just fine."

"The doctors said nothing appeared to be too badly injured," she said, her hands tracing feather-light strokes over his face and head and neck and shoulders. "Other than a few burns where the tree didn't block you. And about a thousand bruises and contusions. They'll want to poke and prod and talk with you, though."

"Not to mention the cops," Colin chimed in. "They're down in the cafeteria, is how we got in here."

"Then we have to hurry," Chase said, trying to hold off the pain as he struggled to pull himself farther up.

Kaitlyn gentled him, pressed one of the buttons, and the bed lifted into a half-sitting position. He smiled his thanks, turned to John Dearfield, asked, "You still want a round with the bad guys?"

"You kidding?"

"Does your company still have that plane?"

"Sitting out there on the Titusville runway," Dearfield replied, eyes glittering with new excitement.

Then to Toby Larrson. "How about going along with John, see if he can dig you up a quote?"

"If anybody's going anywhere," Colin chimed, "you better count me in."

Chase started to object, saw the silent appeal. He turned instead to Samantha, was relieved to see her smiling at her husband. "Is he up for this?"

"If you think you can stop him," she replied, "be my guest."

Chase turned to John. "Think your secretary might call the lieutenant governor's office and say one of the chamber board members has come up with some news, something so big he had to immediately fly up and deliver it in person?"

"Big news," Toby Larrson grinned. "I like it."

"I just thought," Chase said, "it might be nice to sort of let him know in person what we've found." When Dearfield had made his call, Chase outlined what he had in mind, was rewarded with a trio of genuine smiles. "Just promise me you'll call as soon as you find anything out."

"Natch." Colin shepherded his charges toward the door, grinning at all and sundry. Stopped to kiss his wife, give Kaitlyn a wave with his good arm, tell Chase, "Hang in there, Slim."

Chase looked at his old friend and saw genuine happiness where before had only been the burden of unending fatigue. "What's gotten into you?"

Colin held the door with one hand, said to

Chase but with his eyes on Samantha, "I'll tell you how it is. My memory banks've been on overload for too long. Only way to straighten things out was by turning away for a while."

"All my man needed," Samantha agreed, "was something to make him feel like all the pain had been worthwhile, all the lessons there for something good."

Colin nodded gravely, his eyes making sparks across the distance separating him from his wife. "Yessir, Slim. You might've just given me what I been looking for all those days and didn't know it."

"What's that?"

He turned back to the door. "A purpose."

After the cops were done with him, Chase spent the hours dozing and watching the television and just relishing the comfort of lying there with Kaitlyn by his side. Which is how Matthew found them. He walked in and nodded to Kaitlyn and then caught sight of Lamar Laroque giving one of his televised proclamations.

Matthew made a face. "How can you stand to watch that drivel?"

"Just studying the enemy," Chase said. He studied his friend's taut features, carefully groomed black hair, intent dark eyes. "About time you showed up."

"That's what you've been up to?" Matthew slid into the empty seat across from Kaitlyn. "Trying to bring down the lieutenant governor all by your lonesome?"

Chase turned back and heard Lamar say in his rolling drawl, "Our beloved state is falling continually further behind. The miracle of growth is fading. No longer do we lead the nation in anything except crime statistics. No longer are we the preferred destination of vacationers. Why should we be, when our past and our prejudices chain us, lock us into patterns which leave us behind. How do we expect to compete, when all around us neighboring states are racing forward, taking advantage of our mule-headed, foot-dragging, ultraconservative attitudes."

"He's wrong, you know," Chase said. "Florida is doing pretty well, all things considered. We continued to grow every year throughout this latest recession, and things are picking up even more now. We're just not growing as fast as we once did, which to my mind isn't all bad. We're moving at a pace now that we can live with for a long time to come. Before, it was like trying to control a brushfire."

Matthew gave his friend a long, thoughtful glance. "Sooner or later you're going to have to go into politics, old son."

That turned him around. "Me?"

"You know it as well as I do, Slim. It's only a matter of time."

"I hate politics and always have. Just the thought of campaigning gives me the hives."

Matt nodded slow approval. "That's why you'll be good."

Lamar Laroque finished with, "I therefore urge you to cast aside both the chains of our fundamentalist past and the barriers of your political leanings and join together with me in a consensus of growth. A consensus of progress. A consensus of transporting our great state forward into the twenty-first century. I urge you to permit gaming to take its rightful place in Florida's future prosperity. Write your local representative. Petition the governor. Become a part of Florida's tomorrow."

Matt said thoughtfully to the television, "Lamar Laroque is so full of hot air he could lift the Love Boat higher than the Goodyear blimp all by his bowtied self."

Kaitlyn reached over, turned off the television, said to Chase, "Matthew's right, you know."

"Not you too," Chase complained.

"You're exactly what we need in higher office," Kaitlyn persisted. "A person who truly cares about both people and issues."

"Someone who isn't afraid to take the higher moral ground," Matthew agreed.

Chase shifted deeper in the covers. "Can we please change the subject here before I get sicker than I already am?"

Matthew nodded. "How much did you tell the cops?"

"Not a lot. All they were really interested in was the house." He inspected his friend's face, saw nothing to indicate the cat was already out of the bag. "What about you? What do you know?"

"Aw, you know local cops. They've got their hands on something big, but they won't give it to us till we've gone through the paper trail, had the ritual head-to-head with the chief, agreed that we'd still be up in Tallahassee sitting on our hands without their help."

"Good," Chase said. "Real good. I was sort of looking forward to telling you myself."

Kaitlyn bent over and kissed his forehead. "I don't need to hear all this again. I'm going to step out for a while, call home and school and work."

When they were alone, Matthew sank into the nearby chair with a sigh of genuine relief. "Glad you're giving me another chance, old son."

"Don't have much choice."

"There's somebody I want you to talk with." He leaned closer to the bed. "He's with a new arm of the Secret Service. Elite computer and telecommunications crime division."

Chase watched him. "How do I know he's going to be any different than the nerd detail you stuck me with last time?"

"Because I checked it out personally. He's the real thing, I tell you. Lean and mean. Ultraprofessional. They have to train on weapons every two weeks."

"Just what I need," Chase said. "A suit with a gun."

"Come on, Slim, this is serious."

Chase shrugged, felt the movement stretch bandages across his shoulders. "Like I said, what choice do I have?"

"Great." Matthew was up and out of his chair before Chase had even stopped talking, came quickly back leading a second man. "This is, well, let's just say a friend. Mr. Burroughs."

"Pull up a chair, Mr. Burroughs. Are you federal?"

"Yes." The man's manner was as clipped as his jawline. Middle age had neither softened his features nor padded his frame. He wore a dark suit with the severity of one more used to uniform.

"You can trust this guy, Chase. Honest."

"Take a seat, Matt. You make me nervous, hovering like that." Chase took a breath, said what he had planned. "Part of my job is to watch over the competitiveness of local Brevard County industry. It has been brought to my attention that one of our companies had been the victim of massive toll fraud."

"Who?" The word was spoken as a command.

"Dearfield Industries. You can contact John Dearfield, he's CEO and the first to bring this to my attention."

Burroughs brought out a pen and pad and made several brief notes. "Toll fraud is a big problem," he said noncommittally. From his place behind Burroughs, Matthew rolled his eyes. Burroughs asked, "Any other names?"

"He is the only one who I know was actually hit," Chase replied. "Anyway, I started checking around, seeing if I could dig up anything."

The quiet man stilled even further, tensing in his seat like a tightly coiled spring. "And?"

"I was able to put together some names. Don't ask me how because I won't tell you. I can't. We have to have that clear before I'll go any further."

Out of the corner of his eye Chase saw Matthew give an almost imperceptible nod.

"We have," Burroughs said slowly, "the power to place you in a witness protection program."

"And force me to leave behind my job and my life? No thanks. This is a take it or leave it situation, Mr. Burroughs."

There was a moment's silence, then, "Agreed."

"Right," Chase sighed. "I have three lists. Well, four really. The first is a list of 800 numbers and their codes. The second list contains mobile phone chip codes. And the third is for phreakers themselves."

He waited, then, "The fourth?"

Chase resisted a glance at the phone. "I'm working on that one."

"When can we have these lists?"

"There's an extra set in my office. Matthew can pick them up when we're finished." When the phone rang, Chase could not help but jump. Expecting it, hoping it would come, but still unable to mask the excitement. "Hello?"

Colin's joy crackled over the wires. "Man oh man, did you ever miss something."

"Tell me." Suddenly out of breath. Turning from the pair of probing gazes. Not wanting to share this with anyone just yet.

"Laroque was in there with our old pal Barry Tadlock, you know, meet the home-boys with their own local representative. Anyway, the guys let Dearfield get about halfway through his little spiel, then Barry proceeds to give us his best impression of a bowl of jello, all boneless quiver. Meanwhile Laroque does a one and a half twist with backward flip, total and complete freak. Right there on his genuine Persian carpet."

Chase found the news extremely satisfying. "You're saying he did not take the news well."

"I mean he went from a normal run-of-the-mill lieutenant governor to a jibbering monkey. All he needed was one of them little red caps and a tin cup, and he'd have been ready for the organ grinder."

Chase permitted himself the first grin of what felt like years. "Sorry I missed that."

"Oh, man, lemme tell you, it was beyooootiful. I'll be carrying that one with me for a long time. Bring me a lot of smiles, that one will. Laroque was a genuine baddie, wasn't he?"

"Bad as they come."

"Even better." Colin listened to voices in the background. "Dearfield says to tell you we're starting back now, we'll come over and give you the blow-by-blow in a coupla hours."

Chase hung up the phone and turned back, relishing what was about to come. Letting the pride of accomplishment glimmer through his rising weariness. "There is just one more thing. I've traced all this back to a company. A Florida group."

The level of both men's focused attention rose to new heights. "Who?"

Chase let the suspense ride for a moment longer, then released. "Omega," he replied. "The Omega Development Corporation of Miami."

18

"You liked that, didn't you." Matthew slung his coat over the bedstead, revealing suspenders of neon red. "Surprising me out of my skin."

Chase made round eyes. "Did I do that?"

"Listen to the man. Omega. Tosses the word out like it was just your basic tidbit, gets to see a pair of hard-nosed prosecution types do imitations of Confederate statues out on the capitol lawn. Turned to stone before his very eyes."

"Hard-nosed," Chase said. "You?"

Burroughs demanded, "Do you have proof of this allegation?"

"Allegations, plural," Chase replied. "Maybe it would be best if I took it from the top."

By the time he was done, his banked-up tension had translated into full-fledged fatigue. Burroughs sat and inspected him, respect tinting the beam from his direct gaze. "I'd like to ask you a few more questions, Mr. Bennett."

"A few, the man says." Matthew's grin lit

up the room. "Try a few hundred thousand."

"Tomorrow," Chase said. "Right now I'm about done on both sides."

Burroughs rose to his feet. "I need to make a couple of calls."

When they were alone, Chase said to Matthew, "From the look on your face I take it your investigations were aimed in the same direction."

"You could say that." Matthew shook his head. "Not to mention the fact that you've just saved us about a hundred billion hours of lawyer and cop and spook time."

Chase found the button, wound his bed down. "So tell me."

"To begin with, we're pretty certain Rochelle is about as Swiss as my Seiko. He started off Columbian, or his family did. Then they discovered what money could do when bank accounts start running to twenty or so zeros. He then went out and bought his passport at the smuggler's five and dime, otherwise known as the Swiss naturalization office."

"And his money?"

"Drugs." Matthew massaged his temples with a force that knotted his shoulders. "See, Slim, when it comes to illegal drug money, almost all our efforts are concen-

403

trated on trying to catch the crooks before they get the funds *out*."

"Laundering," Chase offered.

"That plus a hundred other scams. What's harder for us to track is the cash that's not caught. We figure we're as successful with money going out of the US as we are with drugs coming in, which isn't saying a whole heck of a lot. Call it a success rate of ten, maybe twelve percent. You see where I'm headed? That amount's something the drug kings can figure in as an affordable loss. A risk of doing business. Not to mention how many countries where they're operating nowadays are a lot less worried about chasing down illegal profits than we are. The Columbian cartels are moving into Central Europe in a big way. Spain and Portugal too. Britain's seen a tenfold increase in crack arrests in just three years."

"So what you're saying is that Rochelle is building his developments with drug money."

"What I'm saying is your tying Omega into toll fraud and illegally buying votes for casinos may be the big break we've been looking for."

Kaitlyn came through the door, took one look at Chase, walked up to Matthew and said, "How nice of you to have stopped by.

Please do be sure and come again."

Matthew smiled himself to his feet. "Like I told you the other day, Slim. I do believe you've got yourself a keeper here."

"Any idea how those disks happened to be in Washington?"

"Omega owns a couple of the big Delaware banks, another in D.C. Some of the top guys sit up there and oversee the day-to-day like spiders at the corners of big ol' webs."

"You know the way out, Matthew," Kaitlyn said.

"Probably sending up the final figures to those bank guys," Matthew went on, backing away, Kaitlyn shepherding him toward the door. "You know, let them see just how much it was gonna cost to buy themselves a state legislature."

"Now," Kaitlyn said.

"The telephone codes were probably part of a regular delivery," Matthew said, allowing himself to be gently shoved out, "rerouted from there to all the regional operations."

Kaitlyn shut the door, leaned against it, and crossed her arms. "I suppose there was some reason why you had to sit there and try to give them the whole story in one push."

"You," Chase replied, "are one incredible lady."

Her irritation melted. She crossed the room, sat down, asked, "Where do you hurt?"

"I'm too tired to tell, but I think everywhere."

Her expression was as soft as her caress. "I'm really, really sorry about your home, Chase."

He reached up, grasped her hand, drew it down to his heart, felt the comfort flood through him. "I keep waiting for the bubble to burst, and all the sadness to pour out. But it hasn't happened yet."

"I understand," she said, and with her gaze showed that she truly did. "There's always my place."

"Not likely," Chase said. "I made less than a stellar impression on your mom."

"Dad and I have been talking it over," Kaitlyn replied. "He's taking her back north. See if they can get their life together straightened out. I've agreed to look after Grandpa." Softer now. "If you'll help."

He sighed himself further into the covers, felt the harmony of watching all the pieces of his life brought together before his eyes. "Will I ever."

The employees of Thorndike Press hope you have enjoyed this Large Print book. All our Large Print titles are designed for easy reading, and all our books are made to last. Other Thorndike Press Large Print books are available at your library, through selected bookstores, or directly from us.

For information about titles, please call:

(800) 223-1244
(800) 223-6121

To share your comments, please write:

Publisher
Thorndike Press
295 Kennedy Memorial Drive
Waterville, ME 04901